A Thousand Steps

A Novel

Also by Anita Richmond Bunkley

FICTION:

Black Gold

Wild Embers

Starlight Passage

Emily, The Yellow Rose

Balancing Act

Mirrored Life

Silent Wager

Relative Interest

Between Goodbyes

ROMANCE:

Suite Embrace

Suite Temptation

Spotlight on Desire

Vote for Love

First Class Seduction

Boardroom Seduction

ANTHOLOGIES:

Sisters

Girlfriends

You Only Get Better

NON-FICTION

Steppin' Out With Attitude

A Thousand Steps

A Novel

Anita Richmond Bunkley

Rinard Publishing

Cypress, Texas

www.rinardpublishing.com

Published by Rinard Publishing
Cypress, Texas USA

A Thousand Steps
Copyright © 2012 by Anita Richmond Bunkley

This title is also available as an ebook.

First Printing January 2013

ISBN 10: 0962401234
ISBN 13: 978-0-9624012-3-7

Cover design: Dana Pittman
Cover graphic: Christophe.Rolland1 | Dreamstime.com
Interior Design: Dana Pittman
Printed in the United States of America

A Thousand Steps is dedicated with love and appreciation to my husband, Crawford.

Acknowledgement and thanks to Mr. Richard Fields, Supervisor, Fort Gibson Military Park, and to Mr. Chris Morgan, visitor guide at Fort Gibson for their support of my project.

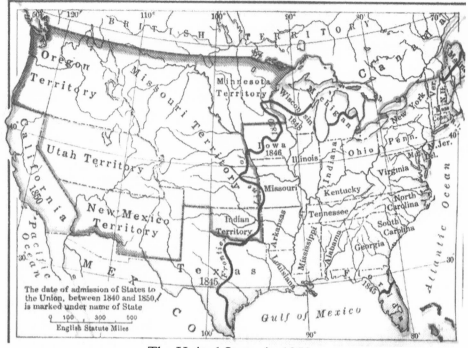

The United States in 1850

S.E. Forman, Advanced American History

(New York, NY: The Century Company 1919)

Foreword

In 1829, Andrew Jackson was elected president of the United States after gaining popularity for defeating the Creek Indians at the Battle of Horseshoe Creek in 1814. For many years afterward he advocated the removal of all Indians to the Indian Territory west of the Mississippi River in order to make more land available for European-American settlers. After the United States Congress passed the Indian Removal Act in 1832, the Creek National Council signed the Treaty of Cussseta, ceding their remaining lands east of the Mississippi River to the government. They accepted relocation to the Indian Territory, and most Muscogee-speaking people were rounded up and marched West in 1834, on what came to be known as The Trail of Tears. However, some Creek remained behind, determined to maintain their traditional way of life, living in small talwas spread along the Georgia and Alabama riverbanks. Such was the clan of the Fox at Great Oaks on the Tallapoosa River.

Chapter 1

Tama

Sampson County, North Carolina, 1855

Smoke as dense and frothy as Carolina cotton sucked air from the room and shadowed the space in a hazy, gray-white veil. It seeped into the cracks of the rough-hewn walls and eased beneath the gap at the bottom of the ill-fitting door, which Master Thorne locked every night to keep his property safe. The sinister, wispy tendrils crawled across the brushed dirt floor and licked the sides of a lumpy cornhusk pallet, where two women slept, unaware of their nighttime intruder. The unwelcome visitor brushed the legs of two ladder-back chairs set before a soot-filled hearth, where a cast iron kettle hung suspended from a fire-blackened hook. Moving on, it swept up the mud-brick chimney and shot out into the thick night air, drawing more of its kind in its wake.

Tama's eyes blinked open, but she quickly squeezed them shut, stung by a burning sensation that pricked her eyelids like a million tiny needles. She opened her mouth to call out, but acrid smoke rushed in and clogged her throat, turning her cry for help into a raspy croak lost to the hiss of the fire. Rolling onto her side, she groped at her mother's shadowy form, grabbed the sleeping woman by the shoulder and shook her hard in an attempt to awaken her, and after coughing up the plug of smoke that trapped her voice, Tama screamed, "Wake up! Mama! Wake up!"

"Humm? Humm? What is it?" Maggie mumbled, finally stirred, groggily awake. She swiped at her eyes with work-calloused fingers, and then latched onto Tama's hand.

"Fire! Mama. It's fire! Come on!" Tama urged, tugging on her mother's arm, frantic to get out of the cabin.

Maggie finally sat up, leaned forward, and struggled to focus on Tama before falling back onto her pallet, too weakened by smoke to push her body up and out of their bed. She shook her head in resignation and released Tama's hand. "You go, child," she hoarsely whispered. "You go. I can't make it."

"You gotta make it, Mama. We gotta get out!" Tama gripped her mother's arm once more, wrapping her fingers over the large half-moon scar near Maggie's elbow as she forced the heavy woman to lift her head. Maggie looked up and gazed at Tama through the hazy fog, fear showing hard and clear on her face. "There's no way ... for me," she managed, words thick with resignation. "You go, Tama. Save yourself. Don't fret about this poor old soul."

"Mama ... I won't ... leave you," Tama objected between spasms of coughs that brought tears to her eyes.

"Yes, you will," Maggie countered in a tight voice that seemed to take the last of her strength. "Do as I say, Tama, and get out of here!" She angrily flailed her hands in front of her face, pushing her daughter away and then threw back the folds of her threadbare quilt and slipped her hand beneath her pallet. "Take this," Maggie urged, tossing a cloth sack to Tama. "Run! Run away from the sun," Maggie commanded in a voice that fell to a whisper. "Don't rest 'til you cross the big mountain." With a slump, she pulled the quilt over her face and hunched her shoulders up to her ears.

The smoke had grown so dark and thick that Tama could no longer see the outline of her mother, but she accepted the bag they had named their "Leavin' Bag"—filled with items tied up in a piece of cloth—ready to snatch if Master Thorne decided to sell her or Tama away from Royaltin Ridge.

A stab of fear laced with anger constricted Tama's heart, squeezing it so hard she winced. Whirling around, she focused on the small window high above the door – the only other way out of the cabin, knowing she had two choices: Remain with her mother and die alongside her, or attempt an exit through the hole in the wall. The sound of crackling fire hissed in her ears as she leaned down, swept her lips across Maggie's soft cheek, and then reached for the hard leather boots that Mistress Irene had given her on the first day of frost. She pushed her bare feet into the shoes, shoved a three-legged stool up against the wall, climbed up, and jammed the sack through the window. Without a moment's hesitation, she heaved her body forward, wiggled through the window, and dropped down onto the frost-covered ground.

Tama lay where she fell, limp with relief, too frightened to stand and run. She rolled onto her back, gasped air into her burning lungs, and listened to the shouts and curses of men as they raced toward the quarters. She could not linger a second longer. If she didn't run, she'd be caught, whipped, and deprived of food for the next five days. Rising to a crouch, she raced into the woods that backed up to the kitchen house, where Tama and her mother worked long hours, peeling, cutting, frying and stewing all manner of food for the master and the mistress of Royaltin Ridge. From the edge of the woods, she stared at the big house, now engulfed in a tower of fire. The top floor of the mansion had collapsed into the center of the house, and its double flank of tall white pillars were

3

reduced to charred black sticks. She watched as a frenzied tangle of flames rippled across the plantation grass and claimed another shabby cabin in the quarters. Explosive bursts of red-orange flames rapidly consumed the rickety huts. Three slave children, who had most likely been pushed through their own cabin windows, wandered in confusion, crying for their mothers.

Clutching the bag that Maggie had thrown to her, Tama watched as Bristo, the burly overseer of Royaltin Ridge, who was hastily dressed and clearly desperate to save Master Thorne's slaves from destruction, began to unlock the cabin doors. Released from their smoke-filled homes, men, women, and children stumbled out just as four white men carrying rifles rode up and circled the perimeter of the quarters, eager to prevent them from running away.

Tears of outrage and sorrow blurred Tama's vision. Suddenly weak with fear, trepidation, and anguish, she wrapped her arms at her waist and shifted deeper into the shadows when she saw Thorne Royaltin, the master of Royaltin Ridge, emerge from the remains of his burning house. He was carrying the limp body of his wife, Irene. Behind him came Old Nip, the Negro houseman who had lived on the plantation all of his life, and he was holding the body of Mistress Carrie, the master's daughter. Tama watched, feeling nothing, as the men placed the women's bodies on the ground, smoke rising from their charred white flesh.

* * * * *

Thorne Royaltin bowed his head, shoved his hands into the pockets of his trousers, and worked his jaw back and forth as Old Nip placed blankets over the lifeless forms lying at his feet.

4

The pain of losing his wife and his only child was so great he could hardly breathe, and a wave of fury coursed through him when the elderly house slave asked, "Is there anything I can do for you, Master Thorne?"

"No!" Thorne snapped, nostrils flaring in icy anger. "Not unless you can bring my wife and daughter back to life!" Brusquely, he shoved the old man out of his way, scanned the wreckage of his plantation, and then scowled at the moon. A sense of utter desolation engulfed Thorne as the reality of his loss sank in. His home, his wife, many of his slaves, and tragically, his only heir had been taken from him. All that remained was the one thousand acre tract of cotton farmland that his father, Horace, carved from the wilderness a generation ago after arriving in America at the age of twelve. Horace had stepped off a leaky, weather-beaten ship from England without a cent in his pocket, but by the time he was old enough to take a wife, he'd carved the Royaltin name into a massive stretch of rich North Carolina farmland that provided his only heir a stream of wealth to this day.

Now, Thorne turned his attention to the burning slave quarters. Was his half-breed, bastard child still alive? Or had he lost her, too? Striding defiantly toward the flaming cabin where Tama and her mother lived, he stood in the open door that Bristo had flung wide and stared into the swirling smoke.

"Tama!" Thorne shouted, peering into the cloudy interior. "Tama! Come out here!" he demanded.

"Nobody in there but Maggie, and she's dead," Bristo called out, running over to Thorne. "Can't find the girl. I'm sure she's run off!"

Thorne clenched the front of Bristo's shirt in a hard grip and yanked the overseer up to his chest. "What do you mean, run off?" He pushed the man away. "Go find her!" he ordered, voice gritty with impatience. "You know how to track darkies. Go north, up across the timberline. Go get her, you hear me? Take men, the dogs, and bring her back here!" He shoved Bristo aside and shouted into the smoky night air, "Tama! If you hear me, listen good! You belong to *me*! And I *will* have you back!"

No, you won't, Tama defiantly vowed. She'd rather die on the run than remain enslaved under Royaltin's brutal control. He might be her flesh and blood father, but he was nothing to her, nothing but a cruel, brutal man who would never lay his lash on her again.

When the bark of excited hounds cracked the air, Tama looked up and studied the sky, relieved to see the faint tinge of daylight emerging above the trees. Recalling her mother's words, she turned away from the rising sun and disappeared into the woods.

* * * * *

Thorne Royaltin, often referred to as the most handsome man in Sampson County, wore his thick black hair combed back from a face that was sharply planed and finely structured. At forty-one, he had not a single gray hair on his head or the shadow of a wrinkle on his milk white skin. His gently muscled physic was the perfect frame for the finely tailored clothing he flaunted, and as the second generation master of Royaltin Ridge Plantation and the owner of the Royaltin Textile Mill, he was one of the wealthiest businessmen in the state of North Carolina. He had married well enough—to

Irene Withers, the daughter of his planter-neighbor, asking her to be his wife, not because she was rich but because she was plainspoken, plain looking, and would never compete with him for anyone's attention. He'd been terribly disappointed that their only child, Carrie, had emerged as a carbon copy of his wife, while his bastard child, Tama, was an exquisitely pretty, dusky-complexioned girl with his violet-gray eyes and wavy black hair.

Now, Royaltin turned his attention on the remains of his home. The four-story mansion with wraparound verandas and filled with European furnishings, was nothing more than a pile of rubble. The huge oak trees that lined the curved brick walkway resembled towers of soot, and the thirty-seven slave cabins, whitewashed the previous fall, glowed orange in the night, like torches set aflame.

Everything Thorne Royaltin loved was gone, and the devastation hurt him to his soul, as did Tama's disappearance. A blind rage swept over him like fire. With a shudder, he curled his lips away from his teeth, incensed that she had dared run off. With fisted hands, he squinted in defiance. No matter how long it took, he would rebuild the big house, replace the furnishings, construct new slave cabins, buy more slaves, and plant more trees. He had the money, slaves, and time to do it. However, the one thing that he could never replace was his family. Certainly, he could take a new wife with whom to live out his remaining years, but he would never father another child. An accidental shooting to the most delicate part of his body – the result of a night of gambling gone bad – had left him sterile, his male anatomy intact.

Though gambling could be a dangerous sport, it was the only vice that Thorne Royaltin embraced. He didn't care much for hard liquor, had only a passing interest bedding loose women, but a gaming table, a deck of cards, and a streak of good luck had been known to keep him away from home for weeks at a time. He had won and lost more money than most of the planters in Sampson County earned in a lifetime of cotton or tobacco farming. He had also made a few enemies due to his suspicious impatience with men he did not trust. After the bloody incident that robbed his fertility, he never again sat down at a poker table without a pistol strapped beneath his finely tailored coat and a back-up dagger stuck into his boot.

His daughter's death was the harshest blow, stripping away Thorne's vision of the future. Carrie had been his assurance that the Royaltin bloodline would continue, that the legacy of his father would continue for another generation. But now she was dead, leaving Thorne with only the land... and Tama ... whose light skin, thick black hair, and violet-grey eyes made her an easy runaway to track. Once he found her and brought her back, he planned to punish her severely. Then he would move her into his newly built home, dress her in decent clothing, install her as the head household slave, and give her the run of his home. He would also make sure she never left the property or mated with a darkie or bore him a black grandson who would dare to call himself a Royaltin.

Chapter 2

Mountains of North Carolina

It wasn't the scurry of rats, the howl of hungry wolves, or the shriek of freezing winds punishing the log cabin that frightened Tama. It was the sound of footsteps, muffled by snow but distinctly recognizable, that made every nerve in her body recoil. She tugged Maggie's threadbare shawl around her shoulders, tucked her chin to her chest, and pressed her nearly frozen body deeper into the corner next to the empty hearth. She curled her fingers into hard fists and listened to the wheezing noise that filtered through the mud-caked walls. It sounded like a person breathing rapidly, as if out of breath, and Tama wondered if it might be Bristo, or one of the men from Royaltin Ridge. Had the overseer tracked her to this remote shelter in the mountains where she took refuge ten days ago? Was he lurking outside, eager to burst in and take her back to Royaltin Ridge?

The thought made Tama's stomach tighten in fear, and, gritting her teeth, she pushed aside an unexpected eruption of memory about the night of the fire: Maggie's tortured face, the screams of the slaves, her master's vow to find her. Tama eased her hand from beneath her shawl and reached for the knife she'd found wrapped in a rabbit skin inside her mother's bag, which had also contained the stub of a tallow candle, a piece of flint, the threadbare shawl she was wearing, a wooden cup, and a metal spoon.

Hefting the knife, Tama pointed it at the door; no match

for a bullet from a rifle, but it was wide, sharp, and could be deadly if used at close range.

But what if it's not Bristo outside? she mused, quivering with cold as her mind suddenly flooded with worry. She was a runaway slave hiding in an abandoned cabin on an isolated mountain ridge. Many dangers lurked outside in the inky night: Crazed mountain men, vicious bounty hunters, and hungry wolves that crept closer to the cabin every night. Angry Cherokee Indians roamed the mountain, too, making sporadic raids for food and livestock to threaten those who lived on land they claimed as theirs.

Shaking off her fears, Tama forced her weariness to subside, relaxed her grip on the knife and tucked her ragged dress around her legs before slipping into a troubled sleep.

When sunlight streamed through the broken shutters covering the cabin window and touched her face, Tama awakened with a start. Moving with caution, she crept from the corner where she'd hidden, crossed the room, unlatched the door, and stood in the entry. Holding firm against the blast of frosty air that swept past her and billowed her tattered dress above her ankles, she looked around. The white glare of glistening snow forced her eyes into slits. She lifted a hand to shade her eyes as she examined the frozen landscape, which lay serene and frigid under the assault of a bright winter sun. Craning forward, she studied a line of tracks embedded in the crusty snow; softly curved, irregular footprints that tracked across the clearing and off into the ice-laced woods. The prints were large, clearly made by moccasins, not boots, and definitely those of a man.

Tama pulled her shawl tighter around her body and stepped outside, praying her night time visitor had moved on, along with the storm that had gripped the land in an icy fist for the last six days. However, a glance at the sky told her that another siege was on its way, and she had better find some food before it settled in. Since escaping the plantation, she had survived on a few handfuls of winter berries and scraps of dried meat she'd foraged from an abandoned hunter's lodge. With her stomach aching from hunger, her mouth as dry as parched corn, and her head buzzing with worry, she left the cabin and started down the steep path toward the trading post she'd spied through the trees while climbing up the mountainside. Going there was risky, but she had no intention of dying from hunger, frozen and alone on a windy mountaintop.

At the bottom of the incline, Tama took the hard-packed trail that led to the rear of the trading post where a hole had been cut to vent smoke from the stove inside. The hole was covered with a scrap of beaver skin, which Tama lifted high enough to peek inside. A stream of warm air, thick with the scent of tobacco, sawdust, and pine, drifted out.

The interior of the post was dim, but Tama could see a shockingly tall man wearing a fox fur vest over a blood red shirt. His skin was dark brown and his hair was coal black and curly, matching the beard that covered his chin. His angular cheekbones and bushy brows created deep sockets that held button-like eyes. He was standing at a wooden table, arranging fat glass jars and square wooden bins filled with goods for trade. Tama watched as he carefully placed a shiny metal pail on top of a round wooden cask, then stepped back to study his display. After a moment of contemplation, he removed the pail and rearranged his display, his slender fingers moving over his goods like sticks of charcoal set to a page.

Suddenly, he looked up, as if alerted by Tama's presence, and stared directly at her—more with curiosity than alarm.

Tama jerked back. He did not break his gaze, seeming to force her to either run away or trust him enough to come inside. When she did not move, he finally crooked his finger and motioned for her to enter, and without hesitating, Tama dropped the beaver pelt back into place and went around to the front of the trading post.

Inside, the trader acknowledged Tama with a somber nod and a slow look-over from head to toe. He took his time inspecting her face, her hair, her dress, her boots, and once he seemed satisfied with what he saw, he leaned over the counter that hogged the center of the store, pushed out his lower lip, and cocked his head to the side. Letting out a slow breath, he grinned, exposing teeth the color of corn.

"Been travelin' long, ha?" he said, in an accent that matched his less than ordinary looks.

"A few days," Tama murmured, praying she had done the right thing by showing herself to this man, that news of the plantation fire and her escape had not reached this isolated post.

"Bet you hungry, ha?" he inquired, stroking the fur on his vest.

Tama lowered her shoulders and nodded her agreement.

Jutting out his bearded jaw, the man curled his lips into a knowing smirk. "Well, t'ain't my business where you come from or where you goin', so I ain't gonna ask no questions." He picked up a clay pipe, stuck it into his mouth, and pulled on it so hard that his leathery dark lips puckered into folds around the stem. Reaching for a basket on a nearby shelf, he scooped out a handful of dried meat strips and stuffed them into a rough bark pouch. Moving among the many tins and casks stacked on the table, he added a fistful of corn, a few apples, two hard biscuits, and a metal scoop of grain. "Here. This might not last long, but it'll help ya go on. I court no trouble, ha?"

Tama hesitated. He shook the pouch in her face. "Go on, take it, and git on your way."

In a swift motion, Tama snatched the bag from the man, tucked it under her shawl, and took two steps back from the table. "I do thank you, sir," she said, relieved that he did not want to know how far she'd come or where she was headed or why she was there at all.

"Go on now," he insisted. "I'm a guessin' you got a fair piece to travel, so you better move outta these parts."

"I'm grateful to you, Mister," Tama spoke up, turning to leave. However, when she placed her hand on the iron latch of the trading post door, the sound of horses whinnying outside stopped her. Tama whirled around and faced the trader, terrified that her short sprint to freedom was about to end.

"Stay," the trader sternly ordered. "Go to the back. Stand at the stove and warm yourself."

Tama hesitated, then swallowed her fear and did as he ordered, slipping into a shadowy space where she would not be seen, but she could see the door.

Footsteps clomped across the wood plank porch, then the air inside the room suddenly cooled when a man entered. Tama flinched, but instead of sinking farther into the shadowy corner, she shifted forward, eager to get a better look at the visitor. The man who entered was not from Royaltin Ridge. He was white, heavily bearded, overbearing in size, and encased in a bearskin coat over heavy woolen trousers tucked into tall scruffy boots.

"Mornin' Clyde," the man greeted the trader.

13

"How-do, Jonas," Clyde replied. "What brings you and the men out in this bad snow we been havin'?"

"Nothin' good," Jonas tersely answered. "Got a paper for you ta post."

"What about?" Clyde wanted to know.

"Fugitive Indian. Attacked a soldier over at Shoulderbone and got away. Dangerous fellow. Fifty dollars in gold to the man who brings him in ... alive."

"Yeah?" Clyde whistled. "The Army been pushin' the Cherokee pretty hard."

"This one ain't Cherokee," Jonas informed. "He's Creek. Told the soldiers he's from down along the Tallapoosa. A place called Great Oaks. He got caught hunting on private land."

"When did all this happen?"

"Two, three days ago," Jonas informed, sounding both solemn and eager. "The injun slashed a soldier's arm with the rusty tin can. Cut him from his elbow to his shoulder, and then ran off. Gashed him so deep the man almost died. Army thinks the fugitive's headed this way. Seen any strange injuns 'round here?"

A beat of silence followed before Clyde answered, "Nope. None I don't know." Then he told Jonas, "Gimme that notice ... I'll post it right now."

A tremor of relief shivered through Tama. She was safe, for now.

After Clyde tacked the Wanted notice on his door, he came back inside. "So you all goin' after him now, ha?" Clyde inquired.

"Yep," Jonas replied. "Hope ta flush him out and turn him

over to the Army. Git that reward money... sure would be nice."

"Which way you gonna go?"

"Over to Shoop Creek. Up to the ridge. Hope the storm ain't covered all his tracks."

"I wish ya luck," Clyde added, sounding genuinely supportive of the mission the man was about to carry out.

After Tama heard the door slam shut, she emerged and turned to Clyde, questioning him with a squint of her eyes.

"Go on now," Clyde told her. When Tama didn't move, he grabbed a rough horse blanket off a shelf and threw it at her. "Take it. And don't tarry 'round here no more. A bad storm's comin' and you ain't nowhere near safe."

Tama snatched the red and white striped cloth, wrapped it around her shoulders, gave him a long look of thanks, and then fled into the woods. Hurrying away from the post, she thought about the noises she'd heard during the night, the footprints in the snow. If the fugitive Indian was lurking around the cabin, maybe she shouldn't return. But where else could she go? She sure as hell wasn't going to set off across the countryside with no certainty of finding another shelter.

Tama cast a worried glance at the thick clouds gathering overhead, stomped her boot-clad feet and then hugged her body with her arms, grateful for the trader's gifts. At least she had a little food, a blanket, and a reprieve from capture. Firming her lips, Tama's nostrils flared in thought as a determined set came to her face. Stepping onto the icy trail, she reminded herself, *I'd rather take my chances with an Indian on the run than freeze to death alone in the woods, wrapped in a trader's horse blanket.*

Chapter 3

Shivering beneath the trader's blanket, Tama chewed on a strip of leathery venison, relishing the meat while trying to warm herself in front of the tiny fire she'd managed to coax to life. Chunks of ice slid off the rooftop and crashed into the snow as a stiff north wind assaulted the leaky shanty. Staring into the flickering flames, Tama turned her thoughts to Royaltin Ridge, to the tiny cabin she had shared with her mother. It had been drafty, sparsely furnished, yet filled with warmth and love. Tears welled in her eyes as she thought about the way she'd left her mother, wrapped in a quilt, veiled in smoke. Had Master Thorne buried her in the slave cemetery behind the horse barn? Did Old Nip, who called himself a preacher, repeat words from the Bible over her? Had anyone made a cross to mark Maggie's grave, so that Tama could find her if she ever dared return? Tama blinked into the fire, wondering if such a day would ever come.

The whispery sounds of labored breathing and soft footsteps suddenly came to Tama once more, bringing her alert. She raised her head and listened closely, recognizing the sounds. More annoyed than frightened, she quickly decided not to hide in fear and wait for the intruder to show himself, but to force an encounter and find out exactly who was stalking her, and why.

With the kitchen knife in hand she eased to her feet, slid back the iron bolt on the door, and cracked it open, sending a shaft of weak light streaming out into the night. The land was a crisp montage of gray and white shapes set against black shadows, everything spiked by the glint of ice. She scanned the bleak scene and immediately saw the figure of a man slip from behind a tree trunk to take cover behind a clump of shaggy brush. Increasing her grip on the knife handle, Tama waited, eyes fastened on a thin shadow that stretched from behind the brush and created a splash of black on the cool white snow. Whoever was lurking out there was also watching her, and waiting.

If this is the Indian who attacked the soldier, I can't act like I'm afraid of him, Tama silently calculated. If he wanted to attack her or kill her he would have already done so. If he came at her, at least she had the knife. But could she really stab a man? Twist the blade so hard it severed his guts? Watch as his blood stained the snow and life drained from his body? Impatient, yet curious, she pushed the door fully open and stood in the entry, trembling more from the cold than from fear. The frigid winter wind stung her cheeks and lifted her woolen dress to her knees, creating a flapping whoosh that vibrated the air.

The figure hiding behind the brush suddenly moved into the shaft of light that radiated from the cabin. *It's the Indian all right,* Tama recognized, and he was standing with his shoulders thrown back, as if hell-bent on taking advantage of her even though he did not carry a weapon.

Tama boldly took a step deeper into the yard, as if daring the man to approach. Her arm began to quiver from the tension in her grip so she slowly relaxed her fingers, but did not lower the knife.

The Indian started walking slowly toward her. Tama sucked in a short breath but did not back up. Standing her ground, she kept her eyes riveted on the man, whose long stride put him, quickly, less than two feet from where she stood. Summoning all of her courage, Tama absorbed his presence. His bearskin cape was heavily beaded down the front and a wedge of silver as wide as the span of Tama's hand gleamed at his throat. Clearly, he was not a common rag-tag Indian out to pilfer food or steal livestock but a man of some stature among his people. When he moved closer, Tama came alert.

"Stay back!" she warned, brandishing her knife at him, assuming he spoke English. Since the arrival of the missionary schools among the Indians, the majority of the Creek and the Cherokee in the Carolina mountains spoke English very well.

Without acknowledging her warning, the Indian rushed past Tama and stormed into the cabin, where he stood and looked around, as if searching for something in particular. Even though he appeared unarmed, she knew better than to relax her guard, so she raised the knife and followed him inside.

"Who are you? What do you want?" she boldly demanded, lifting the weapon to remind him that she was armed. "Are you the Indian that attacked a soldier?" she pressed, letting him know she knew what had happened. "If so, you'd better keep moving because men are on the mountain, looking for you."

"Where is your food? Your guns?" he threw out, as if she hadn't spoken.

"I have no food or guns," she tossed back. "You go! Leave me alone!" She waved the kitchen knife back and forth in a lame attempt to scare him off.

Without comment, the Indian began to search the cabin, kicking at heaps of broken wood and piles of rubbish as he tore through every corner of the shelter. Grunting his displeasure, he headed to the spot beneath the eaves where Tama slept, snatched up her blanket, shook it hard, and dumped the contents of her bag onto the floor. Squatting down, he raked through Tama's meager possessions, making it clear he had no use for the small items he found.

Tama stiffened in disgust, though relieved to have hidden the bark pouch of food beneath the bib of her dress. *If he tries to take it, I will use my knife to slash his throat*, she vowed, keeping her eyes on his back, struck by the star-like pattern of snowflakes on his dark fur cape. His head was uncovered and his shiny black hair was knotted in a tail that lay on his back like a slick black snake.

"They will catch you," she warned, watching the snowflakes melt. "Men with long guns are tracking you right now, and they will turn you over to the Army to be hanged."

For the first time since entering the cabin he actually looked into her face. "I'm not worried about the men who hunt me," he bluntly replied in perfect English. "They track far to the east and will never get to me." His bold assessment of the situation hung in the air, as if he had no fear of being captured.

"Others will come," Tama challenged.

"No one is coming here, you are alone."

"How do you know I'm alone?" Tama snapped. "You've been hanging around here, watching me, haven't you?"

The Indian frowned at her but did not reply. Instead, he shrugged off his thick bearskin pelt and placed it on the floor in front of the near-dead fire. Tama glanced down at her knife, and then back to the fugitive, considering her next move. Throwing the knife at his back would only escalate the situation, which so far did not seem threatening. He wanted food, guns, maybe shelter and warmth, so it might be best to leave him alone and see what he would do.

19

"I will go at daybreak," he stated, kneeling before the fire to press a handful of twigs into the smoldering flames. Immediately, pale yellow light bathed the gloomy space and cast his oversized shadow on the wall. Deciding to ignore him, Tama grabbed her blanket and moved into a corner across the room, but did not let go of the knife. Crouching down, she took her time studying the Indian, taking in the sheen of youth that glistened on his copper profile. Strong arm muscles bulged beneath his oiled deerskin shirt, which was tied at the waist with a knotted hemp belt strung with bits of yellow stone. His leather breeches were well constructed and fit his long legs like a second skin and they showed no scars of wear that naturally adorned the clothing of a more common man. His moccasins, soaking wet and splashed with mud, came nearly to his knees, giving evidence of his arduous journey.

"What is your name?" Tama ventured.

"Hakan," he replied without turning around to look at her.

"You speak English very well."

"It is important to speak the language of those who want to control my fate."

He's smart, Tama decided, struck by a spark of sympathy for him. She hoped he did not sense how truly unafraid she was or how much she welcomed his company. No one had ever turned to her in time of need and asked *her* for help. He was alone, on the run, and hungry. Just as she was. And it was clear he had no intention of harming her. Tama slipped a hand beneath the bib of her dress and removed the pouch of food the trader had given her.

"I do have a little food," she confessed, extending a dried piece of fruit and a strip of meat toward Hakan.

He turned then, a flicker of gratitude skimming his

features as he looked at Tama, then down at the food she was offering. His expression initiated a sense of relief that made Tama begin to relax. "Take the food and warm yourself, but please be gone as soon as light hits the sky."

Hakan accepted the food, returned to the hearth, and sat cross-legged in front of the fire as he bent his head to eat. Tama retreated to a shadowy corner under the eaves and watched him as he ate. Was it bravery, curiosity, sympathy, or stupidity that made her feel so safe? Would she regret her impulsive act of kindness when he attacked her in the middle of the night?

Only time will tell, Tama resolved, suddenly exhausted, even though a calmness settled over her spirit. Sliding down onto the floor, she wrapped her fully clothed body in the striped horse blanket and willed herself asleep.

Like an unwelcome thought, the bark of loud voices broke into Tama's slumber and brought her to her feet. Standing motionless, she glanced around the room. The fire had died down to a smoldering bank of pink-red coals and the lingering scent of Hakan's damp bearskin was the only evidence of his presence.

A sharp pang of disappointment pierced Tama, but her uneasy concern quickly faded when the tramp of horses moving through snow jerked her attention back to the moment. She went to the door, peeked through a wide crack, and was shocked to see a ring of flaming torches, held high by men on horseback. The riders were moving past the cabin, pushing their way through snow that rose mid-leg on their steeds. She recognized the lead horseman as Jonas, the man who'd entered the trading post and vowed to capture the fugitive Indian. He was tugging on a long rope tied around Hakan's neck, and he yanked it hard, forcing the Indian to stumble along behind him.

Shaken by the sight, Tama backed away from the door and pressed a hand to her mouth, her heart pounding in shock and dread. And when she heard a voice shout, "Keep walkin', ya filthy injun!" her heart beat even faster.

"What're we gonna to do with him, Jonas?" another man called out. "Hang him?"

"Naw," Jonas called back. "I'll lock him up in the strong room at the trading post for tonight. Clyde can guard him while I head over to Shoulderbone and get a soldier to come and take him into custody. We'll get that reward money and be finished with this nasty injun."

"Yep, that's 'bout the best thing to do," a companion agreed, sounding very pleased.

Tama's nostrils flared as she closed her eyes and inhaled slowly, trying to calm down. The image of Hakan with a noose around his neck made her heart sink in despair. Hakan had neither threatened nor hurt her. He had not stolen her food or made advances on her. He was not a vicious, wild Indian hell bent on killing soldiers, but simply a man trying to survive in a world that did not want him. Was this why Tama felt no fear or anger toward him, why it pained her to see him with a rope around his neck?

The muffled sounds of horses and men moving through snow grew faint as Tama turned Jonas' words over in her mind: *He'll be held at the trading post until the soldiers come to take him away.*

Sitting in the dark, Tama's thoughts turned back to the

struggle she'd endured since fleeing Royaltin Ridge: a race through forest so dense and wild no sunlight touched her face, a grueling climb up the face of the mountain, a dangerous trek across ice-covered landscapes that showed her little mercy. Discovering the abandoned cabin had been a stroke of luck, but she knew it was time to move on, and was wise enough to know that traveling alone would be dangerous. Perhaps joining with Hakan was her best chance for survival.

Tama packed the remainder of the supplies Clyde had given her into Maggie's leavin' bag, tucked the knife into her boot, and tied the horse blanket around her body. Praying that she had calculated the situation correctly, she plunged into the frigid night and headed down the slippery trail that would take her to the trading post. The path was black and dangerously slick, but she cautiously made her way down the trail and to the post, where all was dark and quiet. Tama stepped onto the wooden walkway and brashly pounded on the door until Clyde yanked it open. He lifted a fat tallow candle stuck into a shallow tin and stared at Tama in disbelief. "What in God's name *you* doin' here, gal?"

In answer, Tama raised her knife and pressed it to Clyde's belly, cutting a slit in the coarse cotton nightshirt he was wearing.

The trader scratched his head, ran his tongue over his lips, and began to back up. "What's this all about, ha?"

"It's about the Indian locked up in your storeroom," Tama snapped in a tone that conveyed the seriousness of her mission. "Open the door and let him out."

"Now, listen here." Clyde put his hand on his hip and scowled, as if Tama were a naughty child trying to put something over on him. "You best go away. I ain't about to get in the middle of the Army's business, and you don't look like the kinda gal who needs trouble from the government, either."

Tama lunged forward, pushing the tip of her knife more firmly into Clyde's stomach, making him jerk back in surprise. "It's sharp and it cuts real good," she informed him as she slit the fabric of his nightshirt. "I could cut you bad, but I don't have to. Not if you do as I say."

"You ain't got it in you to kill me," Clyde stammered, though his voice held a trace of uncertainty.

Tama kicked the door shut behind her and matched his pace, step for step, the knife still glued to his stomach. "Maybe not. But I could put a hole in your gut, and you sure don't want that, do you?"

Clyde shook his head in amazement. "I believe you mean it, gal." He hurried to take a ring of keys from a hook beside the storeroom door, breathing loud and rough as he fumbled with the lock. "What you want with this injun? Huh?" he asked, turning the key with a click.

"Not your concern. Just hurry up and open that door," was Tama's cold reply.

Clyde slid the big iron key out of the lock and pushed the door inward.

Immediately, Hakan, wrapped in his bearskin cape, stepped out, grabbed a coil of rope from a peg on the wall and tied Clyde's hands and feet together, hobbling him like a steer. After shoving a rag into the trader's mouth, he pushed Clyde inside the strong room and re-locked the door. Loud thumping sounds erupted from inside the storeroom as Clyde pounded his feet against the walls. Hakan glanced around the room, still lit dimly by Clyde's fat candle and nodded toward a badly stained shearling jacket that was hanging on a peg by the door.

"Take the coat. Give me your blanket."

Tama immediately dropped the horse blanket to the floor, snatched Clyde's jacket and slipped her arms into the coat. Hakan picked up the blanket and then said, "Give me the knife."

Tama stiffened, wary about giving up her weapon, while fully aware that Hakan could take the knife from her if he really wanted to. She stepped back, the knife now pointed at Hakan. "You can have it ... if you take me with you," she countered, terrified of what would happen to her if she stayed behind. She was a runaway slave, hiding deep in the Carolina mountains. No one cared what happened to her. And now that she'd forced the release of a fugitive Indian who was wanted by the Army, she was a criminal, too. What was the punishment for such a crime? *Death, most likely*, she decided.

"No," Hakan grunted, pushing past Tama. "I must go alone." He yanked open the door and strode outside, leaving Tama to watch him cross the road and take the path toward the icy thicket. However, before he disappeared into the woods, he turned around and looked back at her, his face illuminated by a full white moon that slipped from beneath a drifting winter cloud.

Tama hesitated, fingering the knife, then raced across the road and offered the weapon to Hakan. "Here," she said, letting go of the knife, which dropped to the snow. "Take it. But I will follow you."

Hakan did not speak. He simply picked up the weapon, stuck it into his rope belt, and then plunged into the thicket, leaving Tama to move in behind him and match his steps, taking two to his one to keep up.

"Where are you going?" She had to ask.

"To the village of my people," he tersely replied, throwing words over his shoulder. "A place too far away for you to go." Then he started walking even faster than before.

"I don't care. I'll keep up," Tama countered, hurrying up behind him, not about to ask where his village might be.

After a long stretch of silence, Hakan abruptly stopped walking and turned to face Tama. "You go home." His voice was flat with authority and hard with command.

"I have no home," Tama stated with certainty.

A flicker of understanding flashed across Hakan's face, softening the hardness in his eyes. "Then stay close. Do not speak to me again. We have a long way to go."

Chapter 4

The joint funeral for Irene and Carrie Royaltin took place at the Community Christian Church in the county seat of Sampson, North Carolina ten days after the fire. Nearly every white planter living within fifty miles of Royaltin Ridge arrived to bid the Royaltin women good-bye. They consoled Thorne with gentle words of sympathy, soft pats on his arm, and promises to do all they could to help him recover from his tragedy. Thorne buried his wife and daughter in the family plot on the hillside next to the pile of ashes that once had been one of the most spectacular homes in the state. He marked each grave with a tall marble headstone carved with angels holding trumpets, and placed a spray of winter roses at the foot of each one.

He buried Maggie, along with eight other slaves who died in the fire, in the low country slope behind his barn but placed no markers to identify the graves. As Maggie's body was lowered into the ground, Thorne had stared at the pine box containing the only black woman he had ever lain with, filled with an uneven sense of loss and relief. She'd been a strapping black-skinned beauty in her youth and he'd been unable to resist having her. She fought him like a scalded cat the first time he took her, clawing and hissing until he managed to subdue her, but after his initiation to her body, he enjoyed sexual encounters with Maggie for the next four years, until she became pregnant with his child. Once her belly swelled, he left her alone and never touched her again.

When Tama was born, Thorne acknowledged the child as

his and did as right by the girl as any white planter could. He made sure she got decent food scraps from the kitchen, two cloth dresses and a pair of shoes each year, and when he whipped her for sassing his wife or pilfering food from the kitchen, he gave her half the number of lashes that a field slave would receive. Maybe if he'd been firmer with Tama, she wouldn't have dared to escape. But she was gone, and now he had to find her and drag her back, just as he'd done with Maggie when she ran off fifteen years ago. Thorne tracked Maggie to Ohio, where she was living in squalor, thinking she was free, but he promptly put an end to that foolishness and brought her back to Royaltin Ridge. *That's probably where Tama ran, too,* Thorne decided, fully prepared to travel north and bring his bastard daughter home.

In the days that followed, Thorne posted a reward for Tama's return and sent out men to post notices across the northern counties:

> *Wanted: Runaway Mulatto Girl*
>
> *Goes by the name of Tama*
>
> *Property of Mr. Thorne Royaltin of Royaltin Ridge*
>
> *Sampson County, North Carolina.*
>
> *Twenty years-old. Light-colored skin, long black hair, violet-gray eyes.*
>
> *Five Hundred Dollars for her return - Alive and Unharmed*

In the days that followed, Thorne put his slaves to work on the construction of new cabins, hired carpenters to frame a new main house, and made plans to travel north, not only to search for Tama, but also to establish outlets for the ready-made cloth produced at the Royaltin Textile Mill.

With Old Nip's help, Thorne scavenged usable furniture from the ruins of his mansion and moved it into two rooms above the carriage house. His new living quarters were small, smelly, cramped, and dark: nothing like the luxurious dwelling to which he'd become accustomed. There were no rare oil paintings to gaze at with pride, no imported rugs to caress his feet, and no dutiful wife to sit across from him at table and listen to his account of the day. His meals came to him on a pewter tray, delivered by Old Nip, but Thorne barely touched the food. He had no appetite, did not sleep well, and suffered from headaches that lasted for days. Often, he fell into short periods of depression, countered with spells of rage when he thought of Irene and Carrie lying dead in the ground while Tama ran loose and free.

"It was arson. One of the nigras, I'm sure, set fire to the upstairs parlor, then lit the cabins to burn out the quarters." Thorne shook his head in disgust and then sank down into the chair across from March Collins, his lawyer and best friend.

"You know which one did it?" March asked.

"No, but I whipped every one of them as punishment for not telling."

"And Tama's the only one who ran?"

"That's right, but Bristo's still out after her. If he doesn't find her, I will."

"I bet so," March agreed. He cast a glance out the carriage house window and scowled at the remains of Royaltin's mansion. "I see you got men working on the house already."

"Yes," Thorne replied. "The frame is almost finished. It's going to be an exact replica of the old house." He tapped the blueprint spread out on the table between the two men. "I'm using the original plan for the house, the one my father used when he built the place sixty years ago."

March puffed on his long cigar, hooked one thumb under a wide red suspender strap pulled taut across his protruding belly, and blew a cloud of smoke toward the ceiling. "Bet it's gonna cost a hell of a lot," he cagily observed.

"I don't care how much it costs," Thorne snapped. "I've got the money, I can do what I want, you know?"

"I sure do, Thorne," March agreed, leaning forward as he fingered the bushy whiskers lining both sides of his moon-round face. "But with Irene and Carrie gone and all ... I kinda figured you might want to make do with something less ..." he paused, shrugging as he tapped ash from the tip of his cigar into a thin china bowl.

"Less grand?" Thorne finished, rising from the table. He walked to the large window and gazed at the now-barren cotton fields. Soon, field slaves would be out there preparing the fields for the upcoming planting, and he prayed the crop would be bountiful, supplying a record cotton crop to gin in his new mill. Thorne shifted his attention to the far western edge of the property and focused on the Royaltin family textile mill. His father had used mules and oxen to power the hand-operated jenny mill, producing crude yarn suitable for homespun cloth for use on the plantation. However, when Thorne took over after his father's death, he had installed a cotton-ginning machine and created a more powerful mill that more efficiently processed his cotton crop and created quality cloth for ready-made clothing.

Still staring out the window, he told March, "The cotton crop had better be a good one this year. The demand for quality canvas cloth is thriving. Can't hardly make enough to fill the merchants' demands. You know, they're selling ready-made jackets, shirts, pants, and canvas wagon covers to people traveling west. I'm hoping to get in on some of that business."

"Sounds like a good plan, Thorne. You'll do fine. You got a real head for business, can't nobody dispute that," March commented with a vigorous nod.

Thorne turned, leveling his attention on March. "Well, that's one reason I asked you to come see me today. I'm planning on going to Cincinnati, then on to St. Louis so I can visit some of those merchants who are outfitting the overlanders, and set up my accounts. While I'm away, I want you to take care of things."

"Anything to help. You been through a lot; I'll be happy to do what I can."

"Keep a close eye on my place," Thorne said, lips pursed, both hands stuck into his pants pockets. "I hired a man to replace Bristo while he's out looking for Tama. The new man's name is Orval, and he's got to keep the nigras working on the house and cleaning up the mess left from the fire. He seems a bit lax to me, so you check on him now and then, let him know I got somebody watching, and pay him at the end of the month. I wrote it all down, what he's due," Thorne finished, going to the roll top desk he'd salvaged from his burned-out library. He sat down, picked up a piece of paper, and handed it to March.

"I'll be glad to," March replied shifting in his seat as he perused the document. "But managing blacks is not something I like to do."

"You'll do fine," Thorne said, nodding as he removed a thick brown ledger from the desk's middle drawer. With a flourish he wrote a check for two thousand dollars and handed it to March Collins. "This is for your trouble. I've arranged with the bank for you to draw what you need to pay the men who'll be working on the house while I'm away."

March took the check, sank back in the deep leather chair, and let out a low breath. "You can count on me to make sure all goes well," he told Thorne with a smile of satisfaction. "When will you be leaving?"

"Taking the train out of Raleigh tomorrow. I'll be at the Stanton Hotel in Cincinnati. Send me a telegram if Bristo returns with news about Tama, you hear?"

March traced pudgy fingers over the scarred arm of the chair he was sitting in, a thoughtful expression compressing his features. "You're dead set on bringing that girl back here, aren't you?"

"Yes, I am," Thorne sternly confirmed. "She's my property." Thorne halted, his features hardened with determination.

An uneasy frown crinkled the lawyer's brow, but he nodded in understanding. "I know she's your property, but I thought you might just let her be," he remarked, his voice falling low.

"Hell, no," Thorne pointedly told the lawyer. "I don't give up anything I own that easily. You know that. And besides, she's the only person on this earth, except me, who's carrying Royaltin blood, and I aim to get her back here ...where she belongs."

* * * * *

Saddle sore and weary, Bristo tied his horse to the hitching rail in front of the isolated trading post and clomped up the wood plank steps. With one hand on the door, he paused and swept his eyes across the desolate, snow-laden landscape. The snow storm that blew in a week ago and trapped him and his men in the mountains had finally run its course, but it had left them near starving to death, frost-bitten, and grumbling about his decision to search the western mountains instead of heading north after Tama. Lucky for Bristo, he came across an abandoned cabin where he and his men took shelter from the furious storm that descended on the area.

Now, after two weeks of searching for Tama, Bristo was ready to give up and return to Royaltin Ridge, but before he did, he planned to talk to the man who ran the isolated trading post and get a lead on the runaway mulatto who seemed to have vanished.

Entering the post, Bristo was greeted by a dark-skinned man in a fur vest who pulled his clay pipe from his mouth and said, "Welcome, stranger. My name's Clyde. Come on in and warm yourself by the stove."

CHAPTER 5

Tama blew warm air into the palms of her hands, then brushed bits of dirt and leaves from the front of Clyde's jacket. The heavy coat, lined with thick lamb's wool and far too big for her, did an excellent job of keeping out the cold. The interior of the cave where she and Hakan had taken shelter was dim and damp, but the stench of cold ashes, bat guano, and rotten vegetation barely registered with Tama, who sank to the floor and leaned her head against the smoke-stained wall.

After days on the road, Tama knew the news of what she had done for the fugitive Indian had reached the Army post at Shoulderbone, and she was certain that soldiers, as well as Jonas and his posse, were aggressively looking for them. They had walked without stopping straight through long days, plodding ahead until night fell. They plunged through banks of snow that brushed their shoulders, and crossed ice-edged streams lined with tall cedar trees that threw shadows over the frozen water. Brush encased in crystallized ice snapped and crackled like shattered glass as they pushed it aside and pressed on, moving away from mountains in the east and away from the weak winter sun.

Tama's leather boots, soaked through and muddy, felt like weights attached to her ankles, and the wet lower half of her woolen dress increased the load she had to carry as she struggled to keep up with Hakan. Now, she drew her knees up to her chest and spread her dress out around her, desperate to keep the damp fabric off her legs. Her limbs ached, her head throbbed, and her stomach contracted in hunger.

"Can we have a fire?" she asked Hakan.

"A small one," he replied, carefully examining the dark corners and slippery walls of the cave, picking up twigs and brush to burn. "No one has camped here for many moons," he decided, turning back to look at Tama. "It's safe enough ... for one night."

While Hakan made the fire, Tama removed her shawl from her head and unwound her thick braids, which were as soaking wet as the hem of her dress. With quick movements, she separated the twists in her plaited hair and finger-combed her tresses, creating a cascade of coal black curls around her face. She thought about the days that lay ahead: the arduous trek, the ice-cold rain, damp clothing, hiding in caves, eating whatever they could glean from the harsh winter landscape. However, despite the daunting aspects of the journey, for the first time in her life she felt a raw, and unfamiliar, sense of hope.

Tama's life at Royaltin Ridge had been a forced grind of hard work and mind-dulling routine carried out in subdued resentment. The rigid nature of slavery had lulled her into a muted life devoid of expectation, a listless existence robbed of joy. Now, her mother was dead, and she was on the run with an Indian who barely tolerated her presence. She'd been brave enough, or perhaps desperate enough, to follow him on this dangerous journey, and as miserable as the trek might become, she did not regret her decision. A world of unknowns had opened up before her, providing a chance for a different kind of life.

Tama pushed her hair off her face and leaned toward the flickering fire that Hakan had coaxed into flame. She removed the pouch of food from beneath her coat and set out half a dried apple and the last two strips of stiff meat. Tama broke off a chunk of fruit when Hakan came closer and squatted by the fire. He accepted the food without comment.

"Do you think the soldiers are close by?" she asked.

Hakan answered her with a guttural noise from deep within his throat.

"What if the bounty hunters catch up with us?" Tama pressed.

Hakan chewed the apple in thought, then cast aside her worried remark with a dismissive gesture of one hand. "No one will find us," he finally said. "Not the soldiers who hunt me or the white man who is looking for you."

Tama flinched but held back for a time before saying, "How do you know a white man is looking for me?"

"Why else would a half-breed woman like you hide in the mountains? You wear the heavy boots and rough cloth of the runaways who come to my people's village seeking refuge. Your skin is not dark, and your eyes are light, but you are the property of a white man, I know."

"It's true," Tama acknowledged, surprised that Hakan had actually conveyed his thoughts to her and had used more than two words to do so. "I ran off a cotton plantation on the other side of the mountains. There was a fire. The mistress, her daughter, and many slaves burned to death. Among them ... my mother. While the fire was burning, I ran."

The corners of Hakan's mouth turned down in understanding and he lifted a shoulder to indicate acknowledgement of her confession. "Then, as I said, your master is searching for you."

Tama bit her lip, visualizing Thorne Royaltin's face when he realized she was not among the living or the dead. Had Bristo and his dogs gone north, looking for her? Did Master

Thorne assume she'd taken the same route to freedom that her mother had traveled, only to be brought back in chains? "Let him search," she told Hakan. "I won't go back there. Ever."

"If you stay among my people, you will be safe," Hakan stated with assurance.

"You sound very certain of that."

"I am," Hakan replied, stuffing a piece of dried meat into his mouth. "Many runaways like you live among us. We hide them when the bounty hunters come around asking questions. My family will treat you as one of us."

Tama wanted to take his words of assurance to heart even though she knew how vulnerable she was. At least he hadn't abandoned her along the trail, and for that, she was extremely grateful, and for the first time since beginning their journey, he seemed to be paying real attention to her plight.

Hakan silently worked his jaw, as if churning thoughts in his mind. "Your people are not so different from mine," he finally stated. "We also suffer greatly, enduring pain inflicted by men who seek power over us."

Tama regarded Hakan thoughtfully, impressed by how intelligent and informed he seemed to be. He understood, better than she did, the circumstances of the world they lived in and used clever words to express himself. "Tell me about your village," she remarked, wanting to keep him talking now that he had opened up, hoping to form a picture in her mind of the safe haven he called home.

Hakan moved to the far side of the cave, sat down, removed his wet moccasins and placed them close to the fire. "My *talwa* is on the Tallapoosa River. We call it Great Oaks. There, my mother, my father, and my sister live. We are the Fox, the people of my mother's clan. My father is *mico* of our *talwa*."

"*Mico*.... you mean, the chief of your village?" Tama clarified.

"Yes. My people are Muscogule Creek... among few still living on the river."

"Why were you so far from your village?"

"To hunt."

"But why did the soldiers take you?"

"They said I was trespassing." He paused. "But I was hunting on land where the Creek, and the Cherokee, have hunted for many seasons. The white men say they own the land now and no Indians are permitted to hunt there." Tilting back his head, Hakan stared at the cave wall above Tama's head. "Instead of asking for money, as is the custom for trespassing, the soldier tied my hands and put me in the stockade at Shoulderbone, where I stayed for ten days, waiting to be hanged."

"Hanged? For hunting on their land?"

"Yes. To show my people what happens when the white man's laws are broken."

"But you escaped," Tama whispered, leaning forward.

"Yes, I used a piece of metal to cut the ropes binding my hands. When the soldier tried to stop me from running away, I slashed his arm with it, that is true, but I did not try to kill him. I only wanted to get away."

The fire hissed and crackled, sending ragged plumes of smoke to the roof of the cave as Hakan continued talking. "Strangers build fences and put log cabins on our land, too close to our village. They protect their homes with vicious dogs and long smoking rifles while the Creek are driven into the swamps to live and forage for food like animals." He stopped talking long enough to add a handful of brush to the fire, and then he continued.

"How did this happen?" Tama wanted to know.

"My people signed a treaty with the government long ago to give the white man part of our land ... what remained was divided among the families of the Creek. But the government did not protect my people from evil men who cheated the *micos* and pushed them aside. The Creek were angry, and hungry, so they stole livestock and crops from the intruders. Some even started fires and killed white people in retaliation. That is why the President ordered the Creek to get off the land and go west."

Hakan's words settled in Tama's mind like pieces of a puzzle that finally fit together. Now, her understanding of the Indians' situation was not so faint and incomplete. The white planters who'd visited Master Thorne at Royaltin Ridge had regularly discussed the Indian problem. They talked about sending all of the Indians to a place far away, of taking land that they wanted for themselves. When she'd asked her mother what it all meant, Maggie had told Tama, 'We ain't got time to think on what happens to the red men, it's the black men we gotta worry about.'

"So your people are still there?" Tama ventured, testing her knowledge of the issue.

"Yes," Hakan stated in a low, resentful tone. "My clan refuses to abandon our *talwa*. Our home is on good land; you will see why the white men want it. "

Tama remained silent, sensing Hakan's distress over what was happening to his people. Their suffering at the hands of whites was different from the evils that slaves endured, but it was no less devastating to their lives and their culture. "Perhaps the land in the West is nicer than where your people live now," Tama offered, wanting to express her sympathy.

"The government could never find a place as beautiful as Great Oaks. The resettlement land is hard and rocky, without tall pines or rich black soil. The clear waters of the Tallapoosa River have always provided fish and beaver and turtle to feed every Muscogule living along its banks, but now trappers, hunters, and land-poor whites take more than they need, forcing our men to roam farther and farther away to feed our families. "

Tama remained silent as Hakan expressed feelings that he had, most likely, never revealed to anyone outside of his tribe. His anger was raw, his resistance to relocation was firm, and his love for the Fox was deep and unwavering. There was nothing that Tama could say to make him feel less bitter, but perhaps her willingness to listen made his resentment easier to bear.

Hakan remained by the fire as Tama slept. Owls hooted in the branches of the dark cedar trees outside and the wild wind echoed across the entrance of the cave. Tautly alert, he studied Tama's sleeping form, considering his traveling companion. Until their conversation tonight, he had not thought much of the strange slave girl with dark hair and light eyes who walked with him, but after traveling this far together, he decided it was good to have her company. She was brave, strong, and set on living free. He had spoken more words to this girl than to any woman in his life, and she had paid attention to every word he said. She was easy to talk to and very different from the women of his clan, who remained quiet and did not talk about the affairs of men. Fox women were content to allow the decisions of others to control their fates, but Tama was different. She was not fearful or weak, neither boastful nor shy. She ran away from her master, knowing her fate if caught. And her unusual beauty was intriguing.

Hakan flattened his back against the cold cave wall and quietly pressed his body into the curve of the stone. This girl had saved his life. She was his responsibility now, so he had no choice but to protect her once they arrived at Great Oaks. There, she would be safe among the Muscogule Creek. He owed her that much, didn't he?

* * * * *

They arrived at the Coosa River three days later and pushed across the hard icy shell with their heads bent against the wind, their hands buried deep inside their clothing. Once they were safely on the other side, the thick brush that crowded the riverbank provided sufficient shelter from the wind to stop and rest. Hakan made a spear from a tree branch, punched a hole in the ice and set about catching fish to cook while Tama gathered twigs to make a fire. In a matter of minutes, Hakan presented her with two large trout, which she cleaned and placed on stakes to roast above the flame.

As they ate, Tama asked Hakan to tell her more about his village and his clan, and he was silently pleased that she wanted to know more. Talking to her brought him a great sense of relief, as if telling his thoughts to this girl opened a part of his soul that had been trapped in silence too long.

After eating, they covered the fire with dirt and started off again. They had not gone far when Hakan took Tama by the arm and pulled her off the road. He held up a hand, palm forward, and then whispered, "Stay back. Someone is coming."

Tama slipped into the shadows but kept her attention on the road. Soon, a man driving a wagon filled with Indian women and children appeared.

After a few uneasy seconds, Hakan told Tama, "I have seen this man before. He carries Indians for the government. He calls himself a friend to us, but I don't trust him." Quickly, Hakan stepped onto the road and forced the driver of the wagon to bring his mule to a halt.

Tama shrank back, curious and unsure. She looked into the faces of the women and children who were huddled together in silence in the cart, recognizing the raw fear radiating from their eyes. Their ragged clothing and smoke-stained bodies told the story of their plight.

The wagon driver, who might have been handsome when he was younger and leaner and had less hair on his face, nodded brusquely at Hakan, then hunched forward and scratched his chin, which was barely visible beneath a wiry red-blonde beard. He pushed back the brim of his weathered cowhide hat.

"What're you doing out here? This is private land," he demanded of Hakan.

"I'm going to Great Oaks," Hakan answered in a strong, sure voice.

"And the gal what's hidin' in the brush? Who's she belong to?" the man pressed, turning hard eyes on the spot where Tama was slowly emerging from her hiding place.

"Just a zambo from my talwa," Hakan lied.

"What're you two doin' so far from your village?" The

driver shifted in his seat, as if to ease a sore backside; then he pulled off his dusty hat and wiped his forehead with the back of his hand. He kept his eyes trained on Tama, moving his gaze slowly from her head to her feet.

"Hunting rabbit and fishing for trout," Hakan blithely replied. "We're going to trade the food at Cave Spring for beaver pelts."

"Well, ain't no use going over there. Cave Spring been burned out. Only these here women and children are left, and I'm takin' 'em up to Fort Oglethorpe, turn 'em over to the Army."

Tama flinched, drew in a short breath, and held it in her lungs as the man went on.

"Ain't nuthin left a Cave Spring but a pile o' ashes, so I'm warnin' you and this zambo gal ta move on. I ain't saying something's gonna happen if you stick around here, but I can't protect you. The injuns at Cave Spring were stealing cattle, pilfering food. Generally makin' trouble. Folks 'round here got all riled up and burned 'em out. Best if you clear out, too."

Hakan grimaced in disgust. "If the Indians at Cave Spring stole food or cattle, it was because the locals starved them off their land. They have to eat, too."

"Maybe, but the law gives the government the right to regulate all the land 'round here. You two git going before more trouble starts." Jerking his chin, the man jammed his hat onto his head, slapped the reins against the backside of his mule, and rumbled up the road.

"Hakan, what will happen to those women and children?" Tama asked as soon as the wagon disappeared behind a thick drape of Spanish moss.

"He will dump them on barges and float them down river

or force them to walk to the new homeland."

Tama glanced up and down the road, as if expecting to see soldiers carrying rifles thundering toward her; she saw nothing but wagon tracks in the dusting of snow that settled over the trail. "Do you think the men who burned Cave Spring will do the same to your village?" she asked.

"I hope not," Hakan answered as he leaned into the wind and paced ahead. "The people of my talwa will not be herded like cattle onto small, dry pieces of land to make new homes out of nothing."

Lifting his chin, he threw back his head, and his hair, loose from its braid and flying free, drifted up from his back and floated on the stiff wind that rushed over them. To Tama, he looked as if he represented every proud Creek Indian who had ever lived on the Tallapoosa River, and she knew he would never walk on any other land with the same expression on his face.

When night fell, they stopped to make camp beneath a rocky overhang above the river that protected them from the relentless winter chill. Tama's boots felt like blocks of ice on her feet, and she could not stop her body from shaking. Sinking down by the fire that Hakan coaxed from a tiny flame, she wrapped her arms around her waist and rocked back and forth.

Hakan watched Tama for a moment, then shook out his bearskin cape and spread it over her legs, and she looked up at him in surprise. After an unspoken moment of gratitude passed between them, Hakan moved to the far side of the campsite and sat down in the shadows, and pulled the red striped horse blanket over his body.

Tama clutched Hakan's warm fur cape and stared up at

the stars in the crisp night sky until, finally, her body stopped shivering. "I *am* warmer now. Thank you," she called over to Hakan, feeling obligated to express her appreciation. She had never spent this much time alone with any man, and the sensation of his nearness, of his stoic care for her, was strange, disquieting, yet comforting.

Lying there, her thoughts flitted back to the encounter with the man who'd been driving the wagon, the exchange still sharp in her mind. "Why did that man call me a zambo?" she asked Hakan.

"A zambo is a black person who carries Indian blood or lives as an Indian."

"How many zambos are at Great Oaks?"

"A good number."

"Are they slaves ... or free?"

"Some are slaves ... who belong to the elders. Others are free. But they all do chores and work the land."

"If I stay among your people, will I be free or a slave?" Tama wanted to know.

"The mico will decide," Hakan replied.

Tama could hear him shifting in the dark, before he added, "The mico of the Fox is my father. I will tell him what you did for me, and ask him not to give you as a slave to one of the elders."

"He will do that?" she asked, suddenly frightened by the uncertainty of her situation.

"Yes. To repay you for helping me," Hakan stated with certainty.

Tama pulled Hakan's fur cape up to her chin, shaken by

the possibility of being a slave again, this time among the Indians. However, she had no choice but to stick with Hakan and trust him to protect her. Breathing in the damp, woodsy scent of the river, she watched the fire flames dancing over Hakan's strong, silent face until she fell asleep.

* * * * *

At first, March Collins did not recognize the heavily bearded, wild-haired man who entered his office and spoke to him. Setting aside the stack of legal papers he was checking for a client, March looked at the travel-weary man more closely, and then stood up and called out, "Mr. Bristo!" He removed his wire rim spectacles and placed them on the pile of papers. "I see you have returned."

"Just this morning. Went to the house. Orval told me you're taking care of Royaltin's affairs."

"That's correct. Mr. Royaltin is traveling. What news do you have regarding Mr. Royaltin's runaway slave?"

Bristo removed his hat and slapped it against his thigh. "I got a good idea where she might be," he announced, moving to stand in front of March Collin's desk. "She took off with a Creek Indian. Heard it from a trader at a post in Gap Springs, west of the Ocee Mountains."

"West?" March pressed his teeth into his lips, concerned. "Oh ... well. Mr. Royaltin was certain she would go north."

"Well, she didn't," Bristo countered. "The trader said he met a gal what looked just like Tama, and he knows the Indian, too. Says they ran off together. Quite a tale he told, but I believe he's telling the truth. I gave him a ten dollar gold piece to talk."

"Where're they headed?" March wanted to know.

"Most likely to the injun's village. Down along the Tallapoosa."

"Why did you turn back?" March snapped, not liking what he was hearing. "Why didn't you go after her and bring her here?"

"The snow's too heavy in the mountains right now. Besides, the men and the dogs were near to mutiny, so I decided to come on in and tell Royaltin what I know. In a few days, I'll get supplied, start out again ... and this time I'll track til I get her."

March bit his bottom lip and scratched his cheek, considering Bristo's news. "No, it's best you stay put," he decided. "Wait until I send a telegram to Mr. Royaltin and find out what he wants you to do."

Chapter 6

Great Oaks, one of the few Muscogule talwas remaining in Haralson County, Georgia, spread along the banks of the Tallapoosa River in clusters of sturdy square chickees. The huts, constructed of woven reeds plastered with mud had conical roofs made of bark. The village backed up to a dense forest of maple, pine, cypress, and birch trees that marched up the vine-covered sides of a flat-topped mound. The expansive talwa served as the gathering spot for smaller Muscogule tribes living along the river, who visited Great Oaks for communal celebrations and important gatherings at the Creek's main council house. There, the elders discussed, pondered, and decided issues of importance as they adapted to life among white settlers who pushed closer every day.

The fenced village held fine stock of cattle, horses and hogs, surrounded by fields of corn, rice and potatoes. It was home to over two hundred people, with each family unit maintaining a compound of four rectangular *chickees* that faced a central log fire. All of the structures had wooden, pole frames and bark roofs. The walls were interwoven branches or reeds plastered with mud, and there was a storehouse for holding and preparing food, as well as an open-sided warehouse where blankets, pelts and other necessary supplies were kept.

As word spread through Great Oaks that Mico Blue Waters' son had returned from his journey to the east, members of the Fox clan gravitated to Hakan's family compound, eager to hear news of what was happening on the other side of the great mountains. Tama was surprised to see such a large number of blacks living among the Fox, including many who were clearly mixed-race zambos. Some of the black Creek spoke Muscogule, while others spoke English, or a muddled patois of several languages. A large number of the black Fox dressed in white man's clothing, while others wore traditional Indian attire of deerskin, rough cloth, and fur, and their faces were many shades of brown and black.

The members of Hakan's clan welcomed him with loud cries of relief and boisterous congratulations that he had successfully evaded capture by the soldiers. They looked cautiously at Hakan when an elderly woman with ruddy brown skin and dull black hair streaked with gray stepped forward and planted herself in front of Tama.

"I am Spring Sky, Hakan's mother," the woman said, raking disapproving eyes over Tama's wet, ragged skirt, and boots so covered with mud they no longer had a shape. Tama's thick black hair was matted with chunks of dirt and dry leaves, and her buff-colored skin was blistered from exposure to the harsh winter weather.

"Who is this girl you bring to us? Your slave?" Spring Sky asked, now addressing her son.

"This is Tama, and she is not my slave," Hakan informed his mother, who inched forward to examine the stranger more closely. "If Mico Blue Waters agrees, she will live with us as a free woman and share what we have."

Spring Sky shrugged, making a dismissive gesture with one hand. "My son, if that is what you wish, I respect your decision. But this girl's skin is not dark, though her hair is thick and wavy. She has the blood of the white man, yes?"

Hakan glanced at Tama, who nodded, acknowledging Spring Sky's observation, then lowered her eyes to stare at the ground.

"Yes, that is true," Hakan agreed. "But she is very brave."

Spring Sky lifted her small shoulders, tilted her head to one side, and blinked her flat round eyes, tightening the skin at the corners of her mouth. Adopting a blank expression, she listened as Hakan explained how Tama saved him from certain hanging. When he finished his tale, Spring Sky acknowledged Tama's bravery with a solemn incline of her head and then said, "My son has returned. That is all that matters." Then she spoke to an ebony-complexioned, bird-like woman wearing a head-wrap of thick gray cotton. "Three Winds, take the girl into the sleeping room. Give her water for washing and dry clothing. Make a bed for her so she can rest."

Hakan watched as Three Winds, an elderly zambo who had lived among the Creek for as long as Hakan could remember, led Tama inside his family's second hut, feeling both relieved and proud that Tama had managed the difficult journey so well. They had traveled for many difficult days, from new moon to new moon, covering miles of frozen terrain. She never once complained about the harsh trek, the fast pace he set, or the empty growl of her stomach. Hakan admired Tama's strength, respected her decision to live free, and was surprised by the ease with which he communicated with her. In many ways they were different, yet also alike. Their sense of togetherness on the road created a flux of emotions in Hakan that he did not dislike or want to go away.

"What about Cave Spring?" asked a young man wearing a tall black hat with red feathers sprouting from the side, interrupting Hakan's thoughts of Tama. "Is it true? Everyone is gone? The village burned?"

"Yes, there's nothing left but scarred earth and black

grass," Hakan replied, going on to tell the people about his encounter with the man driving the wagon. "He said he was taking them to Fort Oglethorpe, but I think he will put them on a flatboat and send them up the big river to the new Indian homeland."

Murmurs of disappointment and words of caution slipped from the tongues of those crowded around Hakan. As the people began to disperse and return to their work, Spring Sky led her son away from the gathering and stood with him in front of the log fire that smoldered outside their family's main chickee.

"Where is Suja? And father?" Hakan wanted to know, glancing around the compound.

"Your sister is at the river, gathering wood, and your father is in the council house."

"The council house? Why? Is there a clan meeting today?"

"No. He is alone. Preparing," Spring Sky replied.

"Preparing for what?" Hakan wanted to know, thinking his mother sounded worried.

"Mico Blue Waters is not well ... his time is short," Spring Sky informed her son. "He prepares for a meeting of the elders. The future of the Fox weighs heavy on your father and he has much to settle before he slips away from us and joins the ancestors in the spirit world."

Hakan grimaced, squinting toward the thatch roof rotunda in the center of the village. The building, which was the heart of the talwa, soared high above all others, signaling its importance to the Muscogule Creek. Hakan's chest grew tight and his body tensed to hear his mother's prediction. His father was the oldest male member of the Fox clan, and had served as its leader, teacher, and counselor for many years.

When he passed, Hakan would take on his father's duties, as was the custom in his talwa. For many years, Hakan had sat by his father's side in the council house, where the totem of the upright red fox stood guard at the entry. He had listened to the Mico of Great Oaks conduct discussions with the white men who wanted his people to go away. He had heard his father engage in talks about treaties, decide punishment for disputes within the talwa, and give advice to those who sought it. Mico Blue Waters' responsibilities were heavy, making Hakan pray that when his father was gone and the burdens of the Fox shifted onto his shoulders he would be strong enough to carry them.

"Your father sent word to the clans downriver to come to Great Oaks," Spring Sky continued. "The Wolf, the Bear, and the Turtle must talk, make decisions about the settlers who move closer every day. As you will see, our lands shrink before our eyes."

Hakan inclined his head, knowing how important the council meeting would be, how vital it was for the clan to hold firmly onto what was theirs. The traditions of the Muscogule Creek must hold firm in this time of change and loss, and Hakan understood why his father, in spite of the dark cloud that hovered over him, had called the clans together. "The meeting of the elders is not the only reason the clans up river are coming here," Spring Sky added. "Your father wishes to hold the Red Tail dance."

"Now?" Hakan questioned. "So early before the harvest?"

"Yes, he fears he may not live to see the leaves turn and fall from the trees, or watch as corn is reaped from the fields." Turning thoughtful eyes onto her son, Spring Sky went on. "Soon you will sit in your father's place at the council, so you know what the Red Tail dance will mean."

With a solemn nod, Hakan answered, "Yes, and I am ready."

"Good. I know you will choose wisely."

"I will. But now, I must wash and dress before I talk with father," Hakan told his mother. "I don't want him to see me like this."

Tama awoke with a start, disoriented and unsure, but she remained snuggled in the warm nest of pelts that Three Winds prepared for her. After washing the travel-dirt from her body and putting on the clean clothes given to her, she'd fallen asleep immediately. Now, pale sunlight seeped through jagged cracks in the mud plastered walls, telling Tama that she had slept into the next day. Looking around, she examined the woven grass rug covering the floor and the brightly colored blankets piled in a corner. A clay jar for water and a stack of wooden bowls sat on a shelf near the door, along with an assortment of simple, utilitarian objects necessary for daily life. An unusually pretty shell-encrusted mirror hanging from a peg on the wall brightened the plain decor.

Tama raised her arms, pushed back her hair, and stretched. She was about to get up when a young woman entered the room and took the mirror from the wall. She held it up in front of her face, ignoring Tama completely as she patted her jet-black hair, piled high atop her head in a single coil, secured with two tortoise shell combs. Her plum-colored dress brushed the tops of beaded moccasins and her rough brown cape had long tassels at the back that resembled the tails of a fox. The young woman shared Hakan's rich bronze coloring, had the same keen nose, but her almond shaped eyes were slightly hooded, making her face appear less friendly than his.

She suddenly turned with a flourish, swinging her plum-colored skirt in a swirl, lowered the mirror, and walked over to Tama. She examined the newcomer with a wary expression, not hiding her distaste of the stranger now residing in her family's chickee.

"Are you Tama?" she demanded.

Tama blinked; then swallowed. "Yes, I arrived yesterday with Hakan," Tama answered, sitting up and leaning forward.

"I heard about you. I'm Hakan's sister, Suja."

"I thought so."

"Where are you from?" Suja demanded in a voice that was hard-edged and flat.

"A cotton plantation on the other side of the big mountains. Far away from here," Tama stated, locking eyes with Suja as she raised her chin in anticipation of the next question, not surprised by the interrogation.

"Why did you leave your people?"

"I wasn't happy living there," Tama hedged, not wanting to discuss her life as a slave.

"Hump. You may not be happy here, either," Suja muttered, turning away to flounce out the door.

A flutter of unease rippled through Tama, who rose and shook out the dress Three Winds had given her to wear. The sting of Suja's resentment seeped into Tama's bones. How long would it be before she and Hakan's sister locked horns? Tama wondered, because surely it was going to happen.

The sun was high in the sky when Tama found Hakan sitting with his mother and sister at a long wooden table inside the main chickee. When Hakan motioned for her to sit opposite him, she did so, while wondering what Hakan's father had decided about her fate. Hakan had washed and changed from his travel-worn clothes and was wearing a white wool shirt under a rabbit fur vest, with sturdy black woolen pants. Tama watched as he turned to speak to his mother, his profile as sharp and masculine as the blade of the knife tied at his waist, and she realized that he had little concern or understanding of how handsome he looked with his hair knotted in a single braid that hit mid-waist, entwined with feathers and thin cords of leather.

Tama sat across from Hakan, who looked up at her and smiled ... the first time Tama had ever seen him smile. "You are free to live with my family," he informed Tama, and then he glanced away, his smile vanishing as he looked toward his sister, who handed him a bowl of roasted venison and winter squash.

Tama inclined her head but did not speak, relieved to know she would remain free, and would live with Hakan's family. They ate in silence, scooping the hot meat and vegetables from their bowls with short wooden spoons while the log fire outside hissed and blazed in the bright winter sunlight. When they finished eating, Three Winds removed the bowls from the table and took them outside to wash in the pot of water that was always at the fire. Wanting to prove to Hakan that she was willing to do her share of the work, Tama got up and followed the old woman outside, leaving Hakan alone with his mother and his sister, even though she could hear them talking as she helped clean the bowls.

"Suja, Tama will stay in the chickee with you and

mother," Hakan informed his sister.

"Why?" Suja snapped. "She can sleep outside, at the fire. No nigra girl is going to share my hut."

"She will sleep inside," Hakan firmly told his sister, putting an end to the matter.

"Why do we have to treat her so well?" Suja asked.

"Because she helped your brother get away from men who planned to hang him," Spring Sky interjected.

"That's right," Hakan added. "Tama held a knife on the man who locked me up and forced him to release me," he finished, sounding proud of what Tama had done.

"She was stupid ... not so brave to do that," Suja spoke up.

"She did what was right," Hakan shot back, annoyed by his sister's rejection of Tama.

"I don't understand why," Suja spouted, piercing Tama's heart with the sharpness of her words. "She is not Indian. Her skin may be light, but she is an African slave. A runaway. Why was she so interested in helping you?"

Tama stopped scrubbing a bowl and pulled her shoulders back, sensing Suja's desire to pick a fight.

"Because she knew I would be hanged for defending myself, and it wasn't right," Hakan replied, deflecting Suja's attack. "She took a great risk for me, and she has no home, so I brought her here, where I hope she will be welcome."

Suja remained quiet, but after a few minutes, she burst from the hut, stomped past Tama, and disappeared into the maze of chickees spread along the riverbank.

Tama listened as Hakan launched into a discussion with his mother about the livestock and the state of the talwa.

Listening to their conversation, Tama thought about her mother, lying still and defeated on the cabin floor. At least Tama was free and protected by the Creek. For many days, putting as much distance as possible between herself and Thorne Royaltin had occupied her mind, burying the ache of losing her mother, which now rose in her heart and filled her soul. Tama quickly pushed the pain aside, determined not to break down and show her grief, weakening her position as a free woman. So much had happened so quickly: Maggie's death, hiding in the cabin in the mountains, trekking with Hakan to this Indian village where she felt tolerably safe at last. Though Tama missed her mother terribly, she knew Maggie was looking down on her and was pleased to know that her daughter had found a place where she was welcome, and where she would no longer fear the wrath of their master. Great Oaks was now her home, a shelter from the cruel and stormy life she had endured at Royaltin Ridge. And now, with all of her connections to the past completely severed, she prayed that this place would provide the sense of belonging that she craved, despite the sting of Suja's jealous eyes and the words that flew from the girl's bitter tongue.

The weeks slipped past. Tama worked hard to adapt to life among the Creek. She replaced her hard, misshapen boots with soft deerskin moccasins, and exchanged her coarse cotton clothing for the ruffled skirts and deerskin dresses that the Indian women wore. She grew closer to Spring Sky, and found Mico Blue Waters to be a fragile old man with wrinkled brown skin and cloudy black eyes who, whenever their paths crossed, bowed his head to her in appreciation for what she had done for his son. The Mico was a serious man who rarely came into the family's main compound. He preferred to stay among the men, consumed with preparing for the upcoming council meeting.

Hakan stayed with his father after his return to Great Oaks in a large, thatched roof structure located on the opposite side of the family's log fire, completely separate from the women's quarters. He slept on a mat beside his ailing father, whose health was rapidly deteriorating, and spent most of his time out hunting for game or inside the council house, discussing affairs of the talwa with the elders.

Suja, who remained haughty and difficult, spent most of her time nagging Tama to take on more chores, often fueling division among the other women by making unflattering remarks about the newest member of the clan. She referred to Tama as a lazy half-breed zambo who had no right to live at Great Oak, an intruder who was not welcome.

Ignoring Suja's jealous attacks, Tama worked alongside Three Winds, who took the time to show Tama how to pound corn properly with a mortar, repair a tear in a piece of deerskin, and dig a pit to roast a pig. Tama drew closer to Spring Sky as well and enjoyed going off with Hakan's mother to check the family's beaver traps, or walk up and down the riverbank, spending long hours without talking. She spent her days chopping wood, cleaning and repairing the chickees, cooking meals, skinning animals, and tending the family livestock. Tama took on any chore assigned to her without complaint, her trust and respect for the women of the talwa deepening as they shared the mundane work of feeding their families and maintaining their household units. She did not want Hakan to regret bringing her into his village, and she eagerly tackled whatever Three Winds or Spring Sky asked of her. The hard work took her mind off the uncertainty of her future, and she slowly convinced herself that Bristo and his slave hunting dogs would never find her so far away from Royaltin Ridge.

When winter faded and the first sunny day of late March arrived, Tama went to the sheltered pool at the river where the women customarily bathed. The sun had finally turned the pool of water tolerably warm, and she relished the cool sting as it cleansed away the smoky film of winter fires that clung to everything in the talwa. When she stepped out of the water, her thin cotton under-dress was dripping wet and her black hair was clinging to her head. Standing in a shaft of sunlight as she dried off, she looked up and saw Hakan at the river. He was holding a brace of possum, drinking in the sight of her with such a pointed gaze that Tama shivered under the warmth of the sun. His expression told her that he wanted more than friendship, that he was willing to give her more than gratitude for saving his life. Though unsettled by his intense gaze, Tama was pleased he would look at her that way.

Tama stood completely still and watched as Hakan placed the possum on top of a big tree stump at the water's edge, where the men of the village cleaned fish and dressed game. She did not move when he began walking toward her, moving slowly, the damp earth squeaking as his footsteps crunched the wet river grass, her own breath low in her ears. He had a determined set to his face, a powerful force in his stride. And when he came within an arm's length of her, he simply reached out, placed one hand on her shoulder, the other at her waist, and stared at her face as if seeing it for the first time.

Tama's throat closed. She gulped, but her tongue stuck to

the roof of her mouth as she tried to speak. His hand tightened at her waist, then slipped into the curve of her back, making every bone in her body go as soft and warm as the clover honey that Spring Sky kept in a clay pot next to the hearth. She could easily break free of his grip and run away, and he certainly would not pursue her. But that was not what she wanted to do. She wanted to feel his hands on her, test the depth of his concern and caring, which was all he'd ever professed to feel. Tama leaned away from Hakan, let her body go slack, and waited for him to make the move she silently hoped he would initiate.

He did not disappoint her. With a tug, he pulled her close and pressed his mouth to hers. Tama stilled in his arms, allowing the force of his intentions to find its own momentum. He squeezed her upper arms with both hands, pushed her, almost roughly, toward the ground, and crouched down with her onto the wet grass without ever removing his lips from hers. He capped her knee with strong fingers and moved her leg to the side before settling his body on top of hers. Tama did not resist when he loosened the ties at the front of her wet shift, but she watched his face evolve into a shadowy blur of urgent concentration as he yanked each cotton lace, one by one. Her bare breasts were suddenly his, and she moaned to feel his fingers ripple over them. Heat pulsed through her body, folding into a hot insistent core that burned in the bottom of her stomach. She felt totally disconnected from what was happening, all reasoning vanquished from her mind.

"There you are!" A voice above them shattered the encounter.

Tama pushed Hakan away and hurried to re-tie the bodice of her shift, desperate to hide her naked chest.

"Suja!" Hakan shouted, jumping to his feet.

"You dirty zambo! Get back to the fire and help mother tend the meat," Suja ordered, marching closer, hands on her hips. Hakan gave his sister a calm, but pointed, stare, and then turned his back on her, walked to the tree stump where he'd dropped the brace of possum, and began to skin the animals, as if she were not standing there glaring at him.

Tama dressed quickly and fled back toward the village not daring to glance at Suja as she raced passed the girl. However, she clearly heard Suja's angry voice yelling at her brother when she told him, "Stay away from her! Leave that black slave girl alone or you will regret the day you brought her here!"

Tears stung Tama's eyes and worry clogged her mind. How long had Suja been watching her and Hakan? How far would she go to make sure they stayed apart?

Chapter 7

Elinore

Cincinnati, Ohio
March 24, 1855

Captain Paul Wardlaw
Fort Gibson,
Indian Territory

Dear Paul:

Tomorrow I board the Belle Ohio and leave Cincinnati to begin my journey to be with you. After so long a separation, I can hardly contain my excitement over seeing you again. Little Ben has grown so much, and he looks more and more like his father every day, with your same yellow hair and bright blue eyes. Though he is not yet three years-old, he is my precious little man who gives me no trouble.

I am well prepared for the journey. Against mother's protests, I sewed a pair of sturdy canvas trousers to wear on the overland leg of the trip. All vanity aside, I know comfort and practicality will far outweigh fashion where I am going. I made Ben the cutest rabbit fur leggings with a matching jacket, and added a fox fur collar to the cape of my wool overcoat, so we will be warm aboard ship and on the trail. As you instructed, I also purchased a pair of sturdy leather boots with thick soles and high tops for walking.

When I reach St. Louis, Ben and I will stay with mother's cousin, Vera Findlay. I expect to remain with her for several days until the wagon train is ready to pull out. I received a letter of confirmation from Mr. Lester, the wagon master, who advised me that we will travel to Fort Leavenworth with a larger group heading to California; then our wagon will break off and go south across the Cherokee Strip, then into Indian Territory. I hope nothing delays our departure, as I am very anxious to be on my way to you. I will write again, after my arrival in St. Louis. From what I have read in the newspapers, it seems as if the Indian Removal has become even more controversial. I know that you have a difficult job to do. Maintaining order and expediting the government's policies is not easy, as I hear many of the Indians bitterly oppose what you are doing. Please be careful. In such an emotionally unsettled atmosphere, considerable restraint is required, and the welfare of the Native Americans must be of uppermost importance.

Though it's nearly April, the weather here is still gloomy. Much sleet and bone-chilling rain prevail. However, I have been assured that the Ohio River is passable and our trip by steamer to St. Louis should be without incident.

Your loving wife,

Elinore

Elinore Wardlaw prepared the letter for posting at the telegraph office and placed it in her leather traveling valise, along with her steamboat tickets, two thousand dollars in cash, the keepsake photo album her mother gave her to take along, and the pearl handled pistol that had been a sixteenth-birthday gift from her father. Elinore also owned an old Winchester hunting rifle she had used for hunting rabbit and quail with her father when he was alive, but she'd decided to leave it behind with her widowed mother and purchase a decent rifle in St. Louis.

A sense of nervous anticipation shimmered through

63

Elinore. Tomorrow, she would leave the house she had called home for twenty-five years and start her journey into unknown territory. Her emotions shifted between sadness over leaving her mother, who was not happy that her only daughter and grandson would be living in hostile, scarcely settled land, and excitement over finally becoming a proper wife to Paul.

Elinore was a slim, blonde, green-eyed young woman who, once she made up her mind to do something could rarely be dissuaded. Though attractive and feminine, in a delicate, china-doll manner, her father had often described her as the son he didn't have, calling his daughter too curious and brash for her own good. She could hunt, fish, ride and shoot as well as any young man in Hamilton County, and she had won her share of blue ribbons for marksmanship at the county fair. As a young girl, she had preferred to play stickball with the boys to practicing the piano, and she enjoyed fishing in the river more than stitching a silly sampler. So it should not have surprised her mother or her friends when she decided to go west, referring to the move as the grandest adventure of her life.

Snapping her valise closed, Elinore glanced around the spacious, well-appointed room. *I will miss this house, my mother, and all of my friends I leave behind,* she mused, studying the star and circle patterned quilt on her bed, for which her mother had won first prize at the Hamilton County fair. Moving to one of the floor to ceiling windows that faced the farmland surrounding the house, Elinore gazed out over the wintery landscape of the apple orchard, thinking how beautiful it would look in just a few weeks when the blossoms burst out in a profusion of pink and white. As her gaze drifted over the bare-branched trees, she thought about the importance of this new phase in her life. She was the wife of an Army captain. She was going to live with him at Fort Gibson and share his military experience. It might not be the most glamorous life she was about to embrace, but it was the life she wanted. Just thinking of reuniting with Paul made Elinore's heart swell with love.

Elinore Cummings had been an eighteen-year-old college student when she met Paul Wardlaw at a Valentine's Day dance at Oberlin College. He had been a twenty-two-year-old mathematics teacher from Virginia, visiting his Ohio cousin, John Wardlaw, who was Elinore's date for the dance. When John introduced her to Paul, an immediate attraction sparked between them. Elinore spent the remainder of the evening dancing with Paul, to the bitter disappointment of John, who gracefully bowed out of the picture and allowed his cousin to pursue the beautiful Elinore. Love letters flew back and forth between Ohio and Virginia as the young couple declared their feelings for one another, and by the time Elinore graduated from Oberlin, Paul had moved to Cincinnati to teach math at the Southern Ohio Military School for Men.

Paul and Elinore's courtship moved quickly, even though her father had been cool toward his future son-in-law, doubting that a Southern-bred young man whose family owned slaves and reaped the benefits of the oppressive system was the right man for the daughter of an active abolitionist like himself. However, Paul eventually won Mr. and Mrs. Cummings' trust by convincing them that he was very much against slavery and was happy to have left the South. After Paul passed the son-in-law test, he decided to enter into active military service and work his way up in the ranks, rather than continue to teach mathematical calculations to young men.

Their wedding took place at the Asbury Methodist Church in Cincinnati where Elinore was baptized as a child. Two months after their wedding, Elinore's father died in a boating accident and Paul received orders to report to Fort Gibson as manager of the military accounting division for the territory. Elinore, who was two months pregnant, agreed to remain in Ohio and join Paul once their child was old enough to travel.

Elinore had been a married woman without a husband for nearly four years, and she was eager to join the man she loved, even though she would be far removed from the comfortable life she'd enjoyed as the daughter of a successful Ohio farmer. Elinore had always believed that her destiny would not be ordinary, that her days would never be filled with church socials and quilting bees and potluck dinners with people who had watched her grow from a child into a woman. She longed to stand by Paul's side as they made a life together, wherever that might be, and now that little Ben was old enough to withstand the rigors of the trip, it was time for her to leave.

While taking a final look at the land she would most likely never see again, Elinore's eyes connected with the figure of a man who was walking across the southernmost section of the apple orchard. He was carrying a bundle. He paused to look around a few times, as if unsure about approaching the house, and then started walking again. Elinore watched the man carefully, not at all alarmed by the appearance of the stranger but simply curious. She had witnessed such scenes many times before and could almost predict the man's next move. As expected, he began to walk faster, almost running toward the house, and when he reached the root cellar door, he lifted the rock beside the hinge, removed the key beneath it, and opened the lock. Swiftly, he disappeared down the stairs that led into the dark space beneath the house.

Stepping back from the window, Elinore hurried from her bedroom and down the back stairs, where she found her mother, Sara, in the kitchen pouring hot soup into a wooden bowl.

"Mother, someone's in the cellar," Elinore hissed.

"I know. I heard it," Sara Cummings replied, placing a calm hand on Elinore's arm. "And I know whoever it is, is hungry."

Elinore's eyes locked on her mother's gentle face, suddenly worried that after today, she would not be there to help Sara feed and clothe the frightened fugitives who risked their lives for freedom and found shelter in the cellar of their home.

It all began at church services five years ago when Reverend Durton asked his congregation for assistance in housing a young Negro family for one night. The mother, father, and their two children had been on the move for weeks, trying to get to Canada. They were in desperate need of a hot meal and a safe place to stay until they were moved on. Sara Cummings had immediately volunteered to take them in, launching the beginning of her selfless, yet dangerous, involvement in abolitionist activities that gave her a great sense of purpose.

Now, Elinore took the bowl of soup from Sara, nodded toward the door leading into the root cellar, and said, "Let me take it. This will be my last time to help out, you know?"

Sara lifted her chin in agreement, a faint half-smile on her thin pink lips. "There'll be others who'll need your help where you're going," she said in her flat Ohio accent.

"I'm sure you're right," Elinore replied as she stepped onto the stairs leading down into the cellar. When she reached the bottom step, she paused and waited until the man came out of the shadowy corner where he was hiding. He dropped to his knees, still holding the dirty cloth bundle, and sobbed in muffled relief. After he stood, Elinore looked the man over, frowning in despair at the sight of his badly scarred face and his thin wet frame. He wore a tattered brown hat pulled low on his brow and his shoulders poked through rips in the woolen jacket he was wearing.

Elinore placed the bowl of soup on a low table. "Please, sit over there .... on that bench and eat," she offered, indicating for him to place his bundle on the floor. He sat down on the bench, but refused to let go of his package, which he possessively gripped and shook his head, no.

"It's all right. No one will take your things," Elinore gently informed him, knowing how much the fugitives valued the few items they possessed.

The man squeezed his eyes shut and bit down on his bottom lip, his eyes cast to the floor.

"That's all right. My name is Elinore. What's yours?" she asked, hoping to ease his fears and gain his trust.

He flinched, did not look up, but whispered, "Henry."

"What have you got there, Henry?" she probed, certain he was guarding precious scraps of food, a valuable change of clothing, or even a china vase or a mantle clock that had belonged to someone he loved.

"It's my son," the man managed, turning pain-filled eyes on Elinore.

"Your son? Oh, my," she caught her breath, scrutinized the bundle, and waited for him to give her some indication of what she should do.

Henry's shoulders dropped in resignation and he began to breathe fast, drawing audible air in and out of his lungs. "He's new born. Two days ago. I lost my wife along the way."

Elinore's heart lurched. She steadied herself by holding onto the stair rail, then stepped closer and eased down beside Henry. She touched his arm and waited a moment before speaking. "I'm so sorry. Please. Let me take him," she urged, sensing something was not right. The man jerked back, stiffened, and then stared straight ahead, as if dazed, his unblinking eyes frozen in a vacant stare. His arms tightened more fiercely about the bundle he was guarding.

"Don't be afraid," Elinore said. "Let me take the child. I'll tend to him while you eat," she said, gently taking the baby away from Henry. Cradling the child, she began to unwind the dirty rags wrapped around the tiny form. When she finally removed the cloth, Elinore swallowed a gasp, instantly recognizing the mottled flesh and stiff little body as that of a child long gone from this world. She shook her head in dismay, and then told Henry, "He's dead."

"I know," Henry confessed in a voice hoarse with pain. "I couldn't leave him by the side of the road for dogs to tear apart. I had to keep him with me."

Elinore firmed her lips, understanding the hard decision he had made. "Did you name him?"

"Oliver. After my father."

"Well, I'll take care of Oliver, and make sure he is buried properly," she promised.

"You will?" Henry remarked, tears pooling in his eyes. "God bless you, lady. God bless your soul."

"He'll be buried in my church cemetery, and I'll request that a stone marker is put there, too." She placed a hand on Henry's shoulder, and then put the baby's body in a basket at the bottom of the stairs. "Things will get better," she assured him. "How far did you come?" she wanted to know.

69

"Not too far. From south Kentucky. Walked for a lotta of days. Soon as we crossed into Cincinnati, my wife delivered the boy. Oliver was alive and cryin' real loud for a spell, but his momma bled so much she passed on. I met a black woman who helped me bury her. She told me about this place. Said it was a house where a man like me could maybe get some help." Henry stopped talking and studied his hands, which he had balled into fists, propped on his knees.

"You can stay here for a day or two, this is a safe house ... temporary shelter, so you'll have to move on pretty soon."

"That's alright. I do thank you for helpin' me ... and my boy," he replied. A tentative smile of gratitude struggled to touch his lips. "You're an angel. An angel from heaven, you are."

"No, I'm just a woman who tries to do what she can to help those in need." Elinore sighed. "There are blankets in the box in the corner. My mother will bring you a pail of fresh water to wash. Tomorrow, she'll see about finding you a new place to stay." Picking up the basket containing the dead baby, Elinore turned to leave, but stopped when Henry reached out, as if to touch her skirt.

"You're not coming back?" he pressed, sounding nervous.

"No. I'm leaving for St. Louis tomorrow, but my mother is here, she'll help you."

"St. Louis?" he repeated, narrowing his eyes as he watched Elinore closely. "Up river, huh?"

"Yes. I'm going to be with my husband. He's a captain in the Army in Indian Territory. We have a son ... " she stopped, ashamed to be standing there, holding this man's dead child and rambling on about her son and her plans.

"You gonna live with the Indians?" Henry remarked in

70

surprise.

"Yes, I am," Elinore concurred, speaking with a touch of pride.

"You scared?"

"No," she quickly answered. "I'm not scared at all. It's exactly where I need to be."

CHAPTER 8

The Cincinnati port was a bustling tangle of men, women, children, horses, livestock, and brawny dockworkers loading crates and barrels of goods to be delivered up river. The scene was a rough and tumble mix of excited travelers and hardened crew, all eager for the *Belle Ohio* to get underway. The huge steamer, which could accommodate four hundred passengers and twenty tons of goods, gleamed white in the morning sunlight, and resembled a frilly three-tier wedding cake complete with turned spindles and gingerbread fretwork adorning every deck.

Elinore tucked her white lace handkerchief into the sleeve of her charcoal gray traveling coat and lifted little Ben high, propping him up with both of her arms. Leaning against the steamboat's rail, she turned his face toward Sara, hoping to give her mother a final glimpse of the grandson she might never see again.

"Wave good-bye to Gramma," Elinore urged, taking hold of Ben's tiny hand to shake it at her mother, who was frantically waving her own white linen kerchief back and forth as the *Belle Ohio* pulled away from the wharf. Loud cheers erupted from the passengers as the steamer's whistle sounded and its huge paddles groaned to a start, initiating the vessel's journey up river.

"I'll write .... as often as I can...." Elinore shouted down at Sara, screaming over the loud blast from the side-wheeler's horn. The rush of the flat wooden paddles as they churned the river water added to the cacophony of riverfront noise that drowned out her words. For a long time after the triple-tier steamboat slid into the swift moving Ohio River, Elinore remained at the rail, clutching her son, holding back tears, and watching as the crush of people at the dock gradually blocked her mother from view.

Now that Elinore was under way, she was determined not to falter. She had made her decision to abandon the comforts of life in the city with her mother, to leave civilized amenities behind, and there would not be any tears. Her chest grew tight when she thought about the long journey ahead, the dangers that awaited, the tests of will and perseverance that she would surely face, but she refused to let such worries take hold. She'd heard many horror stories about Indian raids, deathly sickness, intense hunger, and backbreaking travel that plagued the men and women who made the trip west, but she could not allow such talk to frighten her or tarnish her determination to be with Paul.

Looking down at Ben's wispy yellow hair, Elinore knew she was doing right by her son by taking him to live with his father. Even though he would grow up far from the tight knit community she loved so much, where he would have been watched over and fussed over and adored by his widowed grandmother, she and Paul would give him a life filled with adventure and love. This was the sacrifice Elinore decided to make the day she married Paul, and if she wanted to hold her family together, this was the course she was willing to take.

The steamboat paddled its way up the river as the restless energy of the long-awaited departure faded. Elinore could hear the crew calling back and forth from the lower deck as they stoked the twin engines with wood, sending sooty plumes of black smoke shooting from the tall smoke stack.

Passengers fanned out to find their assigned quarters, and Ben, dressed warmly in his rabbit fur leggings and jacket, toddled alongside Elinore as they pushed through the crowd of excited passengers. Maneuvering around bales of cotton and crates of produce stacked on the open deck, Elinore reached the stairs that led down to the First Class section of the vessel.

Along either side of the corridor, stateroom cabin doors stood open as passengers stowed their belongings. It took a few minutes for Elinore to locate the cabin she would occupy for the next five days, and was delighted to find that her accommodations were quite luxurious, comfortably arranged, and well ventilated, promising a welcome stay. Though small, the stateroom was neat and clean. The brass bed, covered with a dark green velvet spread that matched the draperies, complimented the richly patterned rug on the floor. A tall privacy screen hid a chamber pot chair, an oval tin tub for bathing, and a washstand hung with fresh white towels and bars of scented soap. A white wicker chair with a tufted red cushion was stationed near the window, where she could sit and read or watch the shoreline slip by. As Elinore had requested, a spindle-side crib for Ben and a table adequate for in-cabin dining had been installed. The cabin attendant she had requested to assist her during the voyage was already there, waiting for Elinore's instructions.

"Well, I hope you're ready to help us get settled," Elinore greeted the Negro girl, who looked to be no older than thirteen. She wore a simple black dress over which she had tied a long white apron, and her head was covered in a dark blue wrap.

"Yes, ma'am," the girl replied.

"What's your name?" Elinore asked.

"Marva."

"Well, Marva. Just attend to my trunk. I'll take care of the baby's things."

"Yes, ma'am," the girl agreed, moving into the room to begin her work.

With great care, she laid out Elinore's silver backed brush and comb, her hand mirror and hand towels for washing. Elinore guided Ben over to his bed, and then told Marva, "I think he's a bit tired. Would you settle him down for a nap while I take a look around?"

"Oh, yes, Ma'am," Marva responded, smiling, and taking Ben into her arms. She picked him up and then sat him on the bed and began to help him out of his warm fur coat.

Elinore went to the window and watched the shoreline sliding past, a great sense of satisfaction coming over her at the enormity of what she was doing. The journey she had planned for and prayed over for so long had finally begun. Taking in a deep breath, she turned and left the cabin, heading toward the upper deck.

After ascending a narrow flight of stairs, she emerged onto the hurricane deck, an open gallery contained by a low railing where passengers could promenade around the boat at their pleasure or sit in the reclining chairs to enjoy the sun and scenery. Elinore walked out onto the promenade, thinking the riverboat resembled an immense floating hotel, filled with all types, colors, and classes of people. The passengers, crew, and shipboard help were a curious combination of people. She saw aristocrats wearing velvet and lace, common folks in denim and coarse cotton, as well as black men and women in rags, and a few in fashionable clothing. There were single women traveling alone and men who studied them from afar. There were those who lived the fast life, the slow life, the busy life, and the lazy life, all under one roof for the duration of the trip.

Elinore made her way to the dining salon, which was a handsome room of great length and good height, fitted with exaggerated decorations that Elinore found both amusing and tasteless. Oil lamps fit with colored crystal shades hung suspended above long tables surrounded by wooden dining chairs. Servers were busy setting the tables for the evening meal, while shooing away hungry passengers.

Continuing on, Elinore came to the Ladies Day cabin, which was well furnished with sofas, rocking chairs, worktables, and a piano. A handsome Brussels carpet covered the floor. Across from the Ladies' Salon was a Smoke Room for the gentlemen, which opened onto the gambling parlor, where a group of men were already seated, cards in their hands, deep into play.

After exploring the ship, Elinore returned to her cabin to write a short letter to her mother, describing the steamboat and her accommodations. While Ben slept, she even took a short nap, awakening refreshed and eager for the evening meal. After washing and dressing, she left Ben sitting in a high chair at the table with Marva feeding him dinner and went into the grand dining salon to eat. She arrived to find the captain, a stocky whiskered man, sitting at the head of an expansive table laden with roasts, vegetables, fish, and a variety of hearty dishes, all steaming hot and fragrant. After taking her seat among the passengers, who had arrived *en mass* to dine, she filled her plate and settled in to enjoy her first meal aboard the *Belle Ohio*.

After dinner, Elinore enjoyed a musical presentation by a trio of fiddle players in the Ladies Lounge, and then took a final walk outside on the moonlit deck. Sitting beneath the gingerbread fretwork, she snuggled into her fur collar coat and stretched her legs in one of the luxurious lounge chairs, feeling rather sleepy after the heavy meal she'd eaten. Content simply to watch the moonlit shore slide past, she let her mind drift, absorbing the feel of the boat as its great paddles pushed the vessel closer to her destination. However, her peaceful setting was suddenly roused by the intrusion of a man's voice at her side.

"Do you mind if I ask you a question?" he asked.

Elinore jerked forward, looked up, and blinked. The stranger was wearing a full-length greatcoat lined at the cuffs with what looked like mink. He removed his tall beaver skin hat to expose a head full of thick black hair, and then he bent at the waist, awaiting her permission to continue. He was handsome, tall, well-dressed, and impeccably groomed. His violet-gray eyes were mesmerizing. *A gentleman*, Elinore decided before telling him, "No, I don't mind. What is it?"

"I do admire your coat," he told her, his wide eyes sweeping the length of her body. "I admired it when I first saw you boarding the vessel, with your adorable young son, I presume?"

"Yes, I'm traveling with my son, Ben." Elinore sat up and swung her feet to the floor but did not stand.

"Well, your double cape, fur-collar coat is very stylish. Might I ask where you purchased it?" he probed.

"Why .... I bought the pelts in Cincinnati and added them to my old lamb's wool coat ... especially for this journey," Elinore confessed, surprised that the man seemed interested in her wrap.

"May I sit?" he continued, easing into the chair beside her before she could answer. He reached into the inside pocket of his luxurious coat and pulled out a small white card. "Thorne Royaltin, Royaltin Textiles," he informed her, handing her the card.

"North Carolina's finest fabricator of textiles, garments, and canvas cloth goods," Elinore read aloud with interest, and then added, "I'm Mrs. Elinore Wardlaw of Cincinnati."

"My pleasure," Thorne said with a dip of his head as he placed his hat on the seat at his side. "My family's mill produces durable cloth, for harsh wear. I'm always interested to see new, stylish clothing, and I haven't seen a lady's coat quite like yours. So practical, yet quite fashionable."

"Thank you," Elinore replied. "I wanted warm outerwear for my trip, so I took on the task of re-making my old coat."

"Are you visiting family in St. Louis?" Thorne casually inquired.

"No, though I do plan to spend some time with relatives of my mother," Elinore answered, going on to tell him about her journey to Indian Territory to be with her husband at Fort Gibson.

"Ah, your husband is a lucky man. I understand a soldier's life, especially in the territory, can be extremely harsh and lonely. Having his lovely wife and young son with him will certainly make his tour of duty more bearable." Thorne paused to shift deeper into his chair. "You appear to be a woman of quality, not accustomed to the kind of living conditions I'm sure you'll find at Fort Gibson. I doubt it's a place for the faint-hearted or those who can't do without the everyday conveniences we take for granted."

"Oh, well, I'm not worried," Elinore protested, slightly offended that this stranger would assume she had not pondered this move for months, had not taken seriously Paul's warnings about what to expect. He'd written to her about how overcrowded the fort was, how whites, blacks, Indians, and even a few Chinese were pressed together behind its protective walls. How buffalo hide tipis and crude lean-to shanties were scattered across the fields surrounding the fort. Provisions were rationed, travel was restricted, and angry Osage raided other Indian camps, taking captives to ransom for horses or guns from the Army. Her new living quarters would consist of one or two rooms within the officer's complex, where she would share communal necessary facilities with others. She was under no delusions that her life would be easy, but as long as she was with Paul, she was prepared to endure any inconvenience to bring her family together.

"I'm aware of the dangers, as well as the lack of civilized amenities, Mr. Royaltin. I may appear fragile, but I am a very strong woman," Elinore challenged.

"I'm sure I spoke out of turn," Thorne apologized.

"No harm," Elinore said. "Will you be in St. Louis long?"

"Perhaps. I'm hoping to establish an outlet there for my cloth and canvas goods, especially made for those headed West," he finished, smiling broadly at Elinore.

"I'm sure you will do fine," she commented.

A beat of silence followed before Thorne spoke again. "It's good you have relatives to stay with in St. Louis, Mrs. Wardlaw," he continued in a more earnest tone. "I understand the city is very crowded ... with it being the jump off spot for all points west, you know? I heard there's rarely an empty hotel room in town ... and for a quality lady traveling alone ...well, be careful. "

Elinore nodded; then she smiled at Thorne. "Thank you. I will."

When Elinore stood, Royaltin quickly rose to his feet.

"It's been a long day," she told him, extending her hand, which he took and shook rather firmly. "It was a pleasure talking with you, Mr. Royaltin. I must retire now."

"The pleasure was mine, Mrs. Wardlaw," Thorne replied, tilting forward in a goodnight bow.

As Elinore walked away, she sensed his eyes on her back, and though she paused at the top of the staircase, she did not turn around to confirm her suspicion. However, she did sweep a hand over her sleek fur cape collar, wondering if the coat, or something else, had attracted Thorne Royaltin's attention.

Thorne watched Elinore disappear down the stairwell, disappointed that he had miscalculated her status. She was attractive, cultured, and a pleasant conversationalist. He had hoped she might be a widow traveling with her son, and accepting of Thorne's company to pass the time. With a shrug, Thorne left the deck and went into the Gambling Parlor. He stopped at the shiny mahogany bar and ordered a glass of beer, and while the bald-headed bartender splashed amber liquid into his glass he took his time surveying the place, calculating his odds for the night. A fairly competent piano player was pounding out a jaunty tune on an upright in the center of the room. Nearly every seat was filled with men eager to lay down money for a chance at easy wealth. Cigar smoke curled around low hanging oil lamps that cast a yellow glow on the faces of the men. Huge mirrors set in ornate gilt frames hung on the walls at each end of the room, reflecting the scene back to Thorne, who smiled at what he saw. He picked up his beer and headed toward a vacant seat at a poker table.

"Got room for one more?" he inquired of the man who was shuffling his cards. The pile of chips in front of him was proof of his success so far.

He nodded at an empty chair. "Take a seat. Maybe you'll have more luck than the fella who just got up."

"I hope so," Thorne replied, settling down to play.

A steady stream of men came and went throughout the evening while the mound of chips in front of Thorne grew higher with each hand. His lucky streak was like none he'd ever experienced before, and he was determined to run it out as long as he could. Toward dawn, after a long night of tense play, he was edgy, anxious, and fully aware of the rising resentment among those at his table. Thorne intently studied the cards in his hand, wondering if he had pushed his luck too far. Was trouble brewing? Was anger building on the faces of the players at his table? Thorne had sat much longer and played for higher stakes in gaming parlors all across the country, and he knew it was time to leave. He folded his cards, stood, and was about to gather up his winnings when the man to his right shot to his feet. Startled, Thorne eased away from the table, but the man raised his gun and held it on Thorne.

"Not so fast, Mister. You gotta give me a chance to win my money back."

"I don't think so," Thorne calmly tossed out, continuing to pick up his winnings.

"Sit down," the man ordered, waving his weapon.

When Thorne ignored the unwelcome command, the man fired at him, but missed, shattering the mirror on the opposite wall.

Without flinching, Thorne snatched his pistol from beneath his coat and sent a bullet straight into the man's chest.

81

The piano player halted his performance in mid-tune, creating a pause filled by the thud of the card-player's body as it hit the floor. All laughter and frivolity immediately ceased, and the room fell as silent as the inside of a church during prayer meeting. All eyes swung to Thorne.

"I had cause," was all Thorne said as he gathered up his chips and headed to the payout cage to claim his cash.

Two men rushed forward and quickly removed the corpse. In a matter of seconds, the music started up again and the place returned to normal. Thorne pocketed his winnings and sauntered out the door.

Inside his First-class cabin, Thorne stashed his winnings in the false bottom of his valise, and then stretched out on his bed. Reaching into his vest pocket, he removed a folded piece of paper, opened it, and held it under the bedside lamp. The telegraph from March Collins had arrived for Thorne at the Stanton Hotel in Cincinnati three days earlier, and every time he read it, his blood began to boil anew. He had been certain that Tama fled north from the plantation, but now he knew she had headed west. She was living with the Indians, thinking she was free, believing she had outsmarted him.

"You're not so smart, Tama," he whispered, making up his mind to find her personally and bring her home. As soon as he arrived in St. Louis, he would send March Collins a telegram and advise him to call off Bristo's search. Now that Thorne knew where Tama was hiding, he doubted he'd have any trouble reclaiming her. The Indians would be happy to take his money in exchange for his daughter. "There's no place you can go where I won't find you, Tama, so enjoy your taste of freedom, because that's all you'll ever have. Just a taste."

CHAPTER 9

Julee

St. Louis, Missouri

Daisy Lincoln blew out the tall oil lamp in the foyer of her home and slowly ascended the creaky stairs leading to her bedroom. It had been a long, tiring day, and she was looking forward to pulling her soft Circle and Star quilt over her head and forgetting about all that needed to be done. Six new boarders had arrived that day and she'd had a heck of a time getting them settled without any help. As hard as it was managing a boarding house alone, she damn sure wasn't sorry she'd run Julee off the place, after discovering the girl had taken two large ham hocks from the larder. And Julee had the nerve to sass Daisy about the stolen food, even admitting that she took the meat and gave it to a poor family stranded at the river. It wasn't Daisy's fault that the family lost everything when the steamer they were on caught fire and sank in the middle of the Mississippi River, forcing them to walk from Poplar Bluff to St. Louis to join the next wagon train headed West.

"Them Overlanders and river people ain't gonna get fat off me," Daisy huffed, unable to understand how Julee could do such a thing and not expect to feel her wrath. Daisy fed the girl well enough, gave her a room and a roof over her head. *Ungrateful, that's what she is*, Daisy grumbled, not regretting her decision to dismiss the girl, even though it had left her with a hell of a lot of extra work to do. Now, all she craved was some peace and quiet and a good night's sleep.

After changing into her white linen nightgown and matching sleep bonnet, she climbed into bed and sank down into her chicken feather mattress. Closing her eyes, she let her thick body go limp, eager for sleep to claim her. However, she tossed and turned for more than an hour while the clock on the dresser ticked on toward dawn until she eventually drifted off. However, deep into sleep, while the big old house stood silent, a loud knock on the front door sent Daisy wide-awake.

"Must be Julee wanting back in," Daisy decided, lying back, turning over with a groan, not about to let the sassy, disrespectful thief back inside her house. "She can sleep on the porch for a night or two. That'll show her who's who. She'll be beggin' for me to take her back, but I'll not have her stealing and back-talking to me, not in my house, not another day."

The pounding persisted, growing so loud Daisy worried that her six boarders would wake up and start complaining, so she rolled out of bed, pulled back the lace curtain at the window facing the street, and squinted into the steady rain that had begun to fall. All she could see was the shiny black top of a carriage—a very fine carriage, at that. *Must be someone important, come looking for a room. And just when I'm full up*, she thought, pulling on her peach satin robe and yanking her sleep cap off her gray hair. She hurried down the stairs thinking, *Maybe it's a fine Negro gentleman, a minister or a businessman caught on the road late at night and in need of a room.* After all, there weren't very many boarding houses for colored folk in St. Louis, and *Daisy Lincoln's Boarding House for Negroes* did have the best reputation.

Quickly, she opened the door, expecting to see a person of

color; however, the person staring back at Daisy was not what she expected at all. Her mouth dropped open in surprise, and she let go of the door knob to step back into the hallway, wondering why in the world a white woman with a child in tow would be standing at her door in the middle of the night, as soaking wet as a river rat just come out of the water.

The lady pulled the folds of her wet fur cape collar closer to her neck and spoke first. "Good evening. My name is Elinore Wardlaw and I'm looking for Mr. Timothy Lester. I understand he is staying here?"

Daisy rubbed her eyes, wishing she'd grabbed her spectacles off the bedside table, thinking the lady must be a light-skinned colored woman who'd gotten herself lost. Shrugging her shoulders, Daisy assessed the woman's pale creamy skin, blonde hair that was plastered wet against her forehead, and clothing that bespoke of money, and decided that the stranger was, indeed, Caucasian. "Why do you want to see Mr. Lester?"

"Then he *is* here?" Elinore pressed.

Daisy tilted her head to one side and pursed her lips, trying to calculate how much to tell.

"Why do you want to know?"

"I'm to go West with him in his wagon train... I received a letter from Mr. Lester with this address on it, so I thought..." Elinore paused and began to search her handbag for the letter, stopped and then looked up at Daisy. "Well....what it is, I need a room ..."

"Oh," Daisy started, scrutinizing Elinore. "If it's a room you want, I think you've come to the wrong place, Miss Wardlaw. This here's a boarding house for Negroes." Daisy folded her hands at her waist and waited for the woman to flee back down the steps and run after her now-departing carriage, but the woman did not even blink.

"Really?" Elinore said, disappointed, but not concerned. "I didn't realize. The wind blew down part of your sign."

Daisy leaned past the woman standing on her porch and saw that the sign, indeed, had broken in two, and simply read *Rooms - Daisy Lincoln's.* The *"For Negroes"* part was gone.

"Try Brady's Hotel over on Front Street," Daisy suggested, anxious to get back to bed. She didn't plan to stand there talking to this stranded white woman and miss another minute's sleep. "You come back in the morning to talk to Mr. Lester. Ain't no use in waking him now."

"But you see... I've been to Brady's and every hotel in the city. There are no rooms," Elinore explained. "I planned to stay with a cousin, but she's got the pox fever and her house has been quarantined. If I could just stay here tonight, I would be so grateful. I asked the carriage driver to wait, but as you can see ... he's gone. My boy and I are ..." she faltered and blinked, pressing her lips tight in despair.

"Sorry, I just can't help you," Daisy stated in a very firm tone, not about to risk losing her city license by allowing this white woman to spend a night in a colored hotel. If the law found out, there would be trouble. Her hospitality permit, which she paid dearly for, could be revoked. Her business ruined. She started to close the door, but Elinore moved forward, stopping her.

"I understand your concern about letting me a room, but please. Could we come in to dry off? Only for an hour or so? I don't know where else to go."

Daisy looked down at the little boy hiding behind his mother's wet skirts, suddenly feeling sorry for the child and the frazzled mother, too. Maybe it would be all right to let them dry off by the stove. "Well ... I guess you could sit by the kitchen stove and dry yourselves a bit, but I can't give you a bed." She stepped back to let Elinore and the child pass inside, then set about building up the banked coal embers in the kitchen stove as her mind whirled with possibilities. It could be worth the chance. *Julee's room behind the kitchen is empty,* Daisy thought, calculating what she could get for it. *This storm is pretty nasty, and the carriage driver left this poor woman and her baby stranded. Nothing wrong with being charitable.*

"Well," she began, easing into a conversation. "Mind you .... I have a small space and a narrow bed that might do... to keep you and the little one out of the elements. Used to be my kitchen gal's room, but she's gone now."

"Really? That would be so nice of you."

"Well, I'm a Christian woman. Can't leave you on the porch all night."

"I'd be so grateful. How much for one night?" Elinore asked.

"You can have it for ..." Daisy stopped to think, her small eyes steady on her potential guest. If it was one thing Daisy Lincoln loved, it was money. She charged her boarders two dollars a night for a bed, two dollars a day for three basic meals, and if they wanted a bath, it was fifty-cents extra. She grudgingly provided each person a bar of lye soap and one thin towel to dry off. Because her place was the finest boarding house for Negroes on the river in St. Louis, Daisy felt no responsibility to provide more than the basics, and expected her boarders to respect her prices. "I expect I could let you have the room for ten dollars," Daisy finished, deciding if she was going to risk losing her business over this white woman's misfortune, she might as well make a decent profit.

Elinore blinked, clearly taken back by the exorbitant figure, but she reached into her reticule and drew out a folded bill. "Your kindness is greatly appreciated, Miss Lincoln."

"My pleasure," Daisy said, pressing the money into the pocket of her duster. "Come with me," she told Elinore, shuffling to the stuffy little space behind the kitchen chimney that had been Julee's room, until today. She lit a smoky oil lamp, placed it on the night table, and told Elinore to be gone by dawn, before any of her boarders came down and saw her. Then she left, slipping back upstairs and back into bed.

Once Daisy had left, Elinore looked around the dark, unattractive space, dispirited by her circumstances, but relieved to be out of the rain. She tested the bed, which was as hard as a buckboard and covered with a blanket as thin as a bed sheet. She sighed in resignation and began to undress Ben, who was nearly asleep on his feet. Once she'd gotten him settled on the sour smelling mattress, she carefully folded her coat and removed her wet shoes, then sat on the floor with the lamp drawn near. She took a sheet of paper and her writing case, uncorked a small bottle of ink, filled her pen, and then bent low over the page to write:

April 2, 1855

Dear Mother,

I made it to St. Louis, though upon arrival, I found Cousin Vera ill with pox fever and her home under a strict quarantine. It was a great disappointment and shock to learn how ill she is. I spoke to a neighbor who told me the doctor does not expect her to recover. The city is extremely crowded but I managed to find a room in a small hotel not far from the wagon camp. It's a boarding house for colored, but the proprietor let me and Ben stay for one night. The woman who runs the establishment has been very accommodating, but I pray I will find some place more suitable to stay tomorrow. Finding a room preoccupied my mind to such an extent that I could hardly think of anything else. I met a man on the steamer who complimented me on my coat, so I guess I did all right with the alterations. It is hard to believe that I may never again set eyes on your lovely face or the peaceful serenity of our home. Once I get to Indian Territory, I will send you one of those beautiful Indian blankets you asked for. I don't know how long it will be before I can write again, but I will try. For now, I must close, as it is late and I am very tired.

Your loving daughter,

Elinore

For the first time since boarding the *Belle Ohio*, Elinore felt the true ache of loneliness. During the river trip, comforting little Ben and talking with the various chatty passengers had kept her from missing all she had left behind.

Wearing her still-damp traveling dress, Elinore stretched out on the bed beside her son, too tired to bother with removing the whalebone corset beneath her blue linen traveling frock. She ran her hands over her flat stomach, and then circled her tiny waist, which had recovered quite nicely from the swelling expansion of carrying her first child.

Paul had been right to make her stay in Ohio until Ben was born, but now that she was fully recovered from the rigors of childbirth, she was anxious to be a real wife to her husband in every possible way. Elinore's body tingled with anticipation. How she longed to be with Paul again, to feel his hands on her breasts, his lips pressed to hers in that furtive, desperate way he had of fully claiming her. She felt heat begin to gather between her thighs, and she pressed them together tightly, recalling how wonderful it was to lose herself completely in the act of loving Paul.

* * * * *

At the top of the hill behind the hotel, Julee stopped and turned around. She stared down the slope that ended at the river, where campfires burned among the jumble of wagons and people who were preparing for their long trek into the prairie. It was the most magnificent sight Julee had ever seen, and she yearned to be sitting beneath the flutter of white canvas when the wagons pulled out, listening to the clanking metal, the braying mules, and the river camp songs the people always sang. She was desperate to leave St. Louis but had few options: She could sign on with a white family headed to California, Oregon, or Colorado, but they'd work her harder than Daisy ever did and make her life even more miserable than it already was. She could leave Daisy's house and try to find a real paying job so she could save money to pay her way west. But that would take years, and she didn't want to wait that long.

Turning to face the boarding house, she was surprised to see a dim light shining in the window of her room. *I'll bet Daisy's in there, snooping around, going through my things. Maybe even tossing them out,* Julee calculated, her anger rising to recall how nasty the woman had been to her. The ham hocks Julee had taken to the family on the river had been so rancid they were hardly fit to eat, and the lady at the river had been so grateful she'd cried when Julee handed her the meat. Daisy was just mad because Julee had given the meat away rather than throw it out as she'd been told to do.

Moving faster, Julee headed toward the house, pulling in long breaths, determined to find out what Daisy was up to. The only good thing about living with the cranky old woman was that Julee had a room of her own, even though it was no more than a dark cubbyhole behind the kitchen chimney. Too warm, even during winter months when ice covered the windows and water froze in the pump.

The rain-soaked ground beneath Julee's boots was soft and squishy. Each step she took splashed mud onto her cotton stockings and dirtied the hem of her dress. Reaching into her apron pocket, she pulled out the key to the back door, which Daisy had forgotten to take from her when she ordered her out of the house. Julee slipped into the stifling warm kitchen, rinsed her face and hands in the pail of water by the chimney, and then tiptoed toward her room.

Quietly she turned the doorknob and peeked inside. A lit oil lamp on the floor cast dark shadows over a white woman who was lying on the bed, a letter in her hand. Squinting hard, Julee surveyed the scene, shocked to see a little boy fast asleep beside the woman—in her bed!

"Who are you?" Julee demanded rather loudly, approaching the sleeping woman.

Elinore stirred, opened her eyes, and then sat up. "Oh. I must have fallen asleep."

"I'd say so," Julee remarked, standing over Elinore and looking down at her, upset by this invasion of her space. It wasn't much of a room, but it had been hers for fifteen years and no one had ever slept in that bed but her.

"I'm Elinore Wardlaw. Miss Lincoln let me this room for tonight," Elinore said, standing and brushing wrinkles from her dress.

"Well, I'm Julee and this is *my* room."

Elinore stretched her back and frowned. Her body ached from lying in her corset on the hard bed, and her eyes burned from lack of sleep. "You must be Miss Lincoln's kitchen girl?" Elinore remarked, observing the girl's soft ebony skin. Her hair was a mass of soft, spiraling curls that floated around her face in a dark cloud of tight ringlets. The angular planes of her face, her high cheekbones, and broad forehead contrasted sharply with the rest of her body, which was all curves and softness, evident despite the fact that she was wearing a shapeless homespun shirtwaist, belted with a piece of blue cord, and chunky leather boots that were obviously too big.

"How you know me?"

"Miss Lincoln told me. This was your room, wasn't it?"

"*Was?* You mean, *is.*"

"Oh, she said you left."

"She *would* say something like that," Julee grumbled. "We had a disagreement, like we always do. 'Bout nothing big. She got all uppity and told me to get out. So I went down to the river and hung around there til I figured she was sleep. She puts me out quite regular."

Elinore exhaled, her shoulders sagging in worry. "I was desperate for a room. I arrived on the *Belle Ohio* today, but due to circumstances beyond my control, my son and I found ourselves without a place to stay. I'm grateful to Miss Lincoln for letting me in, but I suppose ... you want your room now?"

Julee shifted her eyes from Elinore to the sleeping child, and then shrugged. "No need to wake the boy. Guess I can sleep in the kitchen."

"I assured Miss Lincoln I would leave early ... before her guests came down," Elinore added, as if to soften the inconvenience she was causing the girl.

With flip of her wrist, Julee snapped, "Don't pay that woman no mind. You and the boy stay for breakfast. I'm sure you paid her enough money to get a meal before you go."

As if relieved, Elinore said, "That would be nice."

"Now," Julee started, pointing to a frayed blanket hanging on a hook on the wall. "If you can please hand me that quilt, I'll get out of your way. You go on back to sleep."

Elinore reached for the faded coverlet and gave it to Julee, thankful the girl was being more than reasonable about the situation.

In the kitchen, Julee went to the pie safe and removed a square tin box from behind the cracker barrel. Spilling the contents into her hand, she counted. Nine dollars and thirty-three cents. Not nearly enough to pay her share of expenses on a wagon going west. The familiar pull of disappointment cut sharp and deep as she curled her fingers over the assorted coins and paper. Her hazelnut hands were covered with rough red patches and there were deep cracks in her skin and fingernails from scrubbing charred pots, washing floors, and cleaning up behind the messy boarders who came and went at Daisy's.

Discouraged, Julee put the money back into the tin, pushed it deep into the corner, and then closed the pie safe door. She refused to keep anything of value in her room because Daisy had no respect for anybody's privacy. If she ever found Julee's money, she'd keep it. Daisy went into any room at will, and most likely through the boarder's things, too. After all, as Daisy always told Julee, didn't everything in the house belong to her?

Well, I don't belong to her, or anyone else, Julee inwardly vowed while spreading the quilt on the floor. She lay down close to the black iron stove and stared into the dark. "But I sure wish I knew where I *did* belong," she murmured, turning onto her side.

The next morning, Julee set the pine trestle table with a service for eight, and when the last fork had been placed beside the heavy china plates, she took a deep breath and pulled her shoulders back, hoping there would be no ruckus with Daisy today.

"Those windows are open too wide," Daisy started right in as soon as she entered the dining room, making no comment about the fact that she had run Julee off the place just the day before. "Close them, Julee." The grumpy woman mumbled under her breath, "Wasting my good coal heat. God knows I can't afford it." She clucked her tongue, pulled out the chair at the head of the table, and sat down just as her boarders drifted in and took their seats. Elinore and Ben were the last to arrive, initiating murmurs of surprise and curiosity among the others. Daisy opened her mouth as if to say something, paused, and then pressed her lips together.

Julee hurried to shut the tall windows at the far end of the room, knowing that if they had been closed, Daisy would have complained of the heat and ordered her to open them. There was never any pleasing the woman.

Standing near the sideboard, Julee bowed her head as Daisy launched into her short, standard prayer in a thin, pitchy voice. "Lord, bless this fare we are about to receive and use it to strengthen our souls." She hesitated, opened her eyes, blinked and then added, "And especially watch over Mr. Lester as he undertakes another brave journey across the plains." Then Daisy cleared her throat and invited everyone to eat.

With a platter of pork sausage and potatoes in one hand, and a bowl of watered-down eggs in the other, Julee served breakfast to the eight boarders who seemed eager to eat. The clatter of forks and knives and spoons hitting china echoed throughout the room as Julee moved around the table, appraising the current group of boarders.

At the head of the table opposite Daisy sat Big Tim Lester, the Cajun trail boss who always stayed at Daisy's between jobs leading wagon trains west. He was handsome, in a rough, craggy way, with keen, intelligent eyes and shaggy brown hair that touched his square, solid shoulders. He carried a rifle, a belt of ammunition, and a quiver of arrows wherever he went, and had them with him now as he sat down to breakfast. His laughter was a cross between a howl and a cackle, and he spoke in a peculiar patois that sounded as foreign and exotic as the alligators, pirogues, Indians, and veiled bayous he wove into the yarns he spun to entertain his fellow travelers. He lived on the open road, traversing the land as he delivered people and parcels to far-flung parts of the country. Whenever his travels brought him to St. Louis, which wasn't very often, Daisy gave him the spacious back room on the third floor with windows facing the river. Julee was always pleased to see Big Tim arrive. She loved to hear his tales about the world outside her cloistered life, and he always brought her a gift, which he would shyly hand to her. This time he'd brought her a palm-size leather coin purse engraved with birds and vines. Once owned by a Cherokee princess he'd said, and Julee didn't doubt it was true. Inside the purse, he had placed a shiny silver dollar, adding to her meager hoard.

"Please, Mr. Lester," Miss Herold, a rail-thin schoolteacher wearing tiny round spectacles, begged. "What happened next?"

"Well, let me finish the story," Big Tim replied, taking up the tale where he'd left off at dinner the night before. "Soon as that shaggy mongrel slipped inside his lair, I drop down, way down, like I'm lookin' for crawfish in a bayou. Then, I ease my way in, jump that wolf from behind, and yank that little girl right out of his jaws. Twisted his head til I hear the bones snap."

"How absolutely ghastly! You broke a wolf's neck with your bare hands?" Mrs. Lintner, the preacher's widow remarked, absently taking the platter of eggs from Julee to serve herself.

"*C'est vrai,*" *Big* Tim tossed back. "*Comme ca!*" he finished, cracking his knuckles, grinning at the loud popping sound.

Julee flinched. Miss Herold gasped. Mrs. Linter covered her mouth with a hand, and Daisy just rolled her eyes. The men at the table guffawed with laughter.

Big Tim tilted his chair back on two legs, swiveled his head from the schoolteacher to Julee, who couldn't help grinning as she tugged at the front of her white head wrap, and then he quickly looked away.

"Wasn't nothin' to it, *mes amis,*" he finished, calmly assessing the horrified expressions of the women at the table. "That wolf been try'n to make me mad too long. Had to go. So I killed him."

Everyone at the table let out a collective gasp, and as Julee moved to refill Big Tim's empty coffee cup, she wished the coffee were stronger, more like the thick rich chicory he said he loved so much.

"Yes, it sounds like something you would do," Daisy huffed suspiciously; then she turned to Elinore, her stiff gray curls dancing around her dark brown face. "Let me warn you now, Mrs. Wardlaw. This man is a real talker. You're gonna have to listen to his stories about thieves, bandits, disease ... and God knows what else, all the way to Fort Gibson."

Elinore smiled, tilting her head to the side with a shrug as her eyes caught Big Tim Lester's. "It'll be entertaining, I'm sure."

"Hump," Daisy grunted. "I wouldn't strike out across those plains for nothin' in the world. Everything I need and want is right here in St. Louis. I'm told it's the devil out there. Folks start off all fired up and excited to be goin' somewhere and don't even live to see the corn in Kansas. You can have it. I came here from South Carolina twenty years ago, and I've come as far West as I care to."

Elinore calmly sipped her weak coffee; then she set the cup aside, and, ignoring Daisy's remarks, directed her question to Big Tim. "Is the wagon about ready?"

"Almost set. Just been waiting for a few supplies, and you and the boy to arrive," Big Tim replied. "Guess your trunks are still at the dock?"

"Yes, they are," Elinore confirmed.

"I'll get 'em right after breakfast. You come on down to the river, and I'll show you how things is all set up."

"Good," Elinore replied, wiping a dribble of milk from Ben's chin.

"You can leave the boy with me," Daisy brusquely offered. "No need in takin him down there among all that trashy rabble if you don't have to, you know?"

"There's no trashy folks down there," Julee quickly interjected.

Daisy shot a fierce glance at Julee, who quickly picked up Miss Herold's cup and refilled it from the pot on the sideboard. As Julee handed the cup back to the woman, she caught Big Tim's eye and spoke directly to him. "Must be wonderful to see all the different people, watch the Indians dance, hear the drums." She paused from stacking dirty plates in her arms and studied Big Tim's bronzed, sun-ravaged face, seeing among the creases all the places he'd been, all the Indians he'd both befriended and killed, all the hardships he'd suffered on his dangerous excursions. "I'd love to see everything you seen."

"Hold up, *Cherie*," Big Tim shot back. "T'aint so pretty a sight out there and no place for a young girl like you. Oh, sometimes it can be nice enough, but mostly, the folks moving out West got a hard life for shore."

"And," Miss Herold started, addressing Julee, "you'd be terrified of the Indians. I hear they scalp people and even eat their brains."

Julee shook her head, dismissing the woman's concern with a frown. "I wouldn't be afraid at all."

"You stop that crazy talk, you hear me?" Daisy ordered, pulling her shoulders back in a huff, glaring at Julee. Firming her jaw, Daisy jumped to her feet and grabbed Julee by the elbow. "You go on." Daisy shoved Julee, causing her to stumble. "You get back in the kitchen where you belong and quit conversatin' with my boarders."

Julee narrowed her eyes at Daisy, cut a fast look at

Elinore, then turned on her heel and left the dining room. Standing inside the kitchen, she listened as Daisy ranted in anger.

"Well, well ... I never," Daisy stuttered. "Please excuse that girl's rude behavior. She's not too bright." Daisy cut her eyes at Big Tim when she said, "I took pity on her cause her mama ran off and left the child. Just a baby she was. Thought the child would be grateful for a decent place to live, but all I get from her is sass."

There was a short uncomfortable silence, and then Daisy turned the conversation. "That's enough talk about Indians and wolves and such. Ain't fit conversation for the breakfast table anyway."

Julee was tying her apron around her waist when Daisy pushed through the door between the dining room and the kitchen and stood there looking at Julee as if she could kill her.

"I'll thank you kindly to keep your mouth shut while serving my guests. How many times do I have to tell you, gal, keep your place!" Daisy's brown face grew darker with rage. "I can't maintain a respectable establishment with my kitchen help showin' out. How dare you insinuate yourself into a conversation at my table?"

"I was just being friendly," Julee snapped, too frustrated to care what Daisy thought.

"People don't come here to be friendly with the help," Daisy fired back. "They come for a decent meal and a clean bed. They're not paying good money to hear your crazy mouth."

"Well," Julee started, deciding to speak her mind since

Daisy brought up the subject. "If you ask me, they pay too much for what they get."

"Nobody asked you. They're glad to have it," Daisy snarled, stepping closer to Julee, who defiantly held her ground. Daisy grabbed Julee by the arm and pushed her face close. "I don't give a rat's damn what you think. You ought to be grateful you're still here. You owe me a hell of a lot for all I've done. "

Julee yanked her arm free and stepped back. "I don't owe you anything. I'm fifteen years old. I do whatever you ask me to do without complainin'. All you care about is how hard you can squeeze a nickel and how much you'd have to pay a new gal to do the work you get out of me for free. I'm crazy, all right. Crazy to stay around here and ..."

Daisy slapped Julee hard on the side of her face; then she kept her hand raised as if to strike her again. "You ungrateful bitch. I won't be insulted in my home. I could have sent you wandering the roads with dirt caked halfway up your legs a long time ago, but I didn't. I committed to giving you a home when I took you in, and now you sashay around here with your nose all turned up as if you're somebody special."

Julee watched as Daisy's large bosom shook with rage until she lowered her arm, yanked out a chair from the kitchen table, and sat down, looking ill. Fearing the old woman was about to faint, Julee ran for a glass of water, but Daisy brushed it aside, spilling the drink down the front of her dress, breaking the glass on the floor.

"Get out," Daisy yelled. "Get out of my sight. I don't need your aggravation ...and you're gonna pay me for that broken glass."

Julee leveled a hard stare at Daisy and then turned away

and pushed through the back door. Stumbling over the low porch steps, she raced from the house and headed toward the campsite spread along the riverbank.

Chapter 10

Elinore pressed through the sprawling, noisy congregation where everyone was busy stowing gear and making ready to pull out. She was amazed by the crush of people, animals, and prairie schooners assembled at the river where more than fifty wagons were jammed together in the camp. The entire area was a maze of rocking chairs, trunks, tin tubs, and crates of china. Men in battered felt hats with shirtsleeves rolled up and suspenders showing were busy harnessing mules or oxen, preparing them for the heavy loads they would pull for the next two months. Others were cleaning their rifles, counting ammunition, steeling themselves for the danger that awaited. Elinore watched women bustling around with sun bonnets hanging by a ribbon around their necks as they stacked food in cook boxes, folded bedding, and repaired torn clothing for the boisterous children who played around the fires, unaware that they were about to start off on the most dangerous journey of their short lives.

After nearly half an hour of wandering, watching, and searching, Elinore finally found Big Tim. He was brushing a sleek black mare tied to the back of a sturdy-looking covered wagon.

"Mr. Lester?" she ventured, stepping closer.

He turned and looked up, squinted at Elinore and then smiled. "Call me Big Tim like everybody else." With a sweep of his arm, Big Tim motioned for her to come forward. Then he pointed at the wagon, which looked strong, light, and made of well-seasoned timber. The wagon's spoke wheels were taller than Elinore, and its high bowed cover created a shady arch above her head. "This here's your home for the next couple a weeks. What you think?" Big Tim stated with pride.

"I think it looks very nice... even better than I had expected," Elinore replied, cautiously eyeing the wagon. When she was planning her journey to Fort Gibson, she had considered traveling by stagecoach on the Butterfield Overland Mail route, a westward conduit for both passengers and the U.S. mail. It departed from St. Louis, continued east to Fort Smith, and then on through Indian Territory. However, even though the lightweight, fast-moving stagecoach would have taken her to her husband in better time than the wagon train, it would not have provided any comfort for little Ben. The Butterfield Overlander made frequent stops along its route, the carriages were cramped, and the small amount of luggage permitted each passenger made the Overland Mail route most undesirable.

Big Tim cocked his head toward the six oxen tethered to nearby trees. "And these strong fellas gonna be pullin' it." He chuckled when one of the animals looked at him and brayed loudly, tossing its head back and forth. "Gonna be yer companions for a long while, so you'll get used to that sound." He walked to the front of the wagon and propped two fists at his waist, sending the fringe on the sleeves of his shirt swaying back and forth. "You might as well start getting familiar with how things are done. Come on. I'm gonna give you a quick lesson on what goes in and how it comes out, then I'm goin' over to the dock to pick up yer trunks." He hesitated, and then said, "Miss Daisy told me about your predicament, so, if you want, you and your boy can sleep in the wagon til we leave. Might as well get settled...no need to go looking for a hotel."

"Oh, very good. Yes! I'd like that," Elinore agreed, relieved that she would not have to take over Julee's room again. Besides, she wanted to get accustomed to sleeping beneath the tall white canvas dome and to the noisy camp life surrounding her.

"You're gonna need proper clothing," Big Tim stated with authority.

"I'm prepared," Elinore replied, going on to describe what she had packed. In addition to her fur cape coat and the canvas trousers she had made, she'd packed a short, sturdy coat made of wool, three dresses suitable for prairie traveling, several flannel shirts, woolen socks, and walking boots that came well up her legs. She'd also brought along a sewing kit containing stout linen thread, several large needles, buttons, a thimble, and lots of pins. "However, I do want a rifle," she added. "I left mine back home in Ohio, so I hope you can help me buy another one."

"Oh? You can shoot?" Big Tim inquired, eyebrows raised.

"As well as most of the men in the county where I was born."

"All right! *C'est bon!*" Big Tim exclaimed with pleasure. "I know just what you need. I'll stop by the gunsmith's after I get your trunks and see what he's got." With that settled, he waved Elinore closer. "*Bien!* Climb inside and let me show you how it all fits together."

The interior of the wagon was cramped and dim but well organized, and much neater than Elinore had expected. Every inch of space was dedicated to a purpose, every surface utilized well.

"Here's bedding for you and the boy," Big Tim told Elinore, showing her two blankets, a comforter, and two pillows which he'd rolled up inside a square of painted canvas that he called, 'gutta percha.' "You gotta spread the canvas under your bedding if you have to sleep on the ground, then roll it all up to stow it away while we're traveling."

Heavy burlap sacks of sugar, salt, corn, coffee, and flour had been stacked between barrels containing preserved bacon, pork, and grease for cooking. Tins of butter, large packets of dried vegetables, and jugs of potable water lined the outer edges of the interior.

"Everything has its place," Big Time explained, moving to the far end of the wagon where an assortment of cooking utensils hung from the wooden rafters of the wagon. "Here's all you need to make a meal, right here."

Elinore examined the contents of her new kitchen: a black iron kettle for boiling water, a coffee pot, tin plates with matching cups, a metal bucket for hauling water, and a skillet for frying corn cakes or bacon.

Her orientation to her new home was brief, and after Big Tim showed her where everything was stored and what she needed to know about properly managing the wagon, he mounted his black horse and set off on the road that led past Daisy's house.

Elinore, happy to be left alone to continue exploring her new home was busy examining the bedding when she heard a voice call her name.

"Miss Elinore?"

Elinore looked up from spreading out a quilt and smiled at Julee. "Oh, hello," she said to the girl.

"This your wagon? When you gittin' ready to leave?" Julee asked.

"In a few days, I hope," Elinore told her, leveling kind eyes on Julee, who had stationed herself in front of the wagon and was peering inside.

"Mighty fine wagon. Looks right comfortable."

"I think it will be adequate," Elinore said.

"Wish I was going someplace."

Elinore sucked in a breath, struck by the longing in the girl's voice. "You don't like working for Miss Lincoln, do you?" she asked.

"Nope, not at all," Julee admitted, taking her eyes off the wagon to assess Elinore's pretty shawl. "But I can't leave here til I save enough money to go someplace else."

"Where would you go?"

"Any place. Far away. Don't matter where, as long as I get outta that house."

"How old are you?" Elinore wanted to know.

"Fifteen, sixteen come October," Julee answered.

Elinore climbed down out of the wagon and motioned for Julee to sit next to her on a log facing the fire Big Tim had left burning. Once they were settled, she said, "Tell me about yourself, Julee. How did you come to live with Daisy Lincoln?"

"Been here all my life. My momma's dead, and nobody ever came looking for me, so here I am. Still waitin'."

Elinore felt the pain in Julee's words and her heart tightened in sympathy. The girl was soft-spoken, polite, and eager to please. She clearly wanted more for herself than life as an unpaid maid in a boarding house.

"You said you have some money?" Elinore asked.

"Yes, nine dollars and thirty-three cents," Julee said, wishing she had more. "Big Tim always give me a dollar or some change whenever he shows up, so I guess he been back here at Daisy's 'bout seven, eight times."

Elinore managed a tight smile of sympathy. "Nine dollars isn't very much. It wouldn't get you out of St. Louis."

"I know, but it's a start," Julee countered, turning to glance at the wagon when she said, "You sure have a lotta room in there, Miss Elinore. Sure wish you could take me along. I wouldn't take up much space at all. You gonna need help with the boy, too. I can cook. Keep the wagon clean, watch over the boy so you can rest. I'd even... " Julee stopped, turned back, and dropped her head as if ashamed of her request.

Elinore worried her teeth over her lips but remained silent for a long moment, truly considering Julee's situation.

"But I'm going to Fort Gibson. To Indian Territory," she finally said, wanting to put things into perspective.

"I know where you're going, and it don't matter."

"But what would you do once you got there? I can't promise I'd take care of you."

"Oh, I'd be fine. I'd do about the same as I been doing here. I'm a hard worker, and I'm sure there'd be plenty of work for me out there."

"I suppose so," Elinore murmured, and then, in a voice tinged with a bit of relief, told Julee, "You would be a great help to me on the road, I agree, but first I'd have to speak to Mr. Lester. He'd have to be agreeable to taking you along. I'm not sure he'd want to do that."

Julee jumped up, her small body quaking with gratitude.

"Oh, he gonna say it's all right. He's a real good man, Miss Elinore. Only person ever treated me nice. I'm a much better cook than you think, too. Daisy never has any decent food to work with, but I'll ... " She stopped talking seeming embarrassed, then pressed her arms to her waist and stepped away, holding her slim body stiffly erect, as if awaiting orders about what to do next.

"All right, now. All right," Elinore said, taking charge of the situation, wanting to calm things down. "Don't thank me yet. Wait until I speak to Mister Lester. For now, you go on back to the house and tend to your chores. I'll let you know what he says."

Daisy stood on her front porch and watched Big Tim ride his black horse toward her house. Before he got close, she shouted down the road at him and waved her arms, signaling for him to come to her. When finally he saw her and waved, she folded her arms tightly across her waist, puckered her lips, and watched him approach. She didn't wait until he halted at the bottom of her steps before launching directly into what was on her mind.

"You're gonna have to give me a lot more money if you want me to keep that gal here much longer."

Big Tim pushed his cowhide hat to the back of his head and up-jutted his jaw toward Daisy. "I pay you good all these years, *non?*"

"Maybe so, but things are different now. Julee is not a baby anymore, and two grown women trying to run the same house don't mix. She's disrespecting me at every turn. Too mouthy and too much sass. This kinda aggravation will cost you more."

"C'est vrai?" Big Tim murmured, stroking his chin. His shoulders dropped and his chest sank back, as if the weight of Daisy's words were heavy. "Paying more money won't change that," he decided.

"But it'll make my burden easier to bear," Daisy challenged.

"I dunno 'bout that." Big Tim hunched forward, gripping the pommel of his saddle, his fingers locked in thought.

Daisy continued to press her case. "Well, it costs me a lot more than it used to, to care for her. All the things I have to buy. The food she eats! Not to mention what she tries to give away to those people on the river. Gonna break me sure enough."

Big Tim studied his hands, then glanced up to study Daisy's face, which was set in a hard, cold scowl. "Well, maybe you got a point, Miss Daisy." His voice turned soft, words evenly spoken. *"Oui.* Maybe it's time for Julee to leave."

Daisy sucked her teeth loudly; then she snapped her reply. "Leave? And where would she go? Who'd take her in?"

"Me," he replied with a firm nod as the wind whistled above his head and he settled the matter in his mind. When he spoke, there was a sureness in his voice that confirmed his decision. *"Oui.* Guess it's time Julee came along with me. You're right. She ain't no baby no more."

* * * * *

"Yessirree, Gus, I think this here Henry will do just fine." Big Tim turned the brand new sixteen-shot, breech-loading rifle over in his hands and examined it with admiration. He owned an old muzzle-loading Hawkins, a Colt six-shooter, a bow and arrow, and two sharp Bowie knives, but he'd never had a brand new Henry. It looked almost too pretty to shoot. "Gimme a good amount of ammunition for this beauty, and a real nice pouch, too." He smiled, and then added, "It's for a lady ... I'm takin' her to Injun Country."

"Oh yeah?" Gus, the merchant, remarked with interest.

"Yeah, and she says she can shoot."

"Well, that Henry will sure 'nuf give her something to test her skill with," Gus replied with a shake of his head as he took the money Big Tim handed to him and stuffed it into a drawer. "Be right back," he said, heading into the back of the store, leaving Big Tim to peruse the variety of weapons and supplies displayed on the gunsmith's shelves.

When the bell above the door to the store jingled, Big Tim glanced up, nodded at the white man who entered, and then resumed his inspection of a black calfskin holster. He needed to replace the one he had worn for so long it was wearing thin at the buckle, threatening to tear apart. While Big Tim was trying the new holster on for size, Gus emerged and began to wrap his purchases in sheets of brown paper. "Want to throw that holster in?" Gus inquired, not looking up from his task.

Big Tim hesitated, thinking it over as he fingered the shiny belt buckle and patted his hip. "Maybe so." But he continued to deliberate, testing the strength of the leg cords, adjusting the tightness of the belt, not quite ready to give up on the one he'd worn so long it was molded to the shape of his body. Breaking in a new holster took time, and he was about to set off on another trip into Indian country. Maybe he'd better pass.

"Mighty fine looking holster," the stranger who entered

the store said to Big Tim. He removed his hat, smoothed back his thick black hair, and walked over to Big Tim. "If you don't buy it, I might."

Big Tim focused more closely on the stranger, feeling a sudden sense of dread that drained through his body and hollowed him to the core. He blinked, unable to believe he was looking at the man he had prayed he would never see again. It was Thorne Royaltin, all right, and he did not recognize Big Tim at all. Fifteen years had passed, so why should this white man remember a dark-skinned man who meant nothing to him at all? A surge of rage hit Big Tim like a flash of lightning, but he inhaled, stepped back, let it pass, and swallowed the curses that rose in his throat. Calmly, he unbuckled the holster.

"You can have it, mister," he said in a flinty tone. "I think I have all I need." Then he handed the pistol holder to Thorne, picked up his purchases, and left the store, his heart pounding, his mind filled with questions he wished he could ask the man he had vowed to kill.

Big Tim strode to his horse, stuffed his purchases into the saddlebags, and climbed into the saddle. He held Elinore's rifle across his lap as he turned his horse around, unsettled by the strange encounter with Thorne Royaltin in St. Louis. Memories flew to the front of his mind. Memories he'd thought were too faded and dusty to ever rear their ancient heads.

Thorne turned to Gus and said, "How much for the holster?"

"Seven dollars, Mister," Gus replied.

"I'll take it."

"Fine. What else can I get for you?"

Thorne looked around. "Oh, let's see," he started, surveying the merchant's shelves. "This is a mighty handsome traveling case. I've been considering buying a new one."

"Take your time," Gus advised, turning away from Thorne to greet two boys who entered the store.

Thorne glanced at the young men, and then looked out the store's large front window. The black man who had given up the holster had mounted his horse and was sitting with a rifle across his saddle. Thorne carefully studied the man, certain he'd seen him before. But where? When? And why did the sight of him make Thorne feel so uneasy?

* * * * *

That night, Elinore hardly slept at all. She lay awake inside her wagon, a scratchy Army blanket spread over her body, her soft yellow hair fanned out on a pillow made from a sack of rice. She stared up at the dull white canvas stretched over the huge bows of wood, feeling safe, protected, and excited. The braying mules, the shouts of drunk men whooping it up one last time before taking to the trail, and the melancholic harmonica music quivering in the air brought Elinore more comfort than annoyance.

By the light of an oil lamp, she wrote her final letter to Paul, which she would leave with Daisy Lincoln to post in the morning. She hoped Paul would receive her correspondence before she arrived at Fort Gibson.

"Dear Paul, I miss you so," she whispered into the shadows as she wrote. "I wish you were here, traveling with me and Ben. I know you have entrusted Mr. Lester with the responsibility of delivering your wife and son safely to you, taking us hundreds of miles into the wilderness, so I am not worried. I met a young Negro girl who is desperate to leave St. Louis and who will be a great help to me, so I agreed to bring her along. I pray I am making the right decision." As Elinore continued to write, her mind turned back to the day Paul left for duty at Fort Gibson, the day Elinore cried so long and hard she was sure her soul contained no more tears. But now, a fresh flood rose: not because she was afraid but because everything was moving so quickly, and the reality of what she had prepared for and anticipated for so long was coming at her in waves, forcing her to believe that all would go smoothly, that soon she would be with Paul, his arms around her once more.

Departure day arrived in a veil of morning fog that cast everything in ghostly shadows. Big Tim introduced Elinore to her wagon driver, a man named Wood. He was short and stocky, with a cap of black curls that framed a reddish brown face, and a spine that appeared to be permanently hunched – the result of long hours driving mule teams across vast stretches of prairie. He was also stone deaf – the result of a blow on the head in a barroom brawl, according to Big Tim, so Elinore communicated with Woods using simple hand movements that he easily understood.

As soon as Elinore, Ben, and Julee were in place, Big Tim rode up, nodded at Elinore, then leveled serious eyes on Julee.

"I shore hope you're ready for what you're heading into, young lady," Big Tim told Julee. "Fort Gibson is rough and wild and not what you been used to." He shifted in his saddle, and then shrugged. "Nothing disrespectful intended, but it's a place where the livin' is hard for whites, blacks, and Indians alike. Most comforts you're accustomed to don't even exist, so be prepared for a hell of a big change."

"I'm not worried, Mr. Lester. I'm just glad you gonna take me along."

Big Tim pulled back his shoulders and smiled at her. "You don't work for Daisy no more, so you can call me Big Tim, *oui?*"

"Okay, Big Tim. I promise you're not gonna be sorry you let me come along," Julee said, grinning in excitement.

"No. I don't expect I will," he agreed, letting his eyes linger on Julee's face for a brief moment. "Now I gotta go check to see that everybody is ready," he told her, riding off to reassure those who had paid dearly for his guidance and protection on the trail.

Elinore clasped Ben's shoulders with nervous hands. "We're on our way, son." She ruffled his fine blond hair. "You feel okay?"

Ben shook his head up and down. "Happy," he told his mother.

"Me, too," Elinore agreed, looking over at Julee, who was sitting tall in her seat, as if about to jump into the road and start walking.

Big Tim's voice boomed out over the crowd as he gave the signal to move out. A bugler sounded his horn, and the wagons pulled into line, their ballooning white tops shaking in the morning light. Elinore took a deep breath, filling her lungs with the sharp smoke of recently extinguished campfires; then she turned around and surveyed the string of wagons snaking along behind her. The ragged curl of fluttering canvas represented desperate dreams that might, or might not, come true. Men were walking alongside mules and oxen, cracking whips and gee-hawing at the unruly animals that balked at the weight of their heavy loads. Sons, brothers, nephews, and uncles prodded herds of livestock to move along, corralling horses, hogs, and family milk cows to stick closer to the wagons. Elinore looked into the faces of the women and easily sympathized with the furrowed worry lines etched on their brows. She understood their unease. Like them, she, too, was leaving everything familiar and cherished behind, and there would be no turning back.

Chapter 11

During the weeks that followed Tama's arrival at Great Oaks, she struggled with Suja's misplaced jealousy. The girl's annoying surveillance and outright resentment of Tama was evident to everyone in the talwa, except Hakan, who urged Tama to ignore his sister's attitude, as well as her threats to turn Tama over to slave catchers. He promised Tama that he would never allow anyone to take her away from his village, that he would protect her as if she were a member of his family.

After their encounter at the river, Tama was careful not to be alone with Hakan, or to place herself in a situation that might provoke another expression of his desire. She knew he wanted her, knew he watched her from a distance and let his eyes linger on her face when they sat across from each other at the family log fire. Tama would lower her gaze whenever he looked at her too long, breaking their magnetic connection. She wished she could think of Hakan simply as her friend and not the man who made her heart turn over and her limbs grow weak whenever they were close.

Tama's life at Great Oaks rolled on without incident until one morning, after nearly two months of living among the Fox, she saw a man on a horse emerge from the fog of mist that hugged the compound in a blanket of gray. The shiny gold buttons on his blue uniform created tiny sparks of light that glistened across the clearing. He wore a tall black hat and a haughty expression on his face, reminding Tama of a child's toy made of brightly painted wood. The rigid line of his back and the important gait of his horse indicated the importance of his mission. Everyone in the talwa stopped what they were doing and gawked at him.

Tama stopped pounding dry corn in a tall wooden mortar and watched as the soldier rode deeper into the village. Without acknowledging those who were staring at him, the soldier rode straight to the council house and brought his mount to a halt.

"He has come before," Spring Sky informed Tama, moving to join her by the log fire. "Always with other men, though, never alone."

"Why has he come? To take me away? Or maybe he is after Hakan?" Tama worried aloud, edging toward the shadows of a large palmetto tree, hoping to fade into the protective shield of its cascading fronds.

"I don't know," Spring Sky murmured, taking hold of Tama's arm, digging her fingernails into Tama's flesh. "But you must go!" she demanded. "Quickly! Find Hakan and warn him to stay away, too."

"Where is Hakan?" Tama asked, aware that Hakan had left the village early that morning but did not know where he went.

"He is in the forest, tracking fowl," Spring Sky hissed to Tama. "Find him! Quick! Keep him away ... until we know what this soldier wants."

Tama didn't hesitate. She fled into the woods, cut through the tangled brambles and raced toward the hunters' chickee, a hut built high on stilts among the tall birch trees, a shady place for the men to rest while tracking game in the forest.

Hurrying along the narrow path, Tama sidestepped pools of oozing mud and thick layers of slick moss, not stopping until she saw the thatched, three-sided hut. Quickly, she scrambled up the makeshift ladder made of vines, and peered inside. All she found was an empty gourd and a broken arrow, left by a previous hunter. Frustrated, she turned and scanned the forest, calling Hakan's name. A flock of birds, startled by Tama's voice, flew out of the trees and scattered just as Hakan came running up the path. He paused at the base of the tree and looked up, puzzled, and then grabbed the rough vines and swung himself upward, dropping easily at her side.

"What are you doing here?" he demanded, entering the lofty hut. Inside, he took Tama's hand and held it rather firmly. "You should not be walking around out here. What if I took you for a deer? I could have shot an arrow into ..."

"There's a soldier in the square ground," Tama interrupted, knowing his firm hold on her was out of concern, not anger. The sexual tension between them was ever-present, ever-shifting, and she knew he felt it as much as she did, even in this time of danger.

Hakan stilled, eyes narrowed. "Only one man?" he cautiously inquired.

Tama inclined her head. "Yes. Your mother says he has come before."

"What did he look like?" Hakan asked, his breathing fast and audible as she described the man and his horse.

"His face is pale, thin, and narrow," she said. "And his scraggly red beard touches the buttons on his coat."

"Fisko," Hakan recognized. "He's not a slave catcher or much of a threat. He comes to Great Oaks every year and tells my father we must leave. And every year we ignore him. He's not dangerous only foolish to think we will do as he says." Hakan made a dismissive gesture with one hand. "The soldier has learned that our mico is ill. He thinks the Fox will soon be weak and easy to persuade. Blue Waters' strength and defiance have kept the Army away, but once my father passes into the afterlife, many soldiers will come to make us leave." Hakan turned, preparing to leave.

"But what if he came for a different reason?" Tama pressed, her tone tight with worry. "Maybe he wants me. I helped you escape. I held a knife on the trader. I ..."

"Shh...don't worry," Hakan softly interrupted, releasing Tama's hand. He placed his fingers on the side of her face and searched her features with a mixture of unspoken affection and tentative caution. "There's no reason to fear," he calmly assured her. "Trust me. I will not let anything happen to you. You believe me, don't you?"

"Yes," Tama murmured, boldly placing her head on his shoulder, praying he would not back away. When he did not move, she pressed even closer, and when his arms firmed around her back, she stood quietly, making the encounter last, drinking in the nearness that she craved.

"I must return to the village," Hakan finally said, separating from Tama. "I will stand with my father and my people as we face this soldier and make our voices heard."

The square ground adjoining the council house filled quickly as members of the Fox clan, anxious to learn what the white man on the big horse would say, drew together. An undercurrent of curious murmurs quickly evolved into a single anxiety-filled voice, which faded as soon as Mico Blue Waters emerged from the council house and approached the soldier. The mico was wearing a patchwork cape of vibrant colors that brushed the ground as he walked. A red headband held his gray hair off his face, and he advanced with the aid of a tall walking stick carved of polished wood. Taking his time, Mico Blue Waters crossed the square ground, greeted the soldier with a formal nod, and then waited as Fisko dismounted and faced him.

From behind the protective shade of a large palmetto tree, Tama watched the scene unfold, holding her breath when she saw Hakan stride proudly across the square and join his father.

"I am Sergeant Fisko, United States Army."

"I know who you are," Blue Waters acknowledged. "Why are you here?"

"I've come with orders from my superior officer."

"The same orders you bring every year?" Hakan interjected.

The soldier raised both eyebrows and frowned at Hakan, sniffed, and then went on with his speech, directing his words at the mico. "You have very little time to prepare," he said.

"Prepare for what?" Mico Blue Waters haughtily demanded, as if he didn't know the answer, as if to force the words from the man's pink mouth.

"For your people's resettlement on land set aside by the government for your new home," the soldier answered before spitting a stream of tobacco juice into the red dirt at his feet.

"We have told you before... we will not go West just because the white man orders us to do so," Blue Waters responded, his words as strong and unmovable as the oak trees surrounding his village.

"You will pack only what you can carry," Fisko ploughed ahead, ignoring Blue Waters' remark. "Women with children will ride in wagons, but all others will walk. You are allowed one horse or one mule per family to carry food and any personal items you wish to take," Fisko instructed.

Hakan stared at the man in disgust, searing his face with hardened eyes; then he boldly strode closer and said, "My father speaks for all of us. We will not voluntarily leave."

"I'd re-think that if I were you. This time there'll be no reprieve," Fisko warned, screwing his lips to one side. "It's time to go. Don't resist or try to run away," he continued, "because more soldiers than you have ever seen will come, with fast horses and long guns. You will perish if you don't do as I say."

A young Creek man dressed in western clothes stepped out of the crowd and faced Blue Waters. "Mico," he said to his leader. "If we must go, is it not better to leave here as a proud people, rather than a conquered one?"

Blue Waters stiffened, anger flaming in his weathered face, a scathing look in his hooded eyes. He scowled at the young man who had spoken and drew himself up to his full height.

"John-Eagle," the mico addressed the young man, "you forget that this land is ours. Where we belong. We will not voluntarily abandon our homes. Never!" Then he turned back to remind the soldier, "The President promised this land to us. He said it would remain always with the Creek. It is written on a paper that holds great importance and you must honor it."

An outcry of agreement erupted from the Fox, who began to chant in support of their leader.

"That agreement is no longer valid. Things have changed. You will not be the mico of your people much longer, so you would do well to urge them to leave," was Fisko's curt reply.

Mico Blue Waters reeled backward as if he had been slapped. "You wait for my death so you can prod my people off our land?" Blue Waters' voice rose in indignation. "You underestimate our strength!" He charged forward, pointing his walking stick at Fisko, and raising his chin, waited for the reply that did not come. The soldier simply smirked, and then licked his thin pink lips.

"What about our livestock? The cows, hogs, turkeys that we've raised?" another of the clan shouted out.

"All that will be left behind," Fisko snapped, his temper clearly beginning to rise, his patience growing thin.

"My people have lived here for many generations, peacefully... farming, raising children, and tending our stock. We have done nothing to provoke you to do this to us," Blue Waters stated, slowly lowering his stick, as if to calm the restless crowd.

"Well," Fisko drew out the word. "I can't say that's true. There's been a lot of stealing food, rustling livestock, and even some harboring of slaves." He stopped talking and glanced around, his probing eyes skimming the faces of the blacks in the crowd. "Any new runaways come here since the last time I checked? I'd bet so," he finished, shooting another stream of tobacco juice onto the ground.

The man's remark sent a jolt of fear into Tama, who shrank into the shadows.

"All slaves living among us were accounted for the last time you came to my village," Blue Waters threw back. Turning to his son, the mico inclined his head, giving Hakan permission to speak in his place.

"You hate us for treating our slaves...African and Indian ... as helpers, as members of our families, while white masters bully and beat their slaves, using them like beasts," Hakan began. "We have no blacks here who do not belong to us."

Sergeant Fisko raised his arm and pointed out over the square, bringing a hush over the gathering. "All this talk won't accomplish a thing. You'll be removed, and soon, so I advise you to start preparing. Might be a few days, or a few weeks, but it'll be soon, and you'll be off this land." Then he mounted his horse and roughly turned it around, spraying dirt and rocks over Mico Blue Waters' colorful robe as he galloped away.

The expressions of fear and outrage that erupted made Tama shudder. The voices of the Fox sounded brittle and torn, stretched taut with anxiety as they railed against the announcement they feared might come true this time.

"Come," Spring Sky said to Tama, taking her hand.

Tama, eager to hear what the mico would say to his frightened people, emerged from the shadows of the palmetto tree and followed Spring Sky across the square ground.

As Mico Blue Waters spoke, she heard sorrow in his words, deep regret laced with concern. "I do not know what will happen next," Blue Waters admitted. "But I know land hungry men wait at the edge of our talwa, anxious to take our land, our slaves, and our livestock. This soldier spoke the same words to us many times. I do not believe him any more than I believe his chief – who has not kept his promises."

Breaking his eyes from his father, Hakan lifted a hand to hush the people and then spoke. "I agree with my father. Our removal will not happen. This soldier came only to frighten us into running away," he stopped to let his words sink in and then continued. "We must never forget about the Lower Creeks, who willingly left their homes and went to live in the new land. They left with heavy hearts and broken spirits because they gave up the struggle too quickly. They did not try to hold onto what was theirs. But we Fox have remained, living peacefully, and we must believe the President's promise not to take our land from us. If we resist, yes, the white man's greed may fall upon us. They may burn our homes, trample our crops, kill our livestock and steal all our possessions. But that may not happen ....it is the chance we have to take." He stopped talking and stepped back, allowing his father to take over.

Mico Blue Waters spread his feet apart, as if to anchor himself to the earth. He lifted both hands to the sky. "Soon our brother clans from downriver will arrive for talks in the council house. We will decide our course of action and deal with this man's threat. Do not let this worry burden you, my people. Know that my son, Hakan, who has returned to his home, will carry you forward in my place when I am no longer with you. Tomorrow we celebrate the Red Tail dance. Hakan will dance for me and replace my weak bones with his strong legs. With food, drink, and dance, as is our custom, we will set aside all matters of bloodshed and heartache for a short time." He paused and took a deep breath, his chest heaving up and down as he struggled to draw in air, his frail condition evident to all. "Return to your homes now. Return to your work. Nothing has changed. The Fox will go on living here even when I am no longer among you."

Spring Sky tipped her head back, exposing a weary expression of resignation that suddenly made her appear very old. The skin at the corners of her mouth tightened, and then relaxed, as if she were struggling to accept her husband's pronouncement.

"Don't worry," Tama heard Suja tell her mother. "Father is right. The festivities will cleanse our minds of worry ...for a

124

short time, at least. It will be good for father to be among the men of the Wolf, the Bear, and the Turtle. Their presence will give him strength to hold on for many years to come."

Spring Sky shook her head in denial of her daughter's optimistic words and then turned and walked away.

Tama pondered Suja's remark, sensing the importance of the upcoming gathering of the various clans of the Creek. In numbers there was strength, perhaps enough to prevent the traditions of the Muscogule Creek from slipping away.

The Fox spent the next three days preparing for the arrival of the expected guests. Tama spent her days cooking, cleaning, gathering, grinding, and weaving—chores that kept her hands occupied, while her thoughts, too often, strayed to her feelings for Hakan. Tama worked alongside Spring Sky and Three Winds as they cleaned the family's huts, cleared old ashes from the hearths, gathered fan palms to place on the ground for sleeping mats, and laid new logs in the fire pits. Suja did little more than boss Tama around, and Tama quickly learned that the best way to deal with Suja's imperious attitude was simply to stay busy and out of her way. The men brewed large quantities of the Muscogean black drink, a strong concoction of cassava to serve to their guests, while the children created huge piles of wood for the communal bonfire that would burn for three nights straight.

The night before the festivities were to begin, Tama lay awake, trying to imagine what the next day would bring. It saddened her to realize that the Muscogule Creek were living in fear of expulsion and had no way of escaping the change that was coming. The words that Mico Blue Waters had spoken to his people were reassuring, but still Tama worried about her place in the complicated web of Indians, soldiers, settlers, and land grabbers. If the Army removed the Fox, she might be captured, returned to Royaltin Ridge, or sold to another master. Her only hope was that Hakan would not let that happen.

Chapter 12

"Get up, you lazy zambo. I want you to do my hair," Suja ordered, thrusting a stiff bristle brush into Tama's hand before she had time to sit up in bed. "Come over here and help me dress. Guests are already arriving." Suja gave Tama a shove on the shoulder and went to the shelf on the wall to select her clothing for the day.

Tama got up from her straw mat on the floor, stuck her feet into the soft animal skin moccasins Three Winds had made for her, and pulled on the faded red dress that had been Suja's before Spring Sky gave it to her. She watched Suja striding importantly back and forth across the room, her neck stretched taut, her back as stiff as the turkey feather broom propped by the door, clearly flaunting her disdain for Tama.

Not about to get into an argument so early, Tama moved quickly. She placed the three legged stool in the center of the chickee and waited until Suja plopped herself down on it, a small mirror in her hand. Tama had learned the hard way that talking to Suja when Suja was in one of her foul moods was like wading into a flood-ravaged creek: She never knew where or when she might lose her footing and plunge into dangerous waters. However, she did her best to be friendly with Suja, who as the daughter of the mico, did deserve her respect.

Suja admired her reflection in the tortoise shell hand mirror as she told Tama, "You will stay at the chickee and tend the food today. Do not speak to any of the guests. The only people you need to talk with today are me, mother, and

127

Three Winds. And especially *not* Hakan. Understand?" Suja threatened in her most important tone.

"Yes, I understand," Tama murmured, a slow burn rising on her face.

"This is a very special day," Suja went on. "The *obanga* is tonight."

"*Obanga*?" Tama repeated, eager to learn the expressions and the words of Hakan's people.

"The dance, you stupid girl. And Hakan cannot be bothered by *anyone*." She paused, tilted her head to one side, and then shifted her position, as if trying to see Tama in the mirror. "Well, maybe he can be bothered by Wyiana," she added with a sly smile. "Everyone knows she will soon become his wife."

Tama stiffened in surprise and stopped brushing Suja's hair. Pausing with her hand in mid-air, she waited as Suja cleared her throat and continued with her chatter, as if in a hurry to divulge enough details to further aggravate Tama. "Wyiana lives among the Wolf. She is my dearest friend, and I sincerely hope my brother chooses her at the Red Tail Dance tonight. It's long past time for him to take a wife," Suja continued, letting out an audible sigh. "With father so ill, Hakan will soon take his place, and when he does, he must have a Muscogule wife at his side."

Tama felt as if she'd been punched in the stomach. She thought about the gentle way Hakan had protected her during their journey to Great Oaks, how he'd kissed her at the river, how he'd caressed her in the hut in the woods. What had those encounters meant to him? Not what they'd meant to her? She let her shoulders drop, knowing she should not be surprised to learn that Hakan's future had long been planned, and that it would unfold according to the traditions of his people. His overtures of affection had simply been the fleeting, impulsive actions of a young man overcome by emotion and not indications of his love for her.

"Take care not to burn the corn cakes," Suja rambled on, jerking Tama back to the moment. "No one wants to eat burned, dry food, so don't you move two paces from the fire, you hear?"

While Suja raced on giving orders, Tama slowly ran the three-prong, deer bone comb through the girl's long black hair, grudgingly admitting that Hakan's sister did have the most beautiful hair in the village. With a twist, Tama swept the heavy tresses to the front and pushed it into a glossy pompadour that stood out over Suja's forehead like a shiny black hat. In the custom of the women of the Fox, it was the perfect style for a day of festivities and reunion.

Though Tama's hands were busily styling Suja's hair, her mind churned with alarm.

If Hakan takes a wife, what will that mean? Tama picked up a spray of dove feathers to place into the crown of Suja's tresses. *Will he lose all concern for me if he has a wife to worry about?* Tama's fingers quivered and her heart beat faster as she tried to pin the feathers in place. *How can I remain with his family once he has a Wolf wife at his side?* Fearful of sticking Suja, she calmed herself down by concentrating on the yelps and cries of the spirited boys who were playing ball in the square ground outside.

After completing Suja's hair, Tama stepped back to admire her creation, steadying her hands in a tight clasp, hoping Suja did not see how nervous she had become.

Suja held the hand mirror up to her face and studied her

129

reflection. "Well, it will have to do," she muttered rather crossly, but looking over Suja's shoulder and into the mirror, Tama could see that she was pleased with the outcome. "I hope the feasting and dancing goes on all night," Suja sighed, squirming in her seat, clearly anxious for the communal festivities to begin. She lowered the mirror, and then she added, as easily as if she were commenting on the weather, "I am certain Hakan will place the red tail at Wyiana's feet." She resumed her assessment of her reflection, pretending to look at herself while her eyes shifted to watch Tama. "Many of the Fox men have two, or even three, wives. But Mico Blue Waters has been satisfied with only one wife ... my mother. And Hakan will do the same. Wyiana is a strong Wolf woman who will stand by Hakan as he leads the Fox in these difficult times. The clan will be happy ... you know, Hakan could never choose a woman who did not have the respect of the clan."

Tama felt the sting of Suja's remark as it burned through her clothes and touched her heart. However, she held her body taut, unwilling to allow Suja's attempt to rile her to take hold. She stared into the shiny oval of mirrored glass, swept her gaze to Suja's forehead, and then down to her chin. When she spoke, she hoped her voice did not sound as thick and unconvincing as she felt. "Hakan is a man who makes wise decisions. I'm sure he will choose a proper woman as his mate."

With a jerk, Suja suddenly thrust the mirror down onto her lap, and swiveled around to face Tama. "Yes, he will... and you will not interfere."

Tama stepped back, alarmed by the spark of dislike in Suja's tone, determined to clear the air. "I would never interfere with anything Hakan wanted to do. I am his friend

..." Tama began.

"No, you're not his friend!" Suja stated in a near-growl, standing so abruptly that the mirror fell from her lap and crashed to the floor in a spray of broken glass. "You're a runaway nigra with no home and no people. Hakan could have left you behind and let your master find you, but he decided to protect you. Why, I don't know. But never forget, Tama ... I can turn you over to a bounty hunter right now, you know? I'm sure it wouldn't be difficult to find out where you came from. Mark my words, you will not find happiness here ... among the Fox. My brother's pity is all you will ever have." Smugly, Suja patted the front of her tall pompadour and twisted her lips into a sinister grin. With a huff of disdain, she snatched a white cape-blouse trimmed in bands of red and green and a matching skirt from a peg on the wall. She threw the clothing at Tama and glared at her for a moment before ordering, "Help me dress." Then she grabbed a pair of knee-high moccasins from beneath the shelf and held them out toward Tama.

Without a word, Tama squatted down to help Suja into the boots, kneeling to let her settle each tiny foot into the soft dusky leather. Tama's hands were shaking badly, and she concentrated on not touching Suja's flesh, which she knew would feel as cold and hard as the words the girl had spewed at her.

After the skirt was in place and the blouse properly fluffed, Suja reached for a small reed box on the shelf. She opened it, removed a thin leather string and held it high, letting the tiny wooden fox that was tied to it, dangle in the air. The figure was not much larger than a ripe walnut, carved of highly polished wood, and surrounded by bits of red animal fur strung with small white shells. She placed the amulet around her neck, and then lifted the tiny fox-shaped charm closer to her face.

"This will bring the Fox good luck," she told Tama, fingering the wooden charm. "Only members of the mico's family are allowed to wear the *culv*, to prevent evil spirits from spoiling the Red Tail Dance. It has great powers ... but only for those who *belong*." A stretch of silence drifted between the two women while Suja ran her thumb and forefinger over the small fox-shaped charm. After a moment, she dropped it against her breast, turned, and tilted her nose up at Tama. "Tonight, Hakan will give his *culv* to the woman he chooses as his wife, when he dances at the mound top ... and you will *not* be there. Your place is here. At the fire. Understand?"

Tama bit her lip and waited for her anger to cool before deciding to speak her mind. Yes, Suja was Hakan's sister, and the daughter of the mico, but that didn't mean she could treat Tama as if she were her slave. Hadn't Hakan promised Tama that she would live free? Be treated as a member of his clan? "I owe my life to Hakan. He helped me find a safe place to live. For his kindness ..."

"His kindness?" Suja interrupted with a snap. "Your mind has been twisted by his kindness." She suddenly laughed, tilting back her head to send her voice into the chickee's rafters. "Hakan is kind to everyone! Even those who would do him harm. You simple girl. You know nothing."

He may be kind to everyone, but does he hold others in his arms and promise to protect them? Tama thought. Kiss them at the river bank with a passion that stops their hearts? In her heart, Tama knew Hakan did not treat her kindly out of pity. She could still feel the heat of his body warming hers when they huddled together in the cave, sense the pulse of her blood rushing to the surface of her skin as it always did when

132

he came too close or brushed his hand against her arm. Now, Tama narrowed her eyes at Suja, who shrugged and bent to pick up the broken mirror.

"You keep in your place tonight," Suja warned, standing erect. "I'll be watching your every move, and if you do anything to offend me or my family's guests, I will arrange for you to disappear from Great Oaks ... forever. Don't test me, Tama, because if you do, you will lose." Then Suja turned in a swirl of colorful ruffles, ducked her head so that her high pompadour would not catch on the palmetto fronds hanging above the entry, and left.

Tama watched Suja swish off into the maze of huts along the river, a swell of fear rising in her chest. Suja was dangerous, crafty, and as the daughter of the mico, powerful. Tama knew she had to be careful if she wanted to remain free, at Great Oaks, and *near* Hakan.

Chapter 13

The ebony sky, strewn with thousands of crystalline stars, lay silent above Tama's head while the earth beneath her feet pulsed with rhythm. The sounds of drums, shells, and flutes, played with great intensity, swept into Tama's legs, up her spine, and directly into her heart. From her hiding spot behind the fringe of shrub pine at the edge of the mound top, she watched the opening of the Red Tail Dance. She had planned to stay at the log fire and help Three Winds prepare the feast that everyone would enjoy after the dancing, doing as Suja had ordered, but the lure of the music and her own curiosity had won out, especially after Three Winds told Tama, "Don't pay no attention to Suja. She just too full of herself. You go on up there and enjoy the music." The old woman huffed her annoyance, and then told Tama, "Besides, you need to learn about the Fox. Natomee, the keeper of our stories is gonna chant the past, so the young people can learn how the Muscogule came to be."

"But I won't understand more than three words of what he'll say," Tama had told Three Winds, who nodded, and then flashed a smile.

"Then listen up and I'll tell you what he's gonna say," Three Winds decided, launching into a quick lesson on the origin of the Creek. "You see the people the white folks call Creeks came out of caves far away, some say as far away as Texas, from a place called the Red River. They walked into the sunrise until they came to this good land along the Tallapoosa. After they settled here, the Shawnee, the Natchez,

134

the Hitchiti, the Yuchi, the Tuckabatchee, and the Alabama Indians arrived and claimed a spot for themselves. So, the white men just called all of the Indians "Creeks," because they lived along the water, but the people were really Muscogule. After a time, everybody married into different tribes, started speaking the same language, and followed the same traditions. So that's how the Creek came to be." Three Winds cocked an ancient eye at Tama. "You look like you got something on your mind."

"Yes, I do. Tell me about the *culv*. I saw the one Suja is wearing tonight. What's so special about it?"

Three Winds scratched her head, scrunched up her lips in concentration. "The way I heard it ...long ago, the first mico of the Fox carved a tiny wooden fox from the limb of a great oak tree that'd been split in two by lightning. He prayed to it when trouble came, and it taught him how to survive in the new land. Since it protected him from harm, he made one for each member of his family. He believed it had special powers, but only for those who belonged to his family – by blood or marriage."

"And what about..." Tama started, but Three Winds cut her off.

"That's all I'm gonna say, so go on up the mound. You just in my way 'round here."

Not wasting a second, Tama climbed the narrow steps on the steep side of the Sacred Mound, steps carved into the hard, red earth generations ago. Once she reached the mound top, she hid, fearful that Suja might see her and send her away.

Now, Tama watched as the visiting micos of the various clans took seats on the ground in front of the blazing ceremonial fire. In unison, they broke into a high-spirited chant as the women, who were standing around the perimeter of the dance ground, began to sway and rock. They shook shells and bones, creating a nearly hypnotic cadence that blended with the crackle of the fire. Soon, men wearing fox masks entered the dance ground and stood in a circle. Tama spied Hakan immediately. His long legs, firm chest, and muscled arms were sheathed in supple deerskin. His feet were encased in knee-high moccasins hung with bits of fur. Each Fox man carried a long spear topped with a fluffy fox tail, hefted high, as each paraded past the women. Dancers from the visiting clans followed, strutting into the arena in full clan regalia to pay homage to the animals from which their clans originated. The Bear wore shaggy robes of bear fur, the Turtle danced in a jerky half-crouch with large leathery shells tied to their limbs. The Wind hoisted colorful kites strung with multicolored-ribbons, and the Deer wore spiky antlers atop their heads. The mixture of song, dance, drum, and flute created a frenzied mélange of colorful movement that lasted until the bellow of stag horn sounded. The men stopped dancing and moved to stand in front of the women, and a sacred hush fell over the mound.

Tama inched forward, shifting her attention to Mico Blue Waters, who arrived on a cypress litter carried by four men whose faces were painted in red and blue. Blue Waters' elaborate headdress, hung with russet-colored foxtails and bright red feathers, dwarfed his moon-silvered figure. His sunken eyes stood out like dark knots on a pine tree, and his beaded shirt, striped with bands of fringe down the arms and across the shoulders, was studded with shiny cowrie shells. A wistful smile touched Tama's lips. She had grown fond of Hakan's father during her short time among the Fox. He was a wise, much respected leader whose time was short, and tonight, he looked as fragile as a dried leaf tossed by the wind.

The men placed Blue Waters' litter on the ground alongside the other micos, and then stepped away, leaving their chief to preside over the evening's events. When a young girl placed a spray of wild cherry branches in Mico Blue Waters' wrinkled brown hands, he nodded in appreciation, then lay back on the red and brown striped blanket that covered his litter and made a gesture with his hand, inviting Spring Sky to take her place beside him.

After Spring Sky sat down next to her husband, an old man came forward and placed a bag of dried maize and a string of fish at Blue Waters' feet, and then he began chanting. Though Tama did not understand what Natomee was saying, she knew it must be the story Three Winds had told her. As the strange words slipped from Natomee's lips, Tama watched Spring Sky, whose long braid lay across her shoulder like a gray-black snake. She was wearing a deep purple cape-blouse, a ruffled skirt, and pristine white moccasins that looked as if they had never touched the ground. Though she was clearly past the beauty of her prime, her eyes were clear. A serene expression claimed her features, revealing her acceptance of Blue Waters' impending death.

When Natomee finished his story, Blue Waters sat up on his litter, coughed weakly, and then spoke in a voice that was surprisingly strong.

"The path from this world to my home in the spirit land is opening wider by the moment," he began. "My aging soul has lost its fire, and I am restless to join the Giver of Breath on a journey I do not fear. When I leave you, as soon I will," he went on, "I pray you will be brave and honorable in all things, even when all is failing around you. When I was a young man, I could see far across the horizon, to villages beyond the great oaks at the foothills, where my neighbors—the Deer, the Wind, the Wolf, and the Eagle live. But now my fragile eyes see only white men crowding us into a corner, making our hunting grounds as small as clumps of buffalo dung. In the days ahead, they will try to take our land, our horses, our women, and even our slaves ... the helpmates we have treated as our own. My prayer to the Master of Breath is that you, my people, will never let them take your soul."

"And your prayers will be answered!" Hakan called out, taking long strides toward his father. "Tonight we celebrate the bonds of the Muscogule as we come together as one clan."

"And you, my son, will place the scepter on the woman of your choice," Blue Waters stated with pride. "Now, go. Let me see you dance with the Fox so I may close my eyes in peace."

The people cheered, giving up the *yahola yell* of approval.

Tama's eyes grew wide and a chill of adoration rooted her to the earth as she looked at Hakan, who removed the Fox mask and threw a red fur cape across one shoulder, its glossy fur shimmering and trailing behind him as he crossed the ground. He resembled a chiseled replica of himself, carved of magnificent hardwood and adorned with the utmost care. His feathers, fur, paint, and beads created a mesmerizing vision that held the attention of every woman at the mound.

"Hakan is very handsome tonight, isn't he?" a voice beside Tama stated.

She whirled around to see Three Winds standing at her side. "What are you doing here? Who's tending the fire?" Tama hissed, alarmed that the feast would be ruined and Suja would blame her.

"Others are watching the boiling pots and roasting spits," Three Winds assured Tama. "I only gonna stay a minute, just to see a little bit of dancin'."

Tama dropped her shoulders and relaxed, glad that Three Winds had sneaked away from her chores to join her.

A horn sounded and the music resumed. Quickly, the men formed a line that wound like a silky dark ribbon around the perimeter of the dance ground. The drums beat faster, the flutes rang out louder, and the rattle of turtle shells churned the night air to a frenzy. The men leapt and floated across the smooth dirt of the arena, strutting like roosters, eager to impress the women, who edged closer, hoping to be pulled into the dance.

"Which one is Wyiana?" Tama asked Three Winds.

"The slender one dressed in the color of violets," Three Winds whispered, pointing a work-worn finger toward a very pretty girl wearing a heavily ruffled dress. Her black hair was thick and loose, framing a slender face the color of almonds. Eyes that were large and dark stared intently at Hakan, as if to force his attention toward her.

"Suja says Wyiana will be Hakan's wife," Tama stated, easing into the subject that had been on her mind all day.

Three Winds simply clucked her tongue and lifted one shoulder.

Tama kept her attention on the girl, who had begun to dance closer to Hakan, even though he looked past her, his eyes sweeping across the clearing, as if searching the crowd for someone. When his gaze swept toward Tama, she jumped back into the shadows and pulled Three Winds with her. "Oh, no. I don't want Hakan to see me," Tama whispered.

"Why?" Three Winds asked. "Hakan would be glad to know you came to witness the dancing. He won't send you away."

"But Suja would. She threatened to turn me over to slave catchers if I didn't stay away."

"She likes to make threats that she rarely carries out. She's always tellin' Hakan that he needs to take Wyiana as his wife, but as you can see, he hasn't paid his sister any attention."

Three Winds' words stuck in Tama's mind. The old woman was right. Hakan had not married yet, so why should Tama be so concerned about what Suja said. She gripped the folds of her skirt, unable to keep her eyes from Hakan. His sleek fox cape swung around him like the wings of a butterfly searching for a spot to land. The Wolf girl, prodded by Suja, soon positioned herself in Hakan's path, her lovely face turned toward him. Hakan jumped high, his foxtail scepter brushing Wyiana's cheek, which initiated a cry of approval from Suja, who clapped her hands and chanted even louder, her blatant delight twisting Tama's heart.

The tempo of the music and pace of the dance rose to a thrilling peak, and then suddenly everything slowed. The men crowded around Hakan to block him from view. The women began to sing what Three Winds informed Tama was the Song of Betrothal. The thunderous beat of thick beef bones hitting taut deerskin stretched atop hollow logs vibrated the air, and soon, the female dancers retreated to the sidelines in a vibrant swirl of feathers and beads. The circle of men around Hakan opened, and he emerged, holding the fox scepter, from which dangled the *culv* he'd removed from around his neck. He threw back his head, stepped to the left, then to the right, toward the Wolf girl, and then away from her. The women squealed in delight at the sight of the handsome, strong warrior, clearly enjoying the drama of the moment. Hakan lowered his chin, paused, and then stared past Wyiana to grace Tama with the same serious expression she had seen on his face when they'd spoken together in the cave. Afraid to move, she stood mesmerized by his strong, sure eyes, now ringed with gold from the firelight.

Hakan grinned in a rather teasing manner, and then he bowed his head at Tama.

The crowd gasped in surprise. The music stopped completely. Only the sound of wood breaking apart in the bonfire broke the silence. Tama's heart climbed into her throat. She turned to flee, but Three Winds grasped her shoulder and held her in place. "Stay!" she whispered. "You have no reason to run."

Hakan raised the fox scepter and pointed it at Tama, his curious smile shifting into a stern expression that turned his lips into a straight line. As he stalked toward Tama, each step sent her mind reeling. Confused and alarmed, she began to back away from him, unsure of why he was toying with her at such a serious time. Was he taunting her to entertain his guests? Making a joke of the zambo girl who should not even be at the mound top? The scrambled thoughts that raced through her mind scattered when Suja suddenly appeared at her side.

"Why are you here?" Suja shouted, jerking Tama away from Three Winds. She pushed Tama hard, making her stumble and nearly fall, but Tama regained her balance and boldly stepped into the circle of light created by the raging bonfire. "Get back to the chickee!" Suja shouted. "Leave the mount top! You shame my family by coming here. This is our sacred ground, and you do not belong!"

The sting of Suja's jealous rant felt like the prick of a thousand wasps, but Tama refused to react to the pain. She would not give Suja a reason to continue her verbal attack, nor would she leave, unless Hakan asked her to go. Forcing her face into an emotionless mask, Tama held her ground, her hands knotted into fists at her sides.

Suja, realizing she would get no fight from Tama, turned on Hakan. She reached out, grabbed the fox scepter, and angrily dashed it to the ground.

A collective gasp of shock flew from the mouths of the people to witness such an unprecedented act of violation. For the daughter of the mico to do such a thing was unheard of, and questioning whispers rippled through the crowd as they watched the scene play out.

Finding her voice, Tama focused on Hakan and finally spoke. "Why are you doing this to me? Why do you ..." she stammered, overcome with confusion.

Hakan did not speak but simply stood in front of Tama, his body quivering, his breath coming hard, perspiration glistening on his bare chest.

Eager to escape the humiliating situation, Tama bent down, retrieved the talisman from the ground, and held it out Hakan. *Let him give it to Wyiana*, she decided. *It was never meant for me.* However, just as Hakan extended his hand to take the precious necklace from Tama, Suja snatched it and held it high, far from Hakan's reach. Tama grabbed Suja's wrist and squeezed it hard, branding her fingers into the girl's flesh, taking selfish pleasure in the horrified expression that came over Suja's face at the strength in Tama's hand.

When the necklace fell from Suja's grip and landed at Hakan's feet, Suja spun on her heel, stalked away to stand at Wyiana's side and glared at Hakan.

"Tama," Hakan finally spoke. "I did not mean to tease you, only to include you. I thought ..."

"It is nothing," Tama cut him off, struggling to control her voice. "Continue with the dance," she said, blinking to clear tears from her eyes. Turning away, she walked stiffly to the terraced path and descended the uneven steps.

At the bottom of the mound, she clamped a hand over her mouth to contain the scream that was bursting inside her. She ran, racing into the woods, where a mist of silver fog had turned the forest into a sea of clouds. Crashing along the familiar path, Tama felt the piercing eyes of every person standing atop the mound burning into her soul, felt the strike of their astonished words flung down at her like arrows shot from a bow. She heard the music start up again and wondered if Hakan was leaping even higher now, twirling even faster, dancing circles around the Wolf girl before placing the scepter at her tiny, moccasin-clad feet.

Why was he so cruel to me? Tama wondered. His teasing antics had ruined her future among the Fox. From now on, every woman in the village would be laughing behind Tama's back, taking pleasure in her disgrace. What Hakan had done would make Tama a joke for a long time to come. How could she ever hope to get along with Suja now? What did Spring Sky think? How could Tama resume her daily work in the village after what Hakan had done?

Tama stopped running long enough to draw in three long breaths; then she pushed on, tearing at the thorny branches in her way. Shameful tears ran from her eyes, clouding her vision and emptying her heart of all feeling for Hakan. The tangled brambles and fat curling vines grew more dense as she went on, testing each step as she tried to avoid pools of oozing quicksand that lurked beneath the cover of dry leaves. When Tama came to the thatched, three-sided hut raised high on four tall poles, she scrambled up the ladder and collapsed inside, too tired to think about the complicated situation. She had to rest. In the morning, she would go away, and she would not stop running until she found a new place to live, a place where she could truly belong. Tama lay down on her side, drew her knees to her chest, and propped her head on one arm. She closed her eyes, wanting nothing more than to fall into a deep sleep and forget about the dance, Suja's meanness, the Wolf girl's beauty, and especially, Hakan's humiliating gesture.

Moments before sleep claimed Tama, she heard the snap of a tree branch in the woods. She sat up, but remained quiet; she was well aware that white settlers, land speculators, and even slave hunters roamed the woods at night. The snap of tree branches grew louder, and then she heard footsteps approaching the hut. Tama eased to her feet, went to the entry of the hut and scanned the area, relieved to see Hakan, bathed in moonlight, emerge from the shadows. He climbed up the vine ladder, entered the hut, and with a shake of his head, told Tama, "I knew I'd find you here." He sat next to her on the floor, and when his knee touched her leg, she shifted away, not wanting to be close to him.

"Look at me, please," Hakan begged.

Slowly, Tama turned her eyes on him and studied his face, still colored with white stripes that glowed silver in the moonlight. She was desperate to know how he felt: Was he irritated, sorry, worried, contrite? She discerned nothing from his somber appearance.

"I only stopped here to rest. I'm leaving Great Oaks," Tama told him. "I can't return to the village."

"That's not true," Hakan replied.

"Yes, it is. How can I live among your people after what happened? Because of me, you shamed your family. Choosing a wife is a serious matter, Hakan, and you should not involve me in your ugly joke." Tama's voice was strong, yet she prayed he could not detect the confusing mixture of disappointment and hope that filled her heart. "Was Wyiana pleased when you chose her?" Tama had to ask.

Hakan rose up on his knees and bent closer to Tama. She inhaled the wood smoke, tobacco, and perspiration that wafted from his body, surprised to see his fox-shaped amulet resting, once again, against his chest. "I chose no one," he firmly replied. "I didn't mean to hurt you by pointing the scepter at you." He placed a hand on Tama's cheek, making her stiffen with longing. "When I danced and looked into the faces of the women, I saw no one but you. I knew at that moment that I did not want the face of a stranger in my lodge. I traveled far with you. I was at ease with you then, as I am now. My father wanted me to choose a wife, but I couldn't. I know now that it could only be you." When he started to remove his *culv*, as if to place it around Tama's neck, she shook her head and shifted farther away from him.

"No. Hakan, please don't," Tama gently refused, putting her hands over the amulet to push it back toward Hakan. "Think about Spring Sky. Your sister. They would hate you for choosing me. They will never accept me as your wife because I am not of your people ..."

Hakan reached out and tried to pull her to him, but Tama resisted, slumping against the wall of the hut. She squeezed her fingers into fists as tears slid down her cheeks.

"Don't cry." Hakan wiped her face with a gentle brush of his fingers.

"What about Wyiana?" Tama asked.

"Wyiana is beautiful," Hakan admitted. "All of the Wolf

women are beautiful, and their mothers would like nothing better than to have their daughters marry the next mico of the Fox. When I imagine my life, with a woman at my side, I see only you. There's no reason why you can't be my wife."

Tama lifted her head. "One of many, I suppose? Many of the Fox men have more than one wife."

"I only want one woman to share my bed and my life, and that is you."

"Please, don't say that!"

"You care nothing for me?" he queried in surprise.

Tama's hands flew around his neck and she pulled him to her, placing her head on his chest, the touch of his skin burning her cheek. "I didn't say that. You fill my mind, my dreams, my heart, and it is true that my soul aches when I think of you with Wyiana. But you must think about the clan elders, Hakan. Surely, they would reject a fugitive mulatto slave as their mico's wife."

"If I am mico, they will accept my decisions."

"And what does Mico Blue Waters say?"

"He no longer has a say," Hakan whispered, lowering his eyes as he took a long breath. "My father's days on this earth are finished. When the dancing stopped, he lay back and closed his eyes. He is gone. The visiting micos have taken his body into the forest, where his resting place will be prepared. My choice of a wife is mine to make and mine to live with. "

"Perhaps," Tama conceded. "But Suja has hatred for me in her heart. I won't come between you and your sister. "

"Tama," Hakan started, stroking her hair, her neck, her shoulders. "I am not the little boy who chased wild turkeys through the woods and shared wild strawberries with my sister. I am a man, and I want to know if you will live with me and bear my sons."

Tama's answer was a soft kiss that lightly brushed Hakan's lips. When he rested his chin on her chest, she wrapped her arms around him, swept with relief and cautious joy. A ripple of apprehension trailed through Tama, but she quickly pushed it away as Hakan maneuvered her down onto the rough palm leaf covered floor. When he pulled her deerskin dress over her head, she shuddered, wanting him with a fierceness that numbed her worries and made her believe she deserved to be loved.

Tama strained to feel every inch of his body against hers. She roamed her hands along the curve of his back, the slope of his shoulders, the solid muscles of his thighs, falling more deeply into the pool of elusive happiness she sought. Returning his kisses with such fervor brought a tremor of shame, but every part of her body was alive and tingling, restless to join completely with him.

When Hakan took her, with a thrust that made her heart turn over, she welcomed the achingly exquisite plateau of pain that forced a cry from her throat. She dug her fingers into his back, as if to match her pain to his, as he fused her hips more tightly to his. Quickly, the pain passed, and soon, she was moving with him, experiencing the joy of an explosion of love that shivered through her body and left her shuddering against his chest.

Chapter 14

Tama awoke. Alone and in the dark. For a moment, she wondered if she had dreamed of Hakan's smooth copper body taut and sleek above hers, had imagined his soft fox cape folded over her naked skin as they lay together and listened to the night sounds of the forest. But when she sat up and felt the supple fur beneath her buttocks, she smiled and pulled it to her nose. Inhaling the scent of their lovemaking brought a great sense of peace, but upon lifting her head, she was startled to detect the sharp odor of smoke in the air.

Tama went to the entrance of the hut and looked toward the sacred burial grounds, where a flicker of light was shining through the trees. She thought the light must be coming from the place of forgotten altars, where shards of sacrificial jars and talismans lay scattered over the black, scorched earth. Blue Waters' body would be lying on a litter while the shaman chanted the ritual to start his mico's journey into the Spirit World. *Hakan must have gone to the burial site to watch the ritual,* Tama thought.

She eased Hakan's fox cape around her nakedness, climbed down the ladder, and followed the smoky scent, weaving through wispy fog that hugged the trunks of the shaggy cypress trees. After walking for a short time, a rustling sound in the bushes up ahead stopped her in mid-step. Frozen in place, she watched as a panther emerged from the forest and held his ground on the path, his round yellow eyes trained on her. He sniffed the air, as if detecting the scent of her joining with Hakan. Tama stood immobile, staring back at the sleek black cat until it swung its small head to the left and sauntered away.

Moving on, Tama walked closer to the light flickering among the trees. She eased the brambles aside, and was shocked to find herself gazing upon a cluster of blue-coated soldiers, rolled into blankets, asleep on the ground. A slender blonde-haired man, who was cleaning his rifle, sat on a log near the blazing fire next to Fisko, the soldier who had come to the village.

The fair-haired soldier lifted a heavy jug to his mouth and took a long pull, then wiped his drooping mustache with the back of his hand. Tama remained as still as a toad warming itself on a lily pad when the pale one's voice floated through the trees.

"They can dance forever, you know," he said to Fisko.

"Yeah, it's always some kind of a celebration going on. They drink that black drink, get all worked up, and dance for days without stopping."

"All that yelpin' and hollerin' and damn, those drums," the blonde soldier added.

Fisko nodded. "Stinking savages, they are. We shoulda set on 'em at first light this morning like I wanted. Now we gotta wait until they sleep off all that rotgut they filled their bellies with."

"Can't wait too long. At daybreak, we go in."

Fisko kept his attention trained on the fire. "Ain't too many left on the Tallapoosa now, and with the old mico dead, there won't be much trouble gittin' this village cleaned out."

"Then we gotta march 'em a hell of a long way," his companion complained. "I ain't lookin' forward to that."

"Me neither," Fisko said. "And I sure as hell hope this is the last of it. Once I get 'em on the boat, I'm going home to see my wife. I sure do miss her cooking. That dog of a cook we got ain't worth the flour he spills on the ground."

"Well, they shoulda left voluntary, like the others," his colleague remarked with disgust. "We warned Blue Waters to take his people and get out before things got ugly."

"He told me he'd rather die where he was than leave."

"Looks like that's exactly what's happened," the soldier added.

"You know, I kind of liked the old fellow," Fisko mused. "But he was so goddamn stubborn. I told him he'd have to change with the times or face up to what was comin'."

"Well, this here land is too good to keep out of white folks' hands," the fair-haired man decided. "The injuns got no rights now. The papers been signed. The government already told them they gotta go, and we gotta make 'em leave."

"Let's just hope they don't put up much of a fight."

Tama clenched her teeth, worried. Fisko and his men were going to raid Great Oaks at daybreak! They'd been spying on the Fox all night, waiting for Mico Blue Waters to die. She swallowed her fear and pulled the fox cape tighter to her body. Hakan told her that Fisko was no threat, but here he was, planning to drive the Fox from their homeland.

Knowing she had to return to the village and warn the others, Tama eased back, poised to run. However, the snap of a twig beneath her foot halted her retreat, forcing her to sink down and press her body flat to the ground.

"Who's there?" Fisko shouted, as he and the soldier probed the bushes with their bayonets.

"Probably a coon. Saw one up in that tree earlier," Tama heard Fisko remark.

When the men went back to the fire and resumed their conversation, Tama knew she had no choice but to stay put and wait until the sleeping men woke up. She hoped the noise they would make as they prepared to enter the village would cover hers as she jumped up and fled.

* * * * *

The insistent clap of flapping wings awakened Tama. Brushing leaves from her hair, she struggled to her feet and looked up into the sky. Moving her head back and forth, she watched as three huge buzzards circled high above the forest, and the dim memory of why she had fallen asleep beneath a thorny juniper bush leapt into her mind.

Fisko! The soldiers! The raid on Great Oaks! Tama yanked the bushes apart and saw that the soldiers were gone. A black hole in the ground was still oozing smoke.

Tama fled back to the hut, scrambled up the ladder, dressed, and then raced toward Great Oaks. Holding onto Hakan's red fox cape, she pushed through vines and brambles, taking a short cut through the woods that brought her quickly to the edge of the village. Terror churned Tama's stomach as she scanned the chaotic scene. When she saw Hakan, her heart lurched in fear.

He and the men of the village were standing shoulder to shoulder in a line of resistance, blocking the point where the main road entered the talwa. They were holding bows fit with arrows, as well as knives, wooden clubs, and a few old muskets, clearly determined to fight the removal. Hakan, positioned in front of the group, made a hand signal to his men, urging them to hold back from launching an assault.

"We will not strike the first blow," he yelled over his shoulder. "But we *will* defend our right to remain on this land."

The soldiers advanced up the road on foot, their military-issue rifles pointed at the Indians. When they had come within an arm's length of the men, they stopped, allowing Fisko to step forward and address Hakan.

"No one will get hurt if you cooperate!" Fisko shouted, his voice rising above the din of frightened cries coming from the women and the children who hovered behind the human barricade that Hakan and the men had created.

"Cooperate?" Hakan shouted back with disgust. "Never! We will not abandon Great Oaks!"

"Then prepare to suffer the consequences," Fisko tossed out, lifting his hand, as if prepared to signal his men to advance. "The government let you remain on this land longer than all the others, but now it is time to go. Your mico is dead. Your people have no leader..."

"That is not true," Hakan refuted. "I am now the mico of the Fox."

"Then tell your people to gather their belongings and get on the road!"

Before Hakan could reply, the young Fox named John Henry broke away from the men and pushed past Hakan, brandishing a wicked hunting knife.

Fisko jerked to the side to avoid being slashed, but he raised his rifle and shot John Henry in the chest. Instantly, the Indians rushed forward, eager to launch their assault, but Fisko fired again, into the air this time. He glared at Hakan and shouted, "Unless you want to see a lot more of your men dead and lying on the ground, you'd better back down. Now!"

Hakan lifted his chin in defiance and narrowed his eyes at the soldier, calculating his next move. When he raised his bow, which was set with an arrow, Fisko leveled his gun on him.

"Killing me won't stop anything," Fisko warned. "I'm only one soldier. The government will send twice as many next time, and they won't be as patient as I've been!"

Hakan hesitated and then lowered his bow and arrow. "You call yourself patient? You are a brutal, evil man who wants to kill us to take our land."

"I'm just following orders. Now, get on the road!" Fisko shouted, raising his rifle to fire three shots into the air. The Indians scattered in all directions, fleeing for their lives. The soldiers ran after them, and began routing people from their chickees. Screams and anguished cries rose from the village.

Hakan spit on the ground, glared at Fisko, and then mounted his pinto horse. "Prepare to leave!" he yelled to his people, who were crowded together in the square ground. Giving up a war cry that split the air, he charged past the tangle of men, women, and children who hurried to obey his command.

Hakan sharply reined in his horse, rattling the deer bones on his vest when he halted in front of Tama. He looked down at her and asked, "Where is Spring Sky?"

"I don't know! What about Suja?" Tama screamed up at him, her words quickly swallowed by the chaos erupting all around.

"Suja is on the road, but mother is probably at the chickee. Please, Tama. Find her and bring her out!" He yanked the reins and turned his horse around. "We must leave before my people are slaughtered, but I will lead the Fox from their home with dignity." Then he thundered away, swallowed up in the sea of confusion.

Fear and guilt propelled Tama into the crush of people. She stumbled, fell, and landed beside a dead body. Jamming her hand over her mouth, she stared at Three Winds', whose head was a bloody mass of hair and bone – laid open and oozing blood. Buzzards were already circling overhead, and, as Tama looked up at them, her mind burned with shame: *I let this happen. I knew the soldiers were coming, but I fell asleep and did not warn the people.*

Rising, she raced to the family chickee, where Spring Sky was frantically rolling clothing into a quilt. She was still dressed in her purple cape-blouse from the night before and her fox-shaped *culv* remained around her neck. Her long braid had come undone, allowing her gray-streaked hair to fly wild about her head.

"Spring Sky!" Tama took Hakan's mother by both arms. "Come! Now! There's no time to pack. Suja is on the road. Hakan is waiting. We must go." Tama urged Spring Sky toward the door, and just as the women emerged from the chickee, a soldier appeared and waved his bayonet in their faces.

"Get out on the road, you two," he commanded, swinging his long rifle back and forth.

Tama stepped forward. Spring Sky, clutching her bundle of clothing, followed.

"Stay close to me," Tama hissed, linking arms with Spring Sky. "If you leave my side, you may be lost."

They made their way across the square ground and out of

the village to join hundreds of other frightened souls gathered in the road. The soldiers were busy dividing the people into unwieldy groups, and when Tama saw Hakan ride to the front of the caravan, she headed toward him, forcing her way through the tangle of animals and people. However, before she could get to Hakan, Fisko rode up and blocked her path. He dismounted and stood towering over her.

"What's your name, gal?" he demanded.

Startled by the man's rough, and unexpected, question, Tama didn't answer.

"Where you from?" he pressed. "I picked up a runaway notice about a slave that fits you."

Tama inwardly cringed, determined not to tell the soldier anything.

"She belongs with the Fox," Spring Sky spoke up, attempting to step in front of Tama. However, Fisko roughly shoved Spring Sky aside.

Tama glanced at Spring Sky, and then back at the soldier, but she kept her mouth clamped tightly shut.

"I asked you where you from," Fisko demanded, giving Tama a hard shove. He pinched her chin between his thumb and forefinger, pulled her face toward his. "Don't act like you don't understand me, nigger. Speak up! I asked, where you came from?"

Unexpectedly, Suja appeared, pushing her way through the crowd with Wyiana at her side. "She's a runaway slave. Came to our village from across the mountains," Suja blurted out.

"That so?" Fisko commented, letting go of Tama's chin to lean back and look her over. "I think you might be worth holding onto."

"Leave her be, please. She belongs with my family," Spring Sky insisted.

"No, she doesn't!" Suja countered, glaring at Tama with fierce disgust.

"Suja! What are you saying? This girl saved your brother's life," Spring Sky snapped, dropping her bundle of clothing to the ground.

"And he saved hers, so he owes her nothing."

"I won't leave her behind," Spring Sky vowed, moving to take Tama by the hand.

Fisko quickly intervened, separating the women. "Stay back, old woman," he ordered, fastening his hand around Tama's wrist. "The zambo girl stays with me 'til I can figger all this out," he said as he started to lead Tama away.

Suja snapped her arms around her mother's waist and urged her away. "Come with me, Mother! Let the soldier have Tama! Who cares what he does with her?"

Spring Sky refused to move. "No, Suja. Tama must stay with the Fox. She is ..."

Fisko swung his bayonet around, as if to threaten Spring Sky into silence, but his swift movement sent the tip of the bayonet into the side of Spring Sky's face, carving a deep gash from her temple to her jaw. Spring Sky fell to the ground without making a sound.

"You horrible man. What have you done?" Wyiana screamed.

"Mother!" Suja cried out, dropping to her knees beside Spring Sky's motionless body.

Tama gasped in horror as blood spurted from the wound

in Spring Sky's head and mixed with the red dirt on the road. She tried to run toward Spring Sky, but Fisko hefted his rifle up and used it to hold her back.

"Speak to me!" Suja shook her mother's limp body. "Open your eyes! Speak to me!" There was no response. Suja whirled around and glared up at Tama. "See what you've done! You evil zambo. Get away from me!" Suja cradled Spring Sky's head in her hands, tears streaming down her cheeks. Wyiana sank down beside Suja and placed a comforting arm around her friend.

Fisko glowered at the scene, frowning as he shouted, "Leave the old woman and get back with your people." Using the butt of his rifle, he forced Suja and Wyiana to abandon Spring Sky to bleed to death in the middle of the road.

The brutality and hatred stunned Tama. All around her, people were dying, animals were being slaughtered, and children were wailing in fear. When Fisko pushed her to move along, she stumbled a few steps forward, but then impulsively turned around and ran back to where Spring Sky lay in the dirt. She grabbed the bundle of clothing that Hakan's mother had dropped and snatched the *culv* from around the dead woman's neck.

Chapter 15

The trail leading across Kansas was wide, well worn, and crowded with settlers, prospectors, opportunists, and adventurers, all determined to reach their destinations before the fine spring weather turned hot and unbearable. The road, scraped and pockmarked by thousands of weary footsteps, held ruts created by overburdened oxen and thick wagon wheels drawing hopeful travelers closer to their dreams.

They had been on the road for seven days, and Elinore still struggled to adjust to the constant jolt of the wagon, as well as the monotonous sound of clanking metal, the annoying creak of leather, and the pant of the hardworking animals. Her body absorbed every bump and rut in the road, but she did not dare to complain. At least she was riding, and not walking, as so many of the women in the caravan had to do. Pushing aside the pain that had crept into the small of her back, she glanced down at Julee, trudging alongside the wagon, her face shadowed by a tattered straw hat the color of the sun. To keep her mind off the miles of dirt and dust that lay ahead, Elinore studied the landscape, admiring the profusion of blooms on the crab apple trees that dotted the hillsides, their pink and white flowers creating a picture-painted image. All along the road, clumps of purple columbine and sprays of early violets were springing up among the piles of trunks, chests, rocking chairs, and tools that travelers had discarded along the route in order to lighten their loads. A ripple of sorrow slid over Elinore's heart when they passed a freshly mounded grave marked with a tiny pair of baby shoes hanging from a cross made of twigs.

By mid-day, the cool of the morning evaporated and the afternoon heat was punishing the travelers. Big Tim passed word down the line that it was time to stop and rest. Woods slumped back on his spine and maneuvered Elinore's wagon into a grassy curve beside the stream of blue water that paralleled the road, stopping beneath a canopy of trees.

Elinore pulled off her hat, wiped gritty fingers across her neck, and then took Ben to the river to wash. When they removed their boots and waded into the water, Julee quickly followed, cooling her tired feet while the horses, oxen, mules, and livestock drank nearby.

After washing off in the river, the women returned to the wagon and began to set out the noon meal. Julee picked up the wicker basket containing the food that she'd prepared, set it on the canvas cloth that Elinore spread out on the ground, and then said to little Ben, "Cold pork, boiled eggs, and bread, comin' up." Smiling, Julee reached into the basket, but quickly jerked back and screamed, "Help! Oh, no!" and dropped the tin of meat. She scrambled away from the basket and shouted, "Big Tim! Miss Elinore! Somebody come get this thing outta the food!" Too frightened to move, she stared in shock at the big black snake coiled around the loaf of bread. It was shaking its pointed tail while its jaws remained clamped around a hardboiled egg.

"Don't move," Elinore advised after coming up behind Julie to see what the ruckus was all about. Calmly, she assessed the situation, then went to her wagon and retrieved the sixteen-shot Henry that Big Tim had picked up for her in St. Louis.

I must make a clean shot, she thought, trying to ignore the squeals of the women, the shouts of the children, and the mumbling surprise of the men who had crowded around to see what she could do. Elinore placed the rifle against her shoulder, relaxing at the press of its butt. A surge of confidence swept through her as she took aim on the snake, drew in a tight breath, and angled the dull metal barrel toward the basket, which lay at Julee's feet. "Hold still," Elinore advised Julee, her voice low. She squinted one eye closed, sighted her target, and then squeezed the trigger, flinching at the resulting boom.

"Oh, my Lord!" Julee hollered, stumbling backward when the food hamper exploded in a shower of straw, bread, and chunks of hardboiled eggs. The bloody snake fell to the ground in a dark, raw heap and everyone gasped in relief.

Julee gaped at the dead snake as one of the men walked up and nudged it with the toe of his boot. Using a tree branch, he lifted it high for all to see. The snake was nearly four feet long, with a small horny tail at the end of its body. Remnants of the egg remained clutched between its visible fangs.

"Got it," Elinore muttered with a rush of relief. After so long without a rifle in her hands, she had not been sure she would hit her mark, especially with such precision. She looked over at Julee and smiled. "That's the end of that critter."

"Thank the Lord," Julee sighed. "I don't know how this coulda happened. I tied down the basket lid real tight."

Elinore braced her rifle at her side. "Probably got in while we were sleeping." She ran trembling fingers through her blond hair, tugging it into damp tendrils that settled like yellow ribbons on her shoulders. "Lucky you saw it before you put your hand in there."

"That's for sure," Julee agreed.

The crowd thinned. Some of the children continued to ooh and aah over the bloodied reptile, amazed by the precision of Elinore's shot. A lanky teenager took the stick from the man and pulled the snake out full-length on the grass, laughing as his friends squealed and poked at the black scaly thing, daring each other to touch it.

"A timber rattler," Big Tim commented, pushing through the knot of children to squat down and examine the kill. "Gonna see a lot more o' these along the way, for shore." He looked it over with interest. "Coulda been with us since St. Louis." He glanced at Elinore. "Mighty fine shot."

"Thank you," Elinore smilingly acknowledged. "Just lucky no one was hurt."

"*Oui,* that's a good thing," Big Tim replied.

The boy used the forked stick to hurl the snake into the river, laughing as it fell like a limp piece of rope into the water. The other children screamed in delight and raced to the stream to watch it swirl away.

Big Tim stood, rolled back his shoulders, and then removed a small leather pouch attached to a cord from beneath his shirt. He held it up for Elinore and Julee to see. "This here's dried turtle blood. The best cure for snakebite there is." He opened the pouch and shook a few dark red scales into his hand, and then used his forefinger to spread them in his palm. "I was out in West Texas a few years back. Stopped by a Comanche settlement for fresh water. I saw a little boy get bit in the arm by a timber rattler. His momma, who was right there with him, grabbed the boy, sucked out the poison, then pulled a pouch from her bosom, just like this one here. She sprinkled the turtle blood on the boy's wound and sent for water. She mixed the blood into a drink and made the boy swallow it all down."

"He lived?" Julee asked, eyes wide.

Big Tim grunted before he spoke. "Live? That child never even cried. Next day, he was playing stickball in the dust with his friends. I tell you ....the blood of the turtle's a mighty precious thing. I'm gonna make up bags for both of you, and I expect you ta carry 'em at all times."

With all the excitement over, everyone went back to eating, resting, and readying themselves for the next hard push, knowing their short stop would not last much longer. Big Tim stretched out his back. "I was mighty anxious to taste that food, but now that's spoiled, what we gonna eat?"

"We'll make do," Julee quickly replied. "I got some Yankee pork and beans with hard biscuits and a jar of bread and butter pickles." She quickly set about pulling together another meal as Big Tim fell into step beside Woods and headed to the river to wash up. Elinore hefted her rifle in her arms, cradling it like a baby, and placed it back on its rack inside the wagon.

It did not take long for Julee to fix another meal and soon everyone had a tin plate filled with beans, biscuits, and pickles. Elinore passed out calico napkins sprigged with daisies, pleased that the men, and Julee, seemed to appreciate her attempt to have a civilized meal. It was going to take a great deal of ingenuity and planning to maintain a proper home where she was going, and in Elinore's mind, manners and decorum were important. Before leaving Ohio, she'd made up her mind not to let her standards slip, and to do whatever she could to make her and Paul's life at the fort as pleasant and comfortable as possible. All she needed, Elinore assured herself, was the ability to look at things in a new light, to treat obstacles as challenges, like a problem that needed a bit of figuring out. She was determined to remain flexible, tolerant, observant, and most of all brave, if she hoped to survive in her new home.

"So what's the trail ahead gonna be like?" Julee asked Big Tim once they'd settled down to their meal.

"Not too hard," he replied, wiping biscuit crumbs from his chin. "Once we get to Fort Leavenworth, Woods is gonna leave us and go on with the folks who're headed to California. He'll take 'em over the Rockies, while we push south to the Shawnee Trail. Maybe three, four days out, we gonna turn south, and I gotta warn you, things are gonna change. The closer we get to Indian Territory, well ... the truth is, the goin' might get a bit hairy." Between bites of his pickle, he continued. "Osage and Pawnee will be hangin' around, watchin' us, testin' us ... but don't worry too much. I know how to deal with 'em."

"And how's that?" Elinore asked.

"We hold firm. Oh, they gonna come around demandin' food, livestock, horses. Just testin' us to see what kinda folks we are. If we don't hold firm, they'll come back and take whatever they want. A slow-moving wagon like ours is a pretty target for a raid, that's for shore," Big Tim stated with assurance. "But don't you worry, Mrs. Wardlaw. I'm gonna get you and your precious boy safely to Fort Gibson, I guarantee."

"That's comforting," Elinore replied, confident that Big Tim's word was good. So far, the trip had been relatively uneventful, but his description of what to expect later on put the potential for danger into focus.

Julee went to the river to wash the tin plates while Elinore checked on Ben, who had fallen asleep soon after eating and

163

was curled up in his bed. She climbed into the wagon and sat beside her son, resting her head against one of the large hickory bows holding the canvas cover in place. She surveyed the sprawling caravan of livestock, wagons, and people. Cattle bawled and children shouted while the women hurried to repack their wagons and prepare for the call to move out. The people had a gritty strength that Elinore admired. They seemed to possess a sense of controlled desperation anchored in hope, linking everyone together. They were one large family, with everyone headed in the same direction: Toward new lives, new lands, and new expectations of happiness.

Big Tim peeked into the wagon and smiled to see that little Ben was fast asleep. "You got a tough little boy, there," he told Elinore, who smiled her agreement. "His daddy is gonna be mighty happy to see him," Big Tim added, moving around Elinore's wagon to inspect the metal rims of the huge wooden wheels and check the security of the fat water barrels tied to the wagon sides. He was tying off a flap of canvas when a young man wearing a flat black hat and a rumpled white shirt came running up to him.

"Mr. Lester. We gotta wait. My wife's havin' the baby!"

Big Tim broke into a wide grin. "That so, Mr. Abbott?"

"Yeah ... we're gonna need about thirty more minutes before we can pull out."

"All right," Big Tim tossed back. "We can wait." He understood the expression of fear and pride on the expectant father's face. "Everything all right?" he asked, hoping the delivery would proceed without complications and they would leave with a healthy baby and a mother who would live to see the end of the trail. This was not the first time a child had been born during one of his trips, and there would probably be several more before the journey was over.

Watching the excited father-to-be race back to his wife sent Big Tim's thoughts back to a time that he rarely brought to mind.

A woman birthing a baby was nothing new or unusual, until Big Tim Lester experienced it for himself. The scene remained vividly clear in his mind—a montage of suppressed pain, palpable fear, and furtive ministrations carried out on a damp cellar floor covered with dirty straw. He did not speak, and she did not cry out as they struggled to bring their child into the world. The heat of the space, the tannic smell of blood, and the cat-like mews of the newborn baby had carved a hole in his heart that never completely healed.

Chapter 16

The Gambling Parlor at the St. Louis Grand Palace Hotel was nothing like the Paradise Club in Raleigh, North Carolina where Thorne Royaltin enjoyed playing cards and placing large wagers while drinking aged brandy and smoking fine cigars in the company of men like himself. At the Paradise Club, no riff-raff, cowboys, niggers, chinks, or Indians were allowed: It was strictly a white gentleman's domain; a discreet place to gamble, drink, discuss politics of the day, and if they chose, to enjoy the company of ladies who stood ready to give them whatever they wanted. Customs differed greatly at the Grand Palace Hotel, where a riotous mélange of men and women from all parts of the country crowded together to try their luck at the tables. In St. Louis, cash ruled, erasing all lines of color and class, as long as the money was good.

Thorne smiled as he ended his night at the tables, pleased to have added a substantial sum to his horde of winnings. He had more than enough money to offer the Indians in exchange for Tama; cash spoke volumes in any language, so certainly, the Creek Indians with whom Tama had settled would not pass up Thorne's offer of cold, hard currency in exchange for property that belonged to him.

After exiting the Gambling Parlor, Thorne entered the hotel lobby, paid the desk clerk for a copy of the *St. Louis Observer*, and then sat down in an overstuffed chair beneath a large fan palm tree, content to remain out of view. He had no interest in engaging in conversation with any of the people who paraded across the bustling hotel lobby: He hadn't come to St. Louis to make new friends.

After shaking out the newspaper, Thorne folded it in half and began to read, eager to catch up on the latest news. He scanned the headlines and then focused on an article at the bottom of the front page that immediately caught his eye: *Last of the Creek Indians Removed from Georgia.* Curious, he sat back and carefully read the article, which detailed the Army's progress on the Indian removal problem, an article that carried much meaning for him. The writer, a well-known chronicler of Indian matters, had written:

> More than 40,000 Indians from the Five Civilized Nations of the East have now been resettled in the Trans-Mississippi West. Along with the Indians, hundreds of slaves and free blacks who live among them have also resettled in the West. Most recently, the Muscogule Creek living along the Tallapoosa River in Georgia, who fought removal for many years, were uprooted and are on the road, headed to Fort Gibson. This group constitutes the final mass migration and the last large group of Indians to be processed at the fort, which is the entry point into Indian Territory.

Tama is surely among them, Thorne silently calculated, tilting back his head, shutting his eyes. A full two months had passed since the fire, and this was welcome news. He knew in his heart that Tama was alive and hiding among the Creek, believing she was far from her master's reach. Thorne opened his eyes and stared at the article in earnest. Had Fate conspired to place him in the right place, at the right time? Was he destined to recover the daughter that dared to run away from him? With a nod, Thorne stood, knowing he was on the right path.

Tossing the paper aside, he smoothed the creases in his

trousers, left the hotel, and went straight away to the Overland Mail office across the street. There, he purchased a ticket to travel on the morning stage to Fort Smith, the closest he was able to get to the entry point into Indian Territory.

St. Louis had been good to Thorne. The contacts he made with merchants who were eager to accept all the cotton and canvas cloth he could provide would pay off. Time away from his plantation had provided him an opportunity to heal from the loss of his home and his family. The city was a bustling flashpoint for people with guts, money, and outrageous dreams, and there certainly was no shortage of beautiful women with whom to pass the night. It had been a good move, coming to St. Louis. He'd won far more money than he'd expected to win at the gaming table, but now it was time to leave, find Tama, and take his daughter home to Royaltin Ridge.

However, even though recovering his property was Thorne's highest priority, tonight his attention was riveted on the luscious little lady standing before him.

With his early departure from St. Louis hastily, but carefully, arranged, Thorne decided to top off his visit to the rough and tumble city by relaxing with a beautiful woman. He braced his back against the cool metal bars of the curved brass headboard and stretched his legs out on the massive, four-poster bed. Reaching to the nightstand, he picked up the remains of his unfinished cigar, lit it, and inhaled as he focused on the buxom woman with flaming red hair and an hourglass figure who was slowly removing her clothing. He lowered his eyes to her dainty bare feet, and then inched his gaze upward, devouring her firm white thighs, the patch of fluffy red hair between her legs, the waist that was no larger than the span of his two hands, and the twin mounds of pleasure on her chest that he was anxious to embrace.

Without speaking, he motioned for the woman standing naked at the side of his bed to climb in. He put down his cigar, shifted to make room for her to lie down beside him, then leaned over to brush her scarlet hair off her face, and absorbed her green-eyed gaze before crushing his mouth over hers. She responded as he'd hoped, arching her soft flesh against him, smothering him in a cloud of sweet perfume that pushed his need for her near to bursting. His movements were swift, almost brusque, as he lifted her hips and plunged greedily into her, pumping toward the climax that he feared might come too soon. The act filled him with a sense of liberation. He had no need for sweet talk, pleasantries, or commitments of any kind. Anonymous, urgent sex with a pretty saloon-hall girl was all that he craved, and all that he planned to pay for.

Thorne awoke with a start in a pitch-black room, and, for a moment, he felt disoriented. He lay still, allowing his mind to clear, recalling his marathon tryst with the red-haired vixen. He'd paid her handsomely for her favors, and then sent her on her way before falling into a deep black sleep. Now, he was alone in the bed but had a definite sense of someone moving about the room. He thought about the money won at the gaming tables, which was stashed inside his valise at the foot of his bed. He listened as the intruder unfastened the straps on the bag and snapped the buckles open with two sharp clicks. Carefully, he eased his hand beneath his pillow and closed his fingers around the pistol he kept nearby. As his eyes adjusted to the dark, he focused on the spot in the room where a sliver of moonlight seeped between the folds of the heavy room-darkening drapes, and when a shadowy figure crossed into the shaft of light, he sat up, cocked his gun, and said, "You'd better not move. If you do, you're dead."

He swung his feet to the floor, lit the bedside lamp, and then stood, naked, in front of his intruder. "What're you're doing here?" he demanded, not completely surprised that the thief who was standing in his room, holding onto his money, was the woman whose sexual favors he'd so recently enjoyed. He could tell that she was naked beneath the pink floral duster she had hastily wrapped around her body.

"Don't shoot me," she pled, dropping the money and raising her hands, sending large paper bills fluttering to the floor.

Incensed that anyone, especially the woman to whom he had just given a substantial amount of money, would break into his room while he slept and try to steal more of his cash, Thorne advanced on her. He pressed the nose of his gun into the side of her face. "I have every right to kill you," he threatened, leaning low to place his lips even with hers.

"Please don't kill me," she begged, her green eyes filled with terror, her breath still sweet with the smell of cheap whisky. "I only need fifty dollars. For a train ticket to El Paso. I want to go home and see ... well, I thought maybe you ..."

"You thought wrong!" Thorne pulled the gun away from her face, lifted his arm and brought the gun down, smashing the handle across her upturned nose. Blood spurted out and dripped over her chin, creating a scarlet trail on her white creamy neck. He reached down, snatched the hem of her pink duster and shoved it into her mouth, stifling the screams he feared would awaken everyone in the hotel. He was livid. He had caught this woman in the act of robbing him, and had every right to settle the matter as he saw fit. "Nobody takes what belongs to me and gets away with it!" He hit her again, this time on the side of her head, creating a deep cut from her temple to her ear. He grabbed both of her wrists with one hand and twisted them until her knees buckled and she sank to the floor. Still holding onto her, Thorne panted in rage, a white-hot hatred boiling his insides.

"You low-life bitch! You tried to steal from the wrong man this time. I detest people who take things from me. You are gonna pay." He yanked her up from the floor, ripped off her robe, and then threw her, face down and naked, across his bed. He slapped her hard across the buttocks, flipped her onto her back, and then mounted her, determined to teach the woman a lesson she would not soon forget. As he pumped into the terrified redhead, she moaned and squirmed, trying to get away, but Thorne kept his large hand pressed firmly and completely over her face until his anger, and his need to punish, were spent.

"Now, get up and get out of here," he snarled, climbing down from the bed. He gave her two hard shoves, but she didn't move. "Get up!" he ordered again, squinting down at her puffy red face. When she did not stir, he jammed three fingers to the side of her neck, felt for a pulse, but found none. He pressed his palm against her left breast, alarmed that blood was dripping from her nose. There were no signs of life. She was dead, and he had killed her. The last thing Thorne Royaltin wanted was trouble with the law, and he knew he had to move quickly. He pulled on his clothing, wrapped the woman's body in his bed quilt –taking care not to get any of her blood on himself—and then heaved the body over his shoulder and eased open the door to his room.

The wide hallway, lit only by a flickering gas sconce on the wall, was empty. He glanced up and down the dim corridor and then cautiously stepped out of his room. He walked to the last door at the far end of the corridor – where he'd seen the redheaded woman enter earlier that evening –and peeked inside, relieved to find it empty. Thorne dumped the dead woman face down in the middle of the bed, pulled a rumpled sheet up to her neck, and then took the key out of the door and locked it behind him when he left.

The Butterfield Overland mail stagecoach was designed to carry four passengers in comfort, but when it left St. Louis, Missouri, on the first day of May, Thorne found himself squeezed into a carriage with five other travelers seated on the worn leather benches. His companions included two soldiers headed to Fort Smith, a widow dressed in black, a wheezing barber clutching a case of barbering tools, and a preacher with a large silver cross hanging around his neck. Outside, riding high above the passengers, were two drivers, who had the responsibility of safely delivering the mail and passengers to their destinations. They slapped the reins against the six-horse team and rumbled off toward the plains.

"First trip on the Butterfield Overland, I reckon?" one of the soldiers remarked to Thorne soon after they got underway.

"Yes," he replied, shifting in his seat. "Glad I was able to get a ticket."

"Yep. The Butterfield's real popular nowadays. Fastest way to get to Fort Smith ... but it can be a challenge, too." The soldier spoke as if he were eager to show off his experience with the journey as he boasted, "I been traveling this route since it first started," he said, and then he lowered his voice, as if to shield his companions from hearing what else he had to say. "This can be a mighty dangerous route. Gotta be prepared to deal with a whole lotta dust, probably some bandits, a lot of stops at dust-bitten towns, and a few encounters with hostile Indians, too. I can tell you now ... expect annoyance, discomfort, and lots of hardships. If you're disappointed, then thank the good Lord," he finished with a grin.

Thorne gave the soldier a solemn glance, not at all concerned with the dangers they might encounter. All he wanted to do was get as far away from St. Louis as possible before someone discovered the dead woman's body and the sheriff started asking questions. He hadn't meant to kill her, just make her understand how much he hated losing what was rightfully his. Fire robbed him of his home, smoke snatched away his wife and daughter as they slept. He wasn't about to let the Indians take Tama away from him, too.

Chapter 17

The soldiers divided the unwieldy throng into four groups of nearly one hundred each. They allowed the Indians to appoint a conductor to monitor their people and keep track of those who died or went missing during the trek. The Indians broke along clan lines, with the Fox, the Bear, the Wolf, and the Turtle creating separate traveling communities. The Indians were permitted to keep their slaves and the zambos who lived with them, so that everyone entering Indian Territory would be accounted for and properly relocated. Only Tama, whom Fisko held at the rear of the caravan, remained separated from the others.

Once all was in readiness, the massive gathering of people and animals stretched out in a line that disappeared around the bend in the road and spilled into the nearby forest. Knots of women and children stood behind the wagons that they would follow on foot, while the various micos and the respected elders of the tribes mounted horses and rode up and down the line, followed by younger men on horseback. The soldiers moved among the refugees and doled out supplies, giving everyone an army blanket, a small black cooking pot, small sacks of flour and corn, salt pork, coffee, and sugar. It was enough to stave off pangs of hunger but not nearly enough to satisfy a soul.

The refugees pushed off, pressing ahead at a grinding pace as they moved across the countryside. The Indians soon learned that there would be no time to forage for food, stop and tend those who fell sick, or bury those who died.

Whenever the caravan came upon other Indian villages along the way, the soldiers quickly forced the inhabitants to join the throng. Sometimes they encountered villages where only shadows and scattered possessions marked the place where a talwa had once existed, but the smoke rising from the log fires made it clear that the people had fled into the forest to hide and escape removal.

Seven days into the journey, the caravan stopped to make camp where the Choccolocco River met the Coosa. The green forest was as dark as night and tall sugar pines rose on both sides of the river, creating a solid wall of impenetrable vegetation. The Indians made sleeping tents from three poles and sheets of canvas, or created conical tipis of deerskin and beaver pelts. The women gathered wood, built fires on the grassy stretch of land along the river, and poked salt pork around in boiling water to create a warm meal.

Tama sat on the ground next to the crude three-wheeled cart where Fisko had ordered her to stay. She rested her head against the rim of the wagon wheel, thankful that Fisko trusted her not to run away.

Why would I chance running now? she thought. Even if I managed to get away from here, where would I go? Not back to Great Oaks. Not to the north or to the east, she knew, where men close to Royaltin were surely searching for her. Besides, running away meant leaving Hakan, and she would never voluntarily part from him. At least Fisko had not struck her, or put her in shackles, or tried to force himself on her even though he looked at her in a way that made her feel as if a million fire ants were crawling over her skin.

Looking out across the surging throng, Tama caught a glimpse of Hakan. He was standing beneath a fringed willow tree, talking with Suja, whose back was to Tama. Suja's head was tilted downward, her shoulders rounded, and it appeared as if she were crying. The sight initiated a surge of pity for Suja, whose mother was dead, whose village had been destroyed, whose clan had been uprooted and turned out on the road. A glimmer of guilt over Spring Sky's death ignited like a flame within Tama's heart, and suddenly she wanted to comfort Hakan's sister in spite of the nasty words they'd flung at one another.

The next morning, they started out before daybreak and continued lumbering southward for the next fifteen days, trekking across the forested hills of Alabama as they trudged through tall grass and forded swollen rivers. When they reached the Black Warrior River, near the town of Tuscaloosa, they stopped and set up camp once again. There, Fisko ordered Tama to strip naked and bathe while he watched. Quickly, more white men came around to smirk and stare at Tama, who turned her back on them and continued to wash the lice and filth and dirt of the journey from her body. After bathing, she opened the bundle of clothing that Spring Sky had dropped in the road and removed a simple cloth shift and a fringed shawl, which she put on. The clean clothes caressed her tired body, and she suddenly felt closer to Hakan, wearing his mother's clothing.

Late in the day, the sky filled with black clouds and a vicious storm blew in, churning the river into tight, choppy waves. Huge raindrops pummeled the earth as lightning sparked the purple sky, sending white-hot bolts of light across the horizon. Torrents of water slicked the tall grass flat to the ground as Tama huddled beneath a wagon and held onto a huge wheel to keep from being washed into the river. A sleek black horse, frightened by the crackling thunder, tore loose from its tether, ran into the surging water, and disappeared beneath the turbulent river. A little boy, curious about what had happened to the horse, fled from his mother's side and raced to the water's edge. Mesmerized by the plight of the animal as it fought the swirling waves, he stepped too close and fell into the river. His screaming mother raced to the riverbank, her cries of distress overtaken by repeated claps of thunder. No one saw the boy again.

By evening, the storm had passed, leaving downed tree limbs and an ocean of mud behind. People crept from beneath their sketchy shelters and began to dry their wet clothing and blankets in front of struggling fires, grumbling at the mess. They sloshed through mud, gathered possessions blown about by wind, and argued over rights to the bits of cloth and scraps of food they found among the storm-ravaged debris.

Tama settled into a quiet spot, built a fire, and boiled a handful of corn in her little black pot. After eating it, she wrapped her body in the army blanket that Fisko had given her and lay down on the still-wet ground. Staring at the cloud-veiled moon, she ached for Hakan. He had not come to her since the journey began, but Tama understood why he stayed away: The burden he carried for his clan deserved his attention and his time.

He will come to me when all this has passed and we are in our new home, Tama told herself, pushing loneliness aside. Closing her eyes, she soon fell asleep.

Deep into the night, after the fires dotting the landscape had burned down to smoldering coals and Fisko was snoring in his tent across the clearing from her, Tama felt a presence at her side, a gentle touch on her arm. Without opening her eyes, she knew it was Hakan.

Tama shifted toward him and tilted her face upward in question. He answered her with a soft brush of his lips across her cheek. Tama's heart swelled to feel him so close, and when he eased down beside her, she kissed him with tenderness, letting him know that she had never stopped thinking about him or believing in his concern for her. Hakan put his arms around Tama, as if silently telling her not to worry, that in the midst of this tragedy he needed to be near her.

Skimming her hands along his back, she sank into his arms and buried her face against his neck. A whispered moan escaped her lips as the tension of the journey drained away. "I'm so sorry about Spring Sky," Tama whispered into Hakan's ear. "I didn't mean for ..."

"Shh. You had nothing to do with what happened," Hakan interrupted.

"Suja thinks otherwise," Tama responded.

Hakan hesitated, and then said, "I know you did not cause our mother's death. The man Fisko did, and he will pay for what he has done."

"Hakan. I cared so much for Spring Sky. She treated me with kindness. Three Winds, too." A beat while she paused to blink back tears. "When I was in the woods, I overheard Fisko talking about his plan to attack the talwa. But I didn't stop him. I waited, I fell asleep."

"You could not stop him," Hakan assured her, easing an arm beneath Tama's head. "This journey has been a long time coming, but now that it has begun, we must face the future with courage. Rest, do not worry." He kissed the top of her

178

head. "I'll stay with you until you fall asleep."

Tama slid down, placed her cheek against the hard surface of his chest, and sighed, treasuring the gift of his presence.

In the pale light before dawn, Hakan eased from Tama's arms, stroked her cheek with the tips of his fingers, and slipped off toward the mottled shadows of the campsite where his clan slept. He walked quietly, his moccasins slithering over the damp grass as he crept past Fisko's tent. He drew comfort from the fact that Tama was holding up well, and would certainly survive the journey. In time, he knew Suja would forgive Tama, who did not cause their mother's death. The fact that Spring Sky now dwelt with his father in the spirit world gave Hakan a small amount of comfort.

Hakan sat before an ember-banked fire near the crude tipi he had erected for himself. He surveyed the camp: Bodies wrapped in Army blankets lay on the ground and beneath wagons. Heaps of clothing, tools, and an abundance of household supplies cluttered the area. The chaotic scene hurt Hakan, even though it brought him an odd sensation of relief: The uncertainty about the future of his people had finally been decided, and there was nothing to do but accept it.

"You look worried," a voice emerged from the darkness.

Hakan swung his head around and saw Wyiana, clutching a fringed blanket around her shoulders. A weary expression claimed her eyes and worry lines creased her forehead. However, she was as beautiful as ever.

"Oh. I see you, too, are not able to sleep," Hakan remarked, moving aside to make room for Wyiana to sit beside him. Her nearness whirled his mind back to the Red

Tail Dance, to the humiliation he'd caused to both her and Tama. He didn't want to talk about the incident, but he knew Wyiana deserved an explanation.

"No, I am too tired to rest," she admitted with a sigh. "My mind will not be still."

Hakan crossed his arms at his waist and leaned closer to the fire. "Then you must stop thinking so much. Let me do the worrying for now."

"You have much to worry about. Our lives will never be the same." She paused, then said, "Hakan, I want you to know that I don't blame you for what happened at the dance. Tama is your friend. I understand ..."

Hakan seized the opening to clear the air by suddenly reaching out to take Wyiana's hand. He held it loosely as he spoke. "Wyiana. I didn't mean to shame you ...I hope you believe me."

"I do." She eased her fingers from his, and then slipped her hand beneath her blanket. "When I arrived at Great Oaks, I was anxious for the Red Tail Dance, to learn of your choice. Now, none of that matters. We have bigger problems to face."

"But I was wrong to taunt Tama and to hurt you, as I did," Hakan admitted.

"I was not hurt, only surprised. Perhaps I had assumed too much," Wyiana softly stated. "The fault is mine, Hakan, for hoping, one day, to be your wife."

"No, it was not your fault, but mine. I ... I changed ... while I was away from Great Oaks." Hakan picked up a twig and snapped it into little pieces, unsure of how to express what he was feeling. "While I was far from home, captured on the other side of the mountains, I began to see things differently and to feel differently about what I wanted. My meeting with

Tama was predestined. She saved my life, and I owe her much gratitude."

Wyiana remained quiet for a moment. "It is easy to lose your way when you are among strangers. However, you are back among your people now, Hakan. You cannot forget who you are," she reminded him.

"I know who I am and I know that my people have no home, no land to call our own," Hakan countered in a voice hoarse with sadness. "We must now live among strangers who will control our lives. The white men have power over everything that belongs to us, and this way of life will be difficult to bear."

"Yes, it will. The soldiers forced us from our homes, but we carry the Creek way of life with us." Wyiana raised a silky dark brow at Hakan as a shadow of a smile touched her lips. "The Creek will start over together in this new land, but I urge you, Hakan ... please put matters of the heart aside and think only of your people."

Hakan traced his gaze over Wyiana's face, absorbing her beauty, her calmness, her truth. She was reserved, attentive, and lovely. She would be a good wife for any man, he knew. However, she did not make his heart turn over the way Tama did. She did not touch his soul with her spirit and set his heartbeat racing. He cared for Wyiana as he cared for his sister, with deep affection borne of common ties. They played together in the forest as children, splashed around in the Tallapoosa River while it still held ice, and caught beaver in traps to sell to traders passing by. He had heard the elders talk of their desire for his marriage to the Wolf girl, but he had never taken them seriously, as apparently, Wyiana had done.

"You should try to sleep, Wyiana. You will need your

strength in the days ahead," he offered, unable to say more.

"And you, too, Hakan. Your people love you, and they want you to lead them during these troubled times." Wyiana placed the palm of her hand on Hakan's knee, held it there for a moment, and then she added, "You are Mico, now ...you cannot fail the clan." Then she rose and went inside her tipi.

Hakan propped his chin on his fist and studied the flames in the fire. The Fox still faced an arduous journey, during which many more elderly, and children, would surely die. Too many had been hastily left behind, unburied, alongside the road. A grimace firmed his lips. He held the great responsibility of ensuring his clan's future, and he could not let his people down. He would not ignore his father's last words of advice: work hard at being a good man, and you will be a good mico. Strengthening the Muscogule traditions that had held the Creek together for generations was Hakan's priority, and as much as it pained Hakan to admit it, Wyiana was right: He must put matters of the heart aside and honor the title bestowed upon him to fulfill his duties as leader of the Fox.

When the bugle sounded at sunrise, Tama got up and prepared to move on. She folded her blanket around her meager belongings, and then looked up. She saw Hakan, mounted on his horse, signaling for the members of his clan to fall into line behind him. When he moved farther up the trail and disappeared from sight, she, too, stepped into the road and steeled herself for the next leg of the journey.

For five treacherous days, they trekked westward at a cumbersome pace, stopping only to eat and sleep. Rising at dawn, they pressed on to the port city of Vicksburg, Mississippi where they waited for flatboats to take them to the mouth of the Arkansas River and join soldiers from Fort Smith who would escort them into Indian Territory.

Once they were encamped on the Mississippi, armed soldiers surrounded the perimeter of the site to keep the Indians from running off and prevent locals from interfering with the removal. Curious people from the surrounding area arrived to gawk at the Indians and point at the blacks, laughing as if they were looking at wild animals on display. Some of them yelled nasty curses and threw rocks at the Indians, others taunted the blacks with long sticks and branches ripped from nearby trees.

Not surprisingly, local planters arrived to look over the Negroes, searching for runaways and blacks to buy. A wealthy sugar cane planter did lay claim to a man he professed to own, and presented a sheaf of papers to prove it. Fisko told the farmer to take his property and go, but as more planters arrived with hard cash to take the Negroes off the Army's hands, Fisko refused their money. The Army wasn't in the slave trade, he told them, and he ordered them to leave.

As everyone settled into yet another temporary campsite, soldiers carrying small notebooks moved among the throng and wrote down the names of people traveling together, listing family units and various clan members in order to document all who entered the territory. Tama watched as a soldier stopped to speak with Hakan about the members of his unit. Tama prayed that he was including her as a member of the Fox. However, she had little time to worry about what Hakan told the soldier because immediately Fisko walked up and said, "Get your things and get on that horse." He pushed Tama toward a wiry brown mare tethered to a tree on the other side of the road.

"Why?" Tama brazenly inquired before taking a step.

Fisko's answer was a hard shove and a slap to the back of Tama's head, sending her stumbling into the road, clutching the bag of Spring Sky's belongings that she'd guarded so carefully since leaving Great Oaks.

"Keep your mouth shut and move!" Fisko shouted at her before turning to mount his horse.

From the riverbank, Suja watched the exchange with great interest, a half-smile of pleasure teasing her lips. Turning to Wyiana, Suja said, "Look....he's taking the zambo girl away. Hakan will need you at his side." Then she walked away from Wyiana and approached Fisko just as he prepared to ride off. Suja stood in his path and crossed her arms at her waist, raising her chin in a self-important manner. "Where are you taking the zambo?" she called up to him, working her jaw back and forth as she glanced from Fisko to Tama and back.

Fisko scowled down at Suja, but gruffly replied, "Someplace where I hope to get a fair price for her." Then he tugged his cap low over his face and kicked his heels into the side of his steed.

The road that Fisko took led away from the river and into a field of tall wiry grass as high as Tama's head. They plodded along until they came to a rundown cotton warehouse in the middle of a field. They dismounted and went inside, where a white man wearing a light brown suit and a pale green, sweat-stained shirt was sitting at a wooden table, writing in a ledger. A filthy cage holding a vibrantly colored bird sat on a box at his side. The man looked up in surprise when Fisko entered. Setting his pen aside, he said, "Bolt the door."

Fisko complied, and then he walked over to the man, leaving Tama behind to shrink behind a bale of cotton. Eyes wide, she clutched her blanket bundle and listened to the exchange between Fisko and the man, whose large head was covered with tight brown curls. He had an elongated chin that protruded from an equally dense beard, and even the backs of his hands were matted with pads of hair, giving him the appearance of a huge brown bear.

"Good to see you looking so well, Zachary," Fisko said.

"How many you got?"

"Just one," Fisko replied. He turned around, saw that Tama was hiding behind the cotton bale, went to her, and pushed her out in front of Zachary. "There's a five hundred dollar bounty on this one," he told the cotton planter.

"Oh, yeah?" Zachary swiped his forefinger over his nose a few times and then slowly turned down his lower lip, studying Tama as if she were a specimen under glass. "Decent looking gal."

"The man what owns her sure wants her back." Fisko pulled a sheet of paper from his jacket pocket and handed it to Zachary, who scanned the document, and then set it aside.

"Sampson County, North Carolina? Don't know if it's worth my time to take this one back, not for five hundred dollars."

"Bet you could get more. Look at her. She ain't like the usual darkies."

"You touch her?" Zachary asked, scratching his hairy chin.

"Naw. Zambo pussy don't interest me."

"How much?" Zachary asked.

Tama shot a glance at Fisko and saw that he was watching her while running his fingers over his thick brown moustache, his head cocked to one side, as if calculating what he could get. She bit her lip, waiting, hoping he might decide to keep her, might let her go back to the Indians and not sell her to this man. He spat tobacco juice onto the dusty floor, then screwed his mouth into a crooked line and said, "Fifty dollars."

Zachary sniffed. The bird chirped and fluttered around in its cage, creating a shower of bird droppings that fell to the floor. "I guess that'll be okay," he said. Reaching over the clutter on his desk, he opened a metal box and counted out the bills.

Fisko folded the money into his pants pocket and then shook hands with Zachary. "Gotta go get this load of injuns set to go up river."

"You going with them all the way?" "No, once I get 'em on the boat, I'm turning back, going home. But I'll be checking with

you when I come back this way." He gave Tama a final once-over and left.

Zachary whistled through his upper teeth and pushed back his chair, as if glad to be finished with Fisko. He propped both feet on the corner of the table and stared at Tama, arms crossed on his chest. "Pete!" he called out. "Pete! Get in here!"

A grizzled old man in sun-bleached coveralls stained with sweat and missing several buttons slowly pulled open the big double doors.

"What you want, Zack?" he asked, giving Tama a lopsided smile as he scratched his sunburned neck. "What's this? A little diversion?"

Tama stiffened as the scruffy, bewhiskered man sauntered closer to gawk at her. He did not smile as he calmly sized her up.

"A diversion? I think not," Zachary shot back, dropping his feet to the floor. He cleared his throat and sat up straighter.

Tama wasn't sure what "diversion" meant, but she suspected, by the lack of respect that flickered in the eyes of both men, that it wasn't something she wanted to be.

"She's a zambo picked up on the way down the Tallapoosa," Zachary told Pete. "An investment," he added. "Take her to the lodge. Put her up in the loft and lock her in. I don't want this one running off."

"Yes, sir," Pete assured Zack. Then he motioned for Tama to follow him out the door to a crude wooden cart pulled by a nearly hairless mule.

The odor of freshly skinned animals hit Tama as soon as Pete drove into the yard and came to a halt outside a rough-hewn structure at the edge of the sprawling cotton plantation. It was a small building made of thick pine logs chinked with mud. It had a tall chimney at one end and a porch that slanted precariously to one side. Tama cautiously eyed a heap of bloody hides covered with flies piled in the middle of the yard. Pete urged her inside the lodge where he pointed toward a ladder and followed her as she climbed into a stuffy space beneath the rafters that was barely large enough to hold one person in comfort.

"I'll get you some water," Pete told her. He shut the door behind him, clomped back down the ladder, and returned with a pail of water and a chunk of hard bread.

Tama bit back the moan of disgust lodged in her throat as she surveyed the cramped space. It had a sharply slanted roof and no windows. The floor was covered in a thick layer of dust, and cobwebs as dense as cotton batting hung like Spanish moss from the rafters. She sat on the floor, beside the trap door, terrified and worried. No one knew where she was. Hakan would go on without her. She might never see him again. Tama wrapped her arms around her knees and held on tightly, telling herself to be brave, not to lose courage. Courage was her fuel, like kindling to a fire, and Tama needed to be courageous if she planned to stay alive.

When Suja saw Fisko come up the road, returning to the campsite, she grinned. Tama was not with him. She hoped he would turn her over to a bounty hunter to claim the reward and take her back to her master. And out of Hakan's life, too. In Suja's opinion, blacks, even mixed-race blacks like Tama, had no place among her people ... unless they were actually slaves. It was foolish for Hakan to make Tama believe she would be accepted as one of the Fox. *At last she's gone*, Suja thought with relief. Setting aside the blanket she was folding, Suja went to speak to Hakan, who was at the dock, talking to a river man about the upcoming journey.

"Yep," the man was saying to Hakan, "you gonna go by steamboat up the Mississippi to Fort Smith, to the spot where the Arkansas and Poteau meet. Then you gotta head northwest, probably in canoes, on up to Fort Gibson, and then you're right smack in Indian country."

"How long will the journey take?" Hakan wanted to know.

"Maybe four days, if the weather don't turn bad."

Hakan nodded thoughtfully, and was about to ask another question, when Suja hurried up and touched him on the shoulder.

"Hakan," Suja said, interrupting his conversation with the river man.

"What is it?" he asked, moving with her to a quieter spot.

"Tama is gone."

Hakan squinted at his sister, confused. "Gone? What happened?" Raising his chin, he surveyed the crowded riverbank, but he did not see Tama among the many women wrapped in shawls who were busy scavenging for food, tending fires, and tying pieces of rope and strips of leather around their possession in preparation for the boat ride up river.

"The soldier took her away," Suja informed her brother, smugly eying him.

"When?"

"Hours ago. I saw them ride away."

Anger flashed in Hakan's dark eyes. "Hours? Why didn't you tell me?"

"It's not my place to keep up with that zambo."

"Suja. This is not good. I have to find her," Hakan shot back, glaring at his sister for a moment. He started toward Fisko, who was standing at the dock drinking coffee with a knot of soldiers.

"Leave it alone," Suja screamed after Hakan. "She's gone, let it be."

Ignoring his sister's advice, Hakan stomped right up to Fisko's face. "What did you do with the mulatto girl you took from our village?"

"Turned her over to a man who's gonna take her back to her master."

189

"Where is she?" Hakan pressed, stepping closer to Fisko.

"Far away from here, and that's all you need to know. Now get back over there with the others."

"Not until you tell me where she is!" Hakan shouted, moving nose to nose with Fisko, who formed a fist and slammed it into the center of Hakan's chest, knocking him to the ground. Then he slashed his arm through the air and shouted, "You stay back! You have no say in this!"

Hakan spat into the dirt, grabbed a thick piece of wood and rolled to his knees. Drawing in a long pull of air, he pierced Fisko with hate-filled eyes, and then swung the club at Fisko's head. The soldier ducked to the side and escaped the strike, then laughed aloud. "Don't make things worse than they are already," he warned Hakan. "You want to wind up livin' in the stockade instead of on your new land?"

Members of the Fox quickly gathered around and urged Hakan to retreat, but he shook them off and held his ground while Fisko simply stared at him, as if daring Hakan to make another move. After a tense moment, Hakan finally stepped back, feeling confused and off-balance, not from the blow Fisko had delivered to his chest but from the realization that Tama was gone, that he had failed to protect her as he promised to do.

After gracing Fisko with a searing glare, Hakan turned and stomped off toward the river, where he hunched his shoulders to his ears and gazed into the swirling water. *Tama is going back to her master, far across the mountains where I will never see her again.* Hakan swallowed the sob that burned in his chest and firmed his lips into a hard, straight line. As the pain of losing Tama swept through him, Wyiana's words of advice slowly shifted into focus: *Matters of the heart must be put aside.*

Concern yourself with the future of the Fox. At that moment, Hakan knew he had no choice but to remove all thoughts of Tama from his mind and purge her from his heart.

Three days later, the steamboat captain's voice cut through the din of preparation and urged the Indians to move faster, to find a spot and settle down so his vessel could pull out. Weary and anxious, the ragged cluster of wretched souls boarded the boat and sank down on the deck, the rising sun on their backs.

Hakan threaded his way through the tangled mass, a hollow emptiness claiming his bones. Flooded with sadness, he stiffened when the steamboat whistle declared the start of the final leg of the horrendous journey.

Chapter 18

Tama crawled to the far end of the loft and placed one eye to a tiny crack between the floorboards. It took a moment for her sight to adjust to the dim candle light in the room below, but she could see the sleeping area of the lodge. Discarded clothing lay strewn across a straw mattress on a narrow bedstead, beside which stood a lidded chamber pot. Pegs on the wall held a flannel nightshirt, a white felt hat that looked brand new, a jacket, and a pair of blue trousers that had served some time on the trail. An old Betty lamp and two half-burnt candles sat atop a wooden crate.

Tama flinched when Zachary suddenly entered the room and quickly shed his clothing. She watched as the naked man knelt before the cold ashes in the hearth – his huge red member stood at attention. Tama had seen naked boys playing in the slave quarters and seen them swim nude in the river at the talwa, so she knew how the member that hung between a man's legs was shaped. Even though she had given herself completely to Hakan, she had never seen his manhood. She had felt it, stroked it, and let Hakan sweep her into a magical world by moving it inside her, but he would never have paraded his nakedness in such a crude manner, not even in the privacy of his own chickee.

Looking down on Zachary's hairy body flamed Tama hot with shame, but as much as she wanted to turn away, she kept her eye trained on him as he placed kindling in the fireplace, then lit the wood with a stubby candle.

His thighs were heavy and corded with muscle, but his stomach hung slack and soft between his legs. His hands and face were as red as bloodroot, but the rest of his body was moon-white.

The fire sprang to life, sending a soft yellow glow from the hearth to color the room and turn Zachary's massive red-tipped tool a brighter hue of scarlet. He could not see her because she was hidden in the crawl space above his head, yet she felt as if he'd reached out and touched her when he swung his head to the side and squinted toward the ceiling. His eyes were bleary with drink, his jowls were flaccid, and he looked even larger and more threatening without his clothes than he had when she first saw him.

"I want you down here!" he ordered, voice sluggish and thick. "I know yer watching me."

Tama dug her fingernails into the splintered floorboards and held her breath as Zachary unlatched the trap door in the ceiling and let it swing down. "Come here!" he roared, much louder this time. "I know you can hear me. Come down!"

Tama knew what he expected, and her heart raced with fear. She crept to the opposite end of the loft and started down the rope ladder, keeping her back to him, not wanting to see his naked body. Reaching the bottom rung, she let go of the rope and dropped down, but she kept her face to the wall. She could hear him moving up behind her, and squeezed her eyes shut, praying he would finish with her quickly, that the liquor he had drunk might make him sleepy and so listless that his time with her would be short. "Take off your clothes," he curtly ordered.

Slowly, she did as he demanded, stepping out of her dirty skirt, pulling her blouse off her shoulders to drop it at her feet. Feeling the heat from the fire on her skin, she concentrated on the relief that it offered her stiff, aching limbs, thinking that, for some reason, the heat made her feel less naked.

"Turn around!"

She turned and was not surprised to see that he was sitting on the edge of his mattress, glowering intently at her. He held a piece of rabbit fur over his still-erect member, and he was gripping a rifle loosely in the other hand – it was not pointed directly at her but clearly visible and threatening. In spite of the situation, she almost laughed. He looked so strange, sitting there with his fur-covered penis poking up between his legs like a ground hog in the middle of the woods. But she was too frightened to do more than remain still and let his eyes consume her breasts, her stomach, the triangle of dark hair below.

"Turn again!"

She turned in a circle once more.

"Come here, real slow."

She obeyed his command and moved closer. She also complied when he ordered her to lift her arms and bend toward him, letting her hair swing down to the floor.

"On your knees! And look at me, when I speak to you!" She knelt before him, her hands pressed into her thighs as she struggled not to think about what he planned to do to her. She cut her eyes toward the single window, contemplating escape. If she managed to get outside, naked and alone, would she run into the arms of some other drunken man who might beat her senseless or shoot her on sight?

Holding back tears, Tama mentally prepared herself for the moment when Zachary would shove her into his bed and take her. But he did not reach for her. He set his rifle aside and eased one hand beneath the rabbit fur covering his crotch. He began rapidly to pleasure himself, startling Tama to see such a thing, but she relaxed, realizing it was not her body that he wanted, but only the sight of her. Despite his order to look at him, she closed her eyes, unable to witness what he was doing to himself.

The sound of firewood breaking apart in the hearth and the chirping of crickets outside in the yard mixed with the grunting pants and moans of satisfaction that came from Zachary's mouth as he moved his hand up and down, up and down, his drunken gaze riveted on her naked body.

He finished quickly, crying out in a series of short, anguished yelps, before he fell back on the bed and closed his eyes. Tama waited until his breathing had calmed, then she pulled on her clothes, climbed back into her hole in the ceiling, and curled into a tight ball. Pressing her forehead to the floor, she cried then, great sobs of weariness and disgust, wishing she could erase what she had just seen. *Be careful,* she reminded herself. *Tonight, he did not touch me, but I cannot trust this foul man to leave me alone forever.*

Fearing what tomorrow might bring, she turned onto her back, tears staining her cheeks, and found a crack in the roof large enough to count the stars.

Early the next morning, Tama heard Zachary moving around in his quarters, heard him slide a sturdy slat into place and barricade her inside the lodge. She did not move until she no longer heard his heavy footsteps as they crunched across the dusty yard.

He stayed away all day. Her only visitor was Pete, who arrived at dusk, climbed the ladder, and gave Tama a tin cup of water, a bowl of corn mush and a piece of rabbit meat that he dropped at her feet. Soon after Pete left, Zachary returned and took to the bottle again. Late in the evening, he forced her to stand naked before him once more as he pleasured himself and drank large amounts of whiskey. For three more nights, the ritual continued, allowing Tama to hold onto the uneasy belief that she was repugnant to him. She was black. She had lived among the Indians. She was a savage in his eyes. He did not want to touch her, but he did want to use her to ease his torment while remaining faithful to the yellow-haired, pale-eyed woman in the small oval painting that rested among the papers on his desk.

On the morning of the fifth day of her captivity, Tama peeked through the crack in the floor and saw Zachary hurriedly packing a bag. He put clothing, books, and the small oval painting of the yellow-haired woman in his leather traveling case, then told Pete that Tama must remain locked in the lodge. Pete was to give her food and water while he was in Hattiesburg for the next two days.

Tama was relieved to learn that Zachary was going away, even though the reprieve would be short.

Heavy rains fell all day, streaming into her space through holes in the roof. She managed to catch a good amount in the cup Pete had given her. She gulped the water down and then slept until Pete arrived with a bowl of corn mush and two hard apples. When he left, he did not slide the trap door back into place, and curious, Tama wondered if he might be setting a trap, enticing her to come down into Zachary's quarters. Was he waiting down there, prepared to pounce on her and take her, as Zachary had not done? After a long moment of silence,

Tama crept down the rope ladder to see if he was there, but found no one in the room. She pulled a chair up to a window and peeked out. The yard was abandoned, too. Without hesitation, Tama slipped through the window, jumped down onto the mud-slicked ground, and ran.

"Stop right there!" Pete yelled, racing from the shadows, holding his rifle high. He sloshed through the mud after her, grabbed her by the shoulder and spun her around. He slapped her hard across the face, and she tumbled to the ground. With his rifle pointed at her head, he shouted, "Where you think you going?" He yanked her up from the muddy yard.

"Let me go!" Tama pulled away, ready to fight, even die, rather than return to captivity in that miserable loft. Twisting from his grasp, she ran again, but Pete caught her with a long reach of his arm and whipped her back toward him.

"You ain't goin' nowhere."

"I won't stay here!" she screamed at him. "Shoot me! I don't care if you kill me. Shoot me! I won't stay."

"Yes, you will, you crazy zambo." He hit her again, this time drawing blood at the corner of her mouth. "You ain't runnin' off. But I won't be the one to kill you. Zachary'll decide what to do when he gits back."

The thought of returning to that rat hole in the ceiling flared in her mind like a freshly lit torch. She kicked fiercely at Pete, determined to get away. He pulled her across the muddy yard and shoved her into a shed partially filled with rough split logs. He fastened iron manacles around her hands and feet, bolted the door, and left her bruised and crying in the dark.

For two days, Tama lay on her back, stiff, depressed and consumed with pain. No one came with food or water or even to see if she was still alive. Aching with hunger, she dug into pockets of rotten wood for ants, crickets, and shriveled grub worms, which she greedily digested. Luckily, rainwater sloshed under the walls of the shed and settled into muddy pools that provided her with water.

On the third night of her capture, the door of the shed finally burst open. Tama stirred, groaned, and then turned her face away from the intrusive lamp light. Her body ached, her head throbbed, and the welts and gashes on her wrists and ankles from the weight of the heavy manacles flared in pain. However, she forced herself to sit up, and then scooted as far into a corner as she could, afraid, yet curious about who was coming through the door.

The shadowy figure held a burning oil lamp that spread light into the dark space. Cautiously, Tama leaned out from the shadows and gasped. Her visitor was a woman – dressed in a coarse cotton night coat over a filmy gown – and her long yellow hair spread over her shoulders. Her pale eyes were set like smooth stones in her stark white face, and Tama recognized her as the woman in the tiny oval painting on Zachary's desk.

"Get up, you whoring slut," the woman demanded, rushing closer. Her opaque eyes flared as she kicked at Tama, using one foot, and then the other to pound Tama's flesh with the hard leather of her shoes. "Get up or I will set this lamp to you and be happy to watch you burn."

With great difficulty, Tama stood, raising dark eyes to the woman's pale ones.

"You'll not be sharing my husband's bed again, you daughter of a dog," she vowed, putting the lamp so close to Tama's face the flame danced around Tama's wildly matted hair.

"I was never in your husband's bed," Tama dared to object, determined to defend her last shed of pride.

"Liar!" Zachary's wife kicked Tama harder, making her cotton night coat flap like the wings of a pigeon as she raised her leg to strike repeatedly. "You stinking savage. I know your kind. Consorting with Indians for food and favors to elevate your stinking half-breed self from the low-life nigger you are. Well, your disgusting behavior with my husband is over." The wife spat into the dirt, then threw a heavy iron key at Tama, striking her in the middle of her chest. Then she grabbed a handful of Tama's hair and pulled her face up to hers. "Unlock your shackles and get the hell off this place," she hissed through gritted teeth. "You take your filthy belongings and your whoring self out of here and get as far away as you can by daylight." She gave Tama's hair another hard yank; then the pale-eyed woman threw Tama's cloth bundle at her. "And you'd better run fast because if you get caught and they bring you back alive, I will personally whip you to death."

Rainwater filled Tama's moccasins, weighing her down, yet easing the pain that was throbbing in her legs. As she sloshed through tall grass, two words bounced around in her head. *Fort Gibson.* She had no idea how far away the new Indian homeland might be, but whether it took a thousand steps or a million steps, she was going to find Hakan and never part from him again. Driven by her love for Hakan and an unflinching determination to remain free Tama continued to walk until her strength gave out. Collapsing beneath a thick-trunked tree, she fell into a near-unconscious sleep.

When daylight touched the land, Tama awakened, feeling unsure of where she was until the sounds of a river came to her. She got up and started toward the river, her body burning with exhaustion, her mind foggy from lack of food. The waterlogged lowland squished beneath her feet, sending streams of mud onto the hem of her dress, ripped and covered with thorns. The slippery grass threatened to trap her, but she pushed through the reeds and continued on, cursing the sodden landscape until she arrived at the riverbank where the Indians had been camped. Nothing remained but fire pits on the ground where the refugees cooked their meals and sat to talk. Disappointed, she pressed her head against the rough bark of the tree and let her sobs fall freely. Her hands shook, her stomach cramped, and her mind groped for answers to solve her plight.

I will rest, get strong, and then I'll decide what to do, she thought, wiping away tears. Giving into her fears would solve nothing; she had to go on, keep searching until she found Hakan.

When the sound of something coming through the grass startled Tama, she tensed, but rather than hide or run, stood prepared to face whatever it might be. When a figure emerged, Tama exhaled a soft breath of relief to see a woman, dressed like a frontiersman, coming toward her. She was wearing men's pants, a snakeskin vest over a flannel shirt, heavy boots that almost touched her knees, and a red woolen cap. Her ebony skin was shiny with sweat, her gait was slow, and she was surprisingly short in stature.

Too weary to do more than stare, Tama remained where she was, watching as the dwarf of a woman came within two arms lengths from her.

The woman tossed a string of fish to the ground and

scowled at Tama. "You be eatin' dinner with me, then, I reckon?"

The kindness in her voice and the gleam of understanding in her eyes made Tama burst into tears of relief. This woman was someone who did not want to hurt her, who might even want to help her, and raising her chin, Tama pulled her shoulders back and said, "Oh, yes, ma'am. I'd like that very much." Smiling her gratitude, she tried to step forward, but her knees buckled, making her collapse.

Later, after the fish had been boiled with wild onions and turnips, the woman, who called herself Cimpi, muttered a short prayer in a voice that suited her size and manner. "Lord, bless this child and strengthen her brave soul for the hard journey she is about to undertake." Then she cleared her throat and motioned for Tama to come to the table and eat.

Tama moved from the corner of the small cabin where she'd been resting and took a seat on the crude bentwood chair opposite her host.

Cimpi forked a piece of fish for Tama and slapped it on a wooden plate, then cocked one eye at her.

"Eat, child. How you think you gonna make it to Indian Territory less you eat?" She chewed thoughtfully, then added, "I been out West, myself. But I wager I won't be going again."

Tama leaned forward, curious. "Can you tell me how to get there?"

"Nope, but I can draw you a map. If you planning on going, you go alone, and don't get mixed up with strangers. Keep to yourself. There's all kinds of bad men, and women, looking for trouble along the way."

"Where do I go from here?" Tama asked.

Cimpi pushed her chair back from the table and shoved aside her empty plate. She took a piece of charcoal from the hearth, picked up a flat piece of birch bark from the stack of wood beside it and began to sketch.

"Not far from here, just beyond that spot where you was sittin' lives a man who says he's my cousin ... but he ain't never been able to prove it. Anyway, just give him this map and he'll tell you which way to go. You go see him tomorrow. Tonight, you rest. No need being too hasty about leaving. You come a long way. No need to hurry now."

That night, as she lay near Cimpi's fire, Tama went limp. Hakan's face swam in her mind. When he saw her again, would he open his arms and welcome her back? Would the Fox be happy to see her? Perhaps even Suja would have a smile for her. Tama hoped so because she wanted very much to heal the old hurts of their past and start over without so much pain. The lonely ache of her separation from Hakan moved into her throat and constricted the sobs she struggled to hold back. Moving to reach for her cloth bag, she removed the culv she had taken from around Spring Sky's neck. Hadn't Three Winds said that praying to the amulet could make troubles disappear? That the talisman could guide a lost soul to salvation? With her hands pressed around the charm, she closed her eyes and silently spoke to it. *Lead me to Hakan. Show me how to find him. And once we are together again, make our lives whole.* Then she slipped the leather string over her head, certain Spring Sky would not mind if, just for now, she put her faith in the small wooden fox.

Chapter 19

After leaving Vicksburg, the Indians traveled by steamboat up the Mississippi to the mouth of the Arkansas River. Ten days later, the caravan arrived at Sallisaw Creek. The Indians were sick, dispirited, and drenched to the bones after a severe spring storm churned the river and tossed the boat about, creating a miserable situation and a deep sense of despair. They disembarked and settled down behind the crumbling, but sheltering, walls of old Fort Coffee, the long-abandoned garrison built by the government to serve as a buffer between the citizens of Arkansas and the first wave of resettled Indians. Exhaustion, hunger, and disease, especially among the children, had mercilessly plagued the Creek, but after a two-day rest, they pressed on toward Fort Smith, the important supply hub for military expeditions, adventurers and explorers, as well as the resettled Indians in the territory. Hakan was actually relieved when a detachment of U.S. troops met the Indians at Fort Smith and took charge of the situation.

The soldiers divided the unruly throng into even smaller divisions, with each clan headed by its self-appointed leader. They traveled by boat to the fork of the Arkansas and Verdigris Rivers, where they finally saw Fort Gibson, sprawled on a rise high above the water.

Hakan concentrated on the timber-walled garrison in the distance as his group disembarked and moved forward. The grounds spread out around the massive log and mud stockade were dotted with hastily built shanties, lean-tos, tipis, and tents, where a large number of soldiers, a scattering of white women, and throngs of Indians were living. Arriving at the main entrance, the boisterous voices of men mixed with the shouts of children and the chatter of women. Hakan paused to listen to the unusual sounds.

In his village, such loud voices and rowdy behavior were not common, even during the merriment of festivals and dances. The Creek spoke in low tones among themselves and tried to maintain orderly calm wherever they lived. A respectful allegiance to the customs and etiquette of the ancestors kept his people in touch with the effects of their behavior on other members of the tribe, and the elders took it upon themselves to teach young people to promote decorum, cleanliness, and quiet in their talwas. Spring Sky used to tell him, whenever he spoke too quickly or intruded on her meditation, that silence was the cornerstone of a man's great character.

Hakan erased all traces of discontent from his face, wanting to present a defiantly controlled facade to those who plotted to destroy his way of life.

The huge doors swung open, allowing the Indians entrance into the military compound. The center of the fort was a dusty expanse of red-brown dirt, stamped with horse tracks, boot prints, and deep wagon wheel ruts. On either side of the front gates stood open-sided sheds where horses were tethered, muddy pails of water on the ground among them. Uniformed soldiers and a scattering of white women were going in and out of large rectangular structures with doors, windows, and mud-stick chimneys. Hakan's eyes darted over the mix of military men, trappers, traders, farmers, and animals crowded into the fort. Three dark-skinned Indian men squatted in the shade of a horse shed, blankets wrapped around their bodies. Hakan had been inside a white man's fort once before, and he did not admire the four-sided barricades that fenced everyone in among horses and cows and dogs – like livestock in a pen. Such restrictive, claustrophobic living was beyond his imagination; no Indian, even while at war, would hide from his enemy behind walls of wood and mud.

"Follow me," barked the soldier escorting Hakan's group across the square. They headed toward a two-story building with an American flag flapping from a pole atop the roof and open shutters of knotty pine that provided a glimpse into the rooms.

Hakan hurried behind the soldier and stepped onto the wide plank porch. After the soldier knocked on the door, a strong voice told him to enter.

Hakan found himself standing in front of a blonde-haired man sitting at a desk holding a feather quill pen between two fingers. The man looked up, fastened inquisitive blue eyes on Hakan, and then said, "Welcome to Indian Territory. I am Captain Paul Wardlaw, and I am in charge of registration. We will supply your people with food, clothing, housing, and the necessary items required for resettlement."

Hakan nodded his understanding, assessing the man who controlled his people's fate.

"Your name?" Paul inquired.

"Mico Hakan. Son of Blue Waters."

"The name of your group?" Paul continued, moving his quill pen over a clean page in his journal.

Hakan touched the *culv* talisman hanging around his neck, and replied, "We are the Fox of the Muscogule Creek from the Tallapoosa River."

Paul scratched the information on the page, then proceeded to ask Hakan additional questions about those who traveled with him from Great Oaks.

Between answers, Hakan took in his surroundings. The rough-cut table-turned-desk where the captain sat took up nearly all the space in the room, which was no larger than the chickee Hakan had shared with Blue Waters. It was crowded with books, crates, trunks, and soldiering gear pushed against the walls and piled on every surface. Hanging on the wall behind the captain was an official-looking document written in a flourishing black script and pinned with a red ribbon seal. At the captain's elbow sat a clay pot holding a long-stemmed pipe adorned with feathers. Hakan wondered if the man had ever smoked it.

"It's important to document every person who enters," Paul said, jerking Hakan back to attention. "Are all of your people, as well as the slaves and Negroes who came from your village, named here?"

"Yes," Hakan replied, swept with emptiness that Tama's name was not among them.

"Good. Because once your residence assignment is made, only those listed here will receive supplies and live on your assigned land." He ran his eyes over several pages covered with tight script, then turned the book around and told Hakan, "Please make your mark."

Taking the quill, Hakan wrote his full name in large cursive letters: *Mico Hakan, Son of Blue Waters of the Muscogule Fox,* causing the captain to smile. "You show good penmanship," Paul commented tightly.

"The English teachers taught me well," was Hakan's droll reply.

Paul jerked his eyes from Hakan's impassive face and settled them on his own slender hands, which he pressed down onto the brittle pages of the journal as he hunched forward, toward Hakan.

"You'll be relocated among the Lower Creeks on the Arkansas River. You'll find the Indians there well settled in. Some live in log houses, but there are still a lot of tipis scattered around. They' built a school ... run by the Presbyterians. There's a trading post and a decent road for access to the Creek Council House. It's good land for farming and grazing livestock. You'll find it quite suitable, I think." Paul signed his name at the bottom of a page in his book and then said, "Get your people together. Tell them they will be given food and will sleep inside the fort tonight." He looked up and signaled to a Negro soldier who had just entered the room. "Canyon, I want you to lead this group out to the Creek settlement in the morning. Their supplies will follow in a separate wagon."

"Yes, sir," the young black man replied; then he locked eyes with Hakan and said, "Gonna take most of the day to get there, so y'all be ready to start at first light, you hear?"

Hakan inhaled deeply, held the air in his lungs for a moment, and then replied, "We will be ready."

"All right. That's all," Paul told Hakan, who turned abruptly and walked out of the office, his spine as straight as the arrows he carried in his quiver.

The Fox arrived at their allotted land at sunset the following day and settled down to begin life in Indian Territory. The women set up the tipis while the children gathered wood and the men took stock of their meager possessions. By the time night fell, most of the Fox were living in some kind of a makeshift home. The land was flat, dry, and without the tall stands of birch, pine and oak trees that had sheltered them at Great Oaks. As Hakan sat before the fire in front of his tipi, he felt exposed, almost naked, as if the stars were boring holes into his head. The bareness of the land left him feeling hollow and alone, longing for the familiar scent of the forest and the sound of the river where he'd lived his entire life.

When Wyiana came to sit beside him, he welcomed her presence. With her, he did not need to talk, did not have to explain what was on his mind. Wyiana knew that Tama was gone, that she was back with her master, and would not live with the Fox in their new homeland. Perhaps he had been foolish to believe that he and Tama could be more than two strangers whose paths had crossed in a very troubled time. She helped him return to his people, and he helped her gain her freedom—even though it had not lasted very long. All he could do now was hold onto the memory of her beautiful face, the softness of her voice, the feel of her hand in his.

A chasm of emptiness gripped Hakan. He'd never felt so alone in his life, not even while he was in the stockade at Shoulderbone. He tilted his face to the stars, thinking that Tama might be looking at them, too. He hoped she knew why he did not come for her, why he had to go on without her.

"She will not follow you to this place," Wyiana said, as if reading Hakan's mind.

With a slump of his shoulders, Hakan looked over at Wyiana and held her eyes with his. "I know," he said. "She is far away by now." When Wyiana did not speak, he covered her fingers with his. "And I know I must forget her," he finished in a tone of resignation.

"Yes, but you do not have to go on alone," Wyiana whispered, her melodic voice sending a shiver through Hakan. He swept her face with an intense gaze, admiring the silver sheen cast by the moon on her softly rounded lips, the sparkle of the stars in the brilliance of her eyes. His hand tightened over hers, his heart pounding like the thump of an axe hitting wood. A gentle wind blew through the camp, sending her womanly scent straight into his heart, creating a dizzy sense of longing, tinged with regret. The journey to this place had been long, hard, and cruel. He had lost his father, his mother, his homeland... and Tama. The most comforting presence he now had were his sister, Suja, and the lovely Wyiana. She was no different from him: she was an uprooted Muscogule Creek who had no choice but to bend to circumstances and start over in this harsh unfamiliar place. He knew she wanted him, and he needed her. There were no questions to be asked or answered because neither knew how the future would unfold. All they had was tonight—this moment, and a chance to face the unknown together.

When Wyiana stood, Hakan did not let go of her hand. When she led him toward her tipi, he did not hesitate to follow. And when she stepped inside and shed her dress and stood naked before him, he did not turn away from her outstretched arms.

Chapter 20

Forty-two days after leaving St. Louis, Big Tim said good-bye to Woods at the Cherokee Strip and took over the job of driving Elinore's wagon. He turned his small party southward to cut through the small town of Nowata and head deeper into Indian Territory. Because the area was a haven for outlaws, horse thieves, murderers hiding from U.S. marshals, and hostile Indians determined to stem the white man's intrusion, Big Tim remained tensely vigilant as they headed south along the Verdigris River.

After a hard drive that took them to the shores of Oologah Lake, Big Tim pulled the wagon close to the water and unhitched the horses. Elinore, little Ben, and Julee moved farther down the lake to wash. After an evening meal of corn cakes, beans, and coffee, the exhausted women settled down for the night in the wagon, anticipating a decent night's rest. Big Tim unrolled his canvas cloth, spread it on the ground, tossed down a rough Indian blanket, and made his bed by the fire.

Staring up into the brilliant splash of stars in the dark night sky, Big Tim focused his thoughts on Thorne Royaltin, something he rarely did. After coming face to face with the man in St. Louis, the pain of their encounter fifteen years ago swelled and filled his body with rage. Big Tim clamped his jaw tight, stretched out his arms, and placed both hands beneath his head, thinking.

He had planned for her to become his wife, with a real

ceremony and registration of their union at the county courthouse. He had promised her they would be together forever. That they would have another child, maybe a boy next time, and that he would build her a house in a free-black community where they would live and grow old together. Their dreams had been rich, full of hope and ripe with joy. And they would have come true, if not for Thorne Royaltin's treacherous interference.

Ever since Julee was a baby, Big Tim had tried to protect her from Royaltin's grasp. But had he done right by the girl? Had he been selfish and cruel to let Julee believe she had no mother or father? Had he been wrong to allow Daisy Lincoln to raise his daughter and treat her like a servant? Regret clogged Big Tim's throat, bringing a sheen of tears to his eyes that forced him to swallow hard and take a deep breath. Now that he'd brought Julee into his life, he had to tell her the truth. He wanted her future to be easier than his, or her mother's, but how could he make that happen?

Big Tim glanced toward the wagon where Julee was sleeping, worried about what would happen to her once they got to Fort Gibson. How would she survive in such a raw uncivilized place? What kind of a life could she have among wild Indians, outlaws, and freewheeling folks from God knows where? Julee was a good girl, a pretty girl, and nearly a woman, too. She deserved a real home, a family, a future with promise, and a chance at love with a man who would care for her in a proper way – better than he'd ever done. A grimace of frustration firmed Big Tim's lips as he fretted over his next move. He had to tell Julee why he abandoned her to Daisy Lincoln's care and refused to tell her the truth about himself. However, he would wait until they got to Fort Gibson, until after he found her a decent place to live. Then he would sit with her and have a long talk, clearing the air and the burden on his heart. For now, all he wanted to do was push the tiredness from his bones and sleep until the dawn woke him up.

However, late into the night, after the fire had burned low and the tree owls stopped hooting, Big Tim heard the vibrating thump of horses' hooves tramping the ground. The dark night was silvered in faint light from a full moon, and the orange glow of simmering embers cast a soft glow over the camp. Sensing trouble, Big Tim reached for his rifle and pulled on his boots. Crouching low to the ground, he crept behind a stand of brush and watched as two men rode stealthily into the camp. They dismounted and then went toward the wagon. The taller of the two was holding a pistol. His companion appeared to be holding a knife.

Anger squelched the flash of alarm that surged through Big Tim. If there was one thing he hated, it was a thief. Thorne Royaltin had stolen his woman and tried to steal his child. Big Tim had fought Royaltin and lost, but this time he wasn't about to lose.

As he suspected, the noise of the men's arrival awakened Elinore, and Julee, too. They immediately stuck their heads out the back of the wagon and looked around, frightened and confused.

"Big Tim," Julee hissed in a loud whisper. "That you?"

"You in the wagon! Get out!" the man with the gun commanded as he advanced on the ladies. Quickly, Julee jumped down, followed by Elinore, who was holding onto Ben.

"Where're the men?" the one with the knife demanded.

Elinore shook her head, indicating the women were alone.

"Git over there by the fire!" the bandit shouted.

Big Tim watched from his hiding place as the women, arms around each other, complied. He saw Elinore frown when she saw his abandoned bedroll, and without comment, placed her crying son on the empty blanket. She watched one man walk to the wagon; then he waved his gun at his companion, motioning him forward. "Get in there and find the valuables. Take the food, too," he said.

"Leave our things alone!" Elinore screamed, rushing toward the men. "Stay away from that wagon!" Her mind went to her new Henry rifle, along with the few things of value she owned. If only she'd thought to grab her gun ... she'd shoot that man dead in his tracks.

Alarmed, Julee raced after Elinore and took her by the arm. "Leave them be! Be quiet or they'll kill us."

Enraged, Big Tim waited until the short man was about to climb into the wagon before making his presence known. Furious, he moved into the moonlight and shouted, "Stop where you are! Drop your weapons! You ain't takin' nothing' from here!" With his old muzzle-loading Hawkins raised, he walked from behind the bushes, keeping a steady aim on the men.

Quickly, the tall one crouched down and fired at Big Tim, who ducked and escaped the bullet. Freezing in place, he remained low to the ground, his breath trapped in his chest, hoping the bandit might think he'd been hit. Big Tim counted to ten, then stood erect and pushed past the women. He fired off a shot at the gunman, who fired back. Again, the bullet missed Big Tim, but this time it hit Julee in the upper arm.

With a shout, Julee dropped to the ground. Little Ben wailed in fear. Elinore screamed, rushing to Julee's side where she put pressure on the bullet wound. Big Tim stepped off to the side, took aim and fired again, hitting his mark. The gunman dropped to the ground with a dull thud, with blood spilling from the bullet hole in the side of his head. Whirling around, Big Tim swept the area for the second bandit, who quickly abandoned his search of the wagon and was racing toward his horse. After squeezing off two fast shots that missed his target, Big Tim raced after the man, who managed to mount his horse and take off into the night.

Julee lay on the ground, blood streaming down her arm and into the dirt. Stunned by the encounter, Elinore tried to comfort Julee.

"Lie still, Julee. Don't try to move. The men are gone. Everything's under control."

Julee coughed, struggled to sit up, but howled in pain, her cries mingling with those of Ben, who was wailing and clinging to his mother's skirt. Big Tim frantically raced back to Julee, dropped to his knees, and tore away the bloody sleeve of her shirt. Gritting his teeth, he looked up at Elinore. "Make a torch for light. Then get fresh water and clean rags!"

Daylight was breaking by the time Big Tim finished applying a poultice of five-finger-grass and chickweed to Julee's wound, using strips of cloth torn from a bed sheet to bind the herbs in place. He created a sling to support her injured arm, thankful that the bullet had pierced the fleshy part of her limb and did not hit the bone.

"It'll heal fine, in time," he reassured Julee, who closed her eyes with a grateful nod, grimacing from the pain. "But we got to keep it clean. An infection could make you lose that arm, and I ain't about to let that happen." He patted Julee on the cheek, his large, rough hand nearly covering her small face as he gazed down at her with fatherly concern. "You gonna be fine, but you need to get some sleep right now." He gently picked her up, carried her to the wagon, and tucked her into her nest of quilts alongside Ben, who was sucking his thumb, deep into slumber once again. Big Tim stood watching over Julee for a long moment before returning to the fire, where Elinore was frying salt pork and making coffee for breakfast.

"You really think she'll be okay?" Elinore inquired, worry threading her words.

"Oh, yeah, I've doctored gunshots a hell of a lot worse than hers, but I gotta admit I ain't never had to do it on a gal as young as Julee."

Elinore placed the coffee pot in the fire, wiped her hands on the apron she was wearing over her canvas trousers, and then stood to face Big Tim. "You know a lot about surviving out here in the wild, don't you?"

"Reckon so," Big Tim murmured, reaching for a tin mug hanging on the side of the wagon, which he handed to Elinore. "Traveling the roads is all I ever done. Life's cheap in the wild. When danger strikes, you gotta act quick. She was losing an awful lot of blood."

"Thank God you knew how to stop the bleeding," Elinore quietly added. "You saved her life, you know?"

A purse of his lips was Big Tim's reply before he murmured, "Maybe so ... but you know what?" He gazed at the fire and took a breath so deep and long Elinore could see his chest expanding beneath his faded plaid shirt. "I saved that little gal's life once before."

Startled, Elinore tilted her head to one side, letting Big

Tim's remark sink in. She didn't respond, giving him time to decide how much, or what, he planned to reveal. She'd quickly learned while on the road with him that he was a gregarious man who loved to tell tall tales in the company of strangers but revealed little about his personal life. She knew he'd been born in the middle of a Louisiana swamp to a Cajun daddy and a Creole-Negro mother, and that he had no brothers or sisters. At the age of nine, he took to the road, doing any kind of work he could find. He traveled the country and lived hand to mouth before he started driving wagons for wages.

"Guess it's time I told somebody the truth," he blurted out, accepting the tin cup of coffee that Elinore passed to him. "Done kept all this to myself so long, I never thought I'd have reason to tell it." He sat down by the fire, leaned back on his elbows, took a draw on the steaming brew, and then gave Elinore a warning. "You can't repeat what I'm about to tell you, 'cause the day might come when what I'm about to say could destroy everything for Julee."

Curious, Elinore assured him she would do as he asked. "I'd never do anything to harm that girl. I care a lot for her, and I know how much you care for her, too. I've seen the way you look at Julee, the way you talk to her, and treat her … well, it's almost as if she's your daughter."

A burning log broke into pieces and hissed as it crumbled, filling the dead space that lingered. Big Tim lowered his head and stared at the ground. "She is my daughter," he admitted, lifting his head, brows raised to emphasize his confession. "And I'ma tell you the truth about how it all came about." He squinted toward the wagon, as if to make sure Julee was not listening. "You see, Julee's mother was a slave on a plantation in North Carolina. Her name was Maggie. She escaped, even though she had to leave her five-year-old daughter … a child

216

she had by her master, behind. Maggie made it as far as Ohio, where she crossed over into freedom. I found her lying on the riverbank, soaking wet, nearly dead. I took her in and kept her with me 'till she got well. Wasn't long before we found we had feelings for each other. A year later, we had a baby girl. Named her Julee. We talked about getting married to make it all legal. Even talked about having more babies. But her master caught up with her, put her in chains, and was dead set on taking our baby, Julee, too. He claimed Julee was the issue of his property, and so she belonged to him. I fought that man hard. Beat him down and stomped him, too. Then I snatched Julee and ran off with her. He shouted after me, promising to find me and kill me ... kill my baby girl, too. I hid in a coal chute and watched while that evil man beat Maggie with a whip; then he took her away. Nothing I could do to save Maggie, but I swore he'd never take our child. So I ran ... headed west. Made it as far as St. Louis, where I got regular work driving stages. The bad part was I had to leave baby Julee at the boarding house with Daisy Lincoln while I was away working. Over the years, I paid her to raise my girl."

"All those years, and you never told Julee the truth? Why?" Elinore pressed, sensing how hard it was for Big Tim to reveal the secret he had kept so long.

"Afraid to. I figgered ... as long as the child couldn't go 'round telling folks who her momma or her daddy was, she'd be safe from Thorne Royaltin's grab. He mighta owned her mother, but he was never gonna take Julee to slave on his plantation, too."

Elinore's head snapped up. "What did you say the man's name was?"

"Maggie's master? Thorne Royaltin, that's who."

The name made Elinore flinch. "Thorne Royaltin?" she held her breath. "I met a man by that name on the steamer from Cincinnati. He told me he owned a textile mill in North Carolina."

"Tall, dark-haired. Good-looking fellow?"

"Yes." Elinore's voice was a ragged whisper. "He told me he was going to St. Louis for business."

Big Tim slowly moved his head up and down. "I know. I saw him in town when I went to buy your rifle. Maybe he *was* in St. Louis on business, I don't know 'bout that. I'm just glad I left him there and took Julee out of his reach, 'cause if he ever came after her, I'd kill him before I'd let him take her away from me."

* * * * *

The long trek into the heart of Indian Territory was a fearful, backbreaking journey. As the days slipped past, rainstorms turned the trail into a muddy river, bringing their progress to a near-halt. At Catoosa, wolves howled at the edge of their campfire, keeping everyone awake most of the night while Julee tossed and turned, burning with fever. Her wounded arm grew hotly inflamed, with a festering boil that was ugly and red. Elinore rubbed Big Tim's herbal compounds into the wound to ease the inflammation, but her ministrations had little effect. With an injured girl and a small toddler to care for, Big Tim and Elinore pressed on toward Ft. Gibson. Along the way, he managed to catch a wild turkey, which they roasted on a spit and ate with relish. Elinore boiled the bones and made a rich broth for Julee, who barely managed to open her mouth to take it in. Elinore sat at her side and prayed aloud, desperate for the girl's fever to break before it killed her.

Finally, fifty-eight days after leaving St. Louis, they arrived at the fork of the Arkansas and Verdigris Rivers. Big Tim looked out across the land and saw, with great relief, the tall timber posts surrounding Fort Gibson in the distance, but he feared his daughter might not live to sleep inside its protective walls.

They traveled down a narrow road, past the Indian agency office at Three Forks, to arrive at the banks of the Grand River at high noon. There was a small gathering of people there, staring across the river, anxious to see who had arrived. Big Tim noted a cluster of neatly whitewashed blockhouses surrounding the palisades of the fort, as well as a tangle of tipis, lean-tos, and canvas tents that provided shelter for those who wanted to remain near the protective walls of the fort.

Big Tim hollered to the soldiers operating the large ferryboat on the opposite side of the river, and they quickly came for his party. While Big Tim swam the horses and the wagon across, Elinore, Ben, and a very sick Julee, crossed in the ferryboat, which was swiftly poled to the opposite shore. Once they were on land again, the crowd gathered close to inspect the new arrivals, offering words of welcome peppered with questions about where they had come from and how long they had been traveling. After a short greeting and a few words about their journey, Big Tim got his passengers re-settled in the wagon and they started toward the tall gates of the garrison.

A stern-faced guard waved them past the heavy gates and into the open parade ground of the fort. Big Tim drove the wagon deeper into the interior, which was as crowded with people as it was thick with flies. The stench of tanning animal skins and fresh horse manure mingled with the heat, creating a most unpleasant odor, prompting Elinore to place her fingers to her nose as she surveyed the scene.

The fort swarmed with activity as soldiers, trappers, Indians, blacks, civilian women, and children went about their daily chores. There were trappers trading skins and furs for fresh supplies, merchants at tables filled with finery for the ladies and utilitarian household supplies. They passed a telegraph office, a mail post building, a bakery, a pump where white women were washing clothes, and a squat red brick structure with bars on the windows. Four men were sitting outside the jail, their heads poking through holes carved into rough boards clamped together. Their hands had been secured in the splintered rail, and one of them looked as if he might be dead. Elinore stared at the torturous contraption, just as Big Tim commented, "That's what the soldiers call a stockade, and sitting in it is a damned degrading form of punishment."

"I can see why," Elinore replied, shaking her head in dismay as Big Tim gee-hawed to the horses, and then he stopped in front of the largest two-story building at the end of the yard. He shouted a greeting to an old-timer he recognized from a previous visit to the fort and jumped down and turned to help Elinore and Ben from the wagon.

With a whoop of joy, Captain Paul Wardlaw burst out of the building and pushed through the crowd, unashamed of the tears running down his face. He hugged his wife, kissed his son, and sobbed aloud as he embraced his family. Holding onto Paul, Elinore went limp, finally allowing the worry she'd carried in her heart since the day she left Cincinnati to float away and disappear. She was in her husband's arms. Her son was with his father. They were a finally a family, and that was all that mattered.

"Got a doctor here?" Big Tim immediately asked Paul.

"You're Mr. Lester, aren't you?" Paul inquired before answering.

"That's me."

"Thank you for delivering my wife and son safely to me," Paul added.

"That's what you paid me to do. But right now, I got a pretty sick gal in this wagon, and she needs a doctor right away."

"Oh? Who? What happened?" Paul looked nervously from Big Tim to Elinore, who placed a hand on his arm and told her husband, "We ran into some trouble, but Ben and I were not harmed. I'll tell you all about it later. Right now, Julee must have medical attention."

"Right," Paul agreed with a jerk of his head. He pointed across the yard to a one-story brick building opposite the jail. "Over there's the fort hospital. The doctor's in there now."

Big Tim circled the wagon, reached inside, picked Julee up, and without another word, carried her across the yard in long determined strides.

"That's the girl I wrote you about," Elinore began to explain.

"What girl? Well, I didn't get the letter," he replied. "Where'd you pick her up?"

"I met her in St. Louis," Elinore replied. "She wanted to leave the city and I needed help with Ben, so I agreed to let her travel with me. I hope she'll be all right. I feel rather responsible for her. Maybe I should go with Mr. Lester, make sure she gets good care. You see, she doesn't have ...."

"No," Paul curtly cut Elinore off. "You've done enough. You surely can't be bothered with the problems of a girl like that."

"Like what?" Elinore tossed back, surprised by her husband's rude remark. She'd hoped he would be glad to know that she'd had someone to help her with Ben while they were on the road.

"Nothing. Forget it. Let Mr. Lester worry about her," Paul remarked, ending any more discussion about Julee. "She'll get good enough care at the hospital. Doc Stewart treats them all. Blacks, Indians, even delivered a baby for a China woman last week. He'll do what he can for the girl. No need for you to be involved." A flash of annoyance darkened his features, perplexing Elinore, who firmed her lips and stepped back a few feet, as if to give Paul space to calm down.

However, Paul paid no attention to his wife's reaction. He slipped his arm around Elinore's waist and hefted Ben into his free arm. "You're here...at last! That is all I care about. I know how tired and anxious you must be, so let's go see your new home."

Paul called for soldiers to bring his wife's belongings, and he then led her across the dirt yard to his quarters.

The barracks for the single soldiers were a series of long, low lodges with sloping shingle roofs, sparsely furnished and utilitarian. The quarters for the married men were not much better, and at the sight of her new home, Elinore struggled to keep her composure. The single room she would share with Paul consisted of a twelve by twelve space with a narrow bed, a chair, a small nightstand, and an oil-burning lamp with a sooty shade. A brass candleholder hung on the wall next to a pegboard holding Paul's nightshirt and extra change of clothes. The wood plank floor was scarred and rough, and the roof had tiny gaps in it, through which Elinore could see the sky. There

222

was one window, a stone fireplace, and a wood box outside the door. After surveying the room, Elinore moved closer to Paul, tilted her face up to his, and gave him a longer, more intense kiss than he'd received outside. She forced a smile and assured Paul, "This is fine. Just fine, but it could use a woman's touch, that's for sure." Then she shooed Paul and Ben outside, and with a contented sigh, watched them walk away, Ben's small hand curled around his father's thumb. *Everything is going to be all right*, she told herself, *now that my family is whole.*

After casting a critical eye around the room, she shed her ragged sunbonnet, removed the pouch of dried turtle blood she'd worn on a cord around her neck since the day Big Tim gave it to her, and then opened her humpback trunk. With a sigh of relief, she began to unpack the small touches of civilized life she had managed to bring along.

The fort hospital was a square, whitewashed building overflowing with patients. Big Tim carried Julee inside and walked directly toward a long table set up behind two giant columns that rose to the ceiling and divided the room in half. A man wearing a white coat and steel rim glasses stood up from the table and met Big Tim in the middle of the room.

"You the doctor?" Big Tim asked.

"Yes, I'm Doctor Stewart."

"A gunshot wound," Big Tim blurted out before the doctor had time to ask what was ailing the patient. "She's burning hot and ain't been able to eat or drink since yesterday. Been asleep for the past two hours. Help her, please. She's mighty weak."

"When was she shot?" Dr. Stewart asked, indicating that

Big Tim place Julee on the nearest empty cot.

"Ten days ago," Big Tim replied, carefully placing Julee down, while explaining what had happened and what he had done to treat the wound.

Quickly, Dr. Stewart bent to examine Julee's arm. He peeled back the poultice Big Tim had applied and peered at the wound with a practiced eye. "Did you get the bullet out?"

"It passed right through. Left that hole in her arm."

"What's her name?"

"Julee."

"Who's she to you?"

Big Tim hesitated, shifted his eyes to the side, and then said, "My daughter."

"Hum," the doctor murmured, keeping his eyes on Julee as he motioned for a woman wearing a long white apron to come and assist him. "Nurse Bowman, antiseptic and bandages, please," he told her before turning back to face Big Tim. "You did a decent job of staunching the blood flow," he stated, nodding in appreciation of Big Tim's efforts. "But that wound is badly infected." He placed a hand on Julee's forehead, and then pressed his fingers to her wrist. "She's got a high fever. Could lose that arm, but I hope it's not too late to save it."

"How long before you know if she's gonna be all right?"

"Can't say. Leave her here. We'll do what we can."

Big Tim scratched the side of his face in concern, but he stepped aside as the nurse arrived and handed a bottle of brown liquid to the doctor. He stood there, watching them swab Julee's swollen, purple flesh until the doctor scowled at him and said, "You go on. Nothing you can do here. Come back in a day or two. This girl needs a good long rest."

Reluctant to leave, Big Tim lingered at the foot of Julie's cot until Nurse Bowman shook a slender finger at him and began to remove Julee's bloodstained dress. With a nod, Big Tim finally put on his hat and left his daughter in the doctor's care.

* * * * *

The Indian blanket that Elinore tacked to the rafters to divide Paul's quarters into two separate, but tiny, spaces created a bit of privacy for her and Paul's reunion. With Ben finally asleep in his crib behind the partition, she stepped from the tin tub of warm water that Paul had managed to secure for her bath, and eased her naked body down into bed beside him. Though still aching from the arduousness of her journey, and her mind still reeling with concern about making a home for her family in this harsh place, she didn't hesitate to respond when Paul slid his arm beneath her shoulders and drew her to his side. With a shudder of relief, rife with desire, Elinore emptied her mind of everything except her longing for her husband's touch. After nearly four years without him, she ached to feel his lean, trim body stretched over hers, his lips pressing her skin as she remembered. During their long separation, Elinore's love for Paul had not diminished, and judging from the way his hands were moving over her body, touching places long abandoned, she knew his love for her had not dimmed as well. As they came together in the dark, initiating a sense of great liberation, Elinore embraced the flood of passion that swept through her and swallowed the cry of joy that threatened to erupt.

* * * * *

When Big Tim returned to the hospital two days after leaving Julee in the doctor's care, he found her sitting up in bed, her arm wrapped in a white cotton sling. She was wearing a blue and white striped nightshirt and her hair had been freshly washed and combed. She looked so pretty and healthy that Big Tim broke into the first smile he'd made since arriving at Fort Gibson. When Julee looked up, clearly pleased to see him, Big Tim's heart was filled with love for the daughter he'd finally claimed. He just hoped that what he was about to tell her would not ruin her good mood but make her face shine even brighter.

"You sure look like the worst is over," he told her, removing his hat, which he circled with both hands as he sat on a stool beside the cot.

"Maybe so, but the doctor says I still gotta stay here for a while. Something about how long it's gonna take for my arm to go back to its regular size." She raised her injured limb, and then winced. "It's as swollen as a whole hog roasting on a spit," she joked, trying to lighten the mood.

"Well, you do as he says. You gotta get well so you can go home."

"Home?" She gave Big Tim a puzzled glance, tilting her head to one side. "Home?" she repeated. "You sending me back to Daisy's?"

"Nope."

"So, just where's *home* gonna be?"

"Where would you like it to be?" he asked.

With a stutter, Julee stated, "Oh, any place, but with Miss Daisy. I'd like to stay with Miss Elinore ... but now she's with her husband, and I doubt he'd want me around."

"I figger you're right ... from the way he acted the first day I met him," Big Tim muttered.

"She's a fine lady, Miss Elinore. Came to see me yesterday," Julee went on. "Told me she met a white woman who's got extra room since her husband died. Maybe I can live in and work for her."

A scowl touched Big Tim's features. "Well, we'll see about that." A moment lapsed while he gathered enough courage to press on with what he was determined to say. "I been talking to a soldier named Canyon. Very helpful fellow. He got me permission to live in a settlement on the river. I already picked out a spot in a nice place not far from the fort and I'm building a house ... well, best call it a cabin right now, but in time it'll be a real house. You'll see."

Julee huffed at him, as if he were talking nonsense, then bit her bottom lip and lowered her eyes as she picked at a loose thread in the quilt. "You mean you gonna stay here, permanent, with the Indians?" She leaned back to get a better look at his face. "I thought you was a travelin' man, Big Tim. You never said nothin' 'bout settling in with the Indians."

Big Tim scooted closer to the side of the bed and sucked in a hard breath. "Never thought I'd want to stay in one place for long, but now ... things are different."

"How so?" Julee wanted to know.

"Now I got to be worrying about you."

"You don't have to worry about me. I'll make out fine. I sure hope I can go live with the widow woman and get some work, too."

"You won't be living with or slaving for any white widow woman," Big Tim sharply countered, suddenly sounding gruff. "*My* daughter's not gonna be washin' clothes or cooking over a hot wood stove for anybody ... 'cept maybe for me." He gave her a timid smile and held his breath, watching Julee closely.

She laughed and clucked her tongue. "Your daughter? What you talkin' about Big Tim? You know I ain't no kin to you."

"You're wrong." He let a moment pass before going on. "You're my flesh and blood, all right. I know I got a lot to explain, but hear me out before you go getting mad at me for not telling you before now."

Julee squinted at Big Tim but remained silent, listening to his story.

"Your momma was a slave named Maggie," he began. "She ran away from her master and came north from Carolina. I met her, we liked each other right off.... so we decided to stay together. Then you were born, and we were real happy ... until Maggie's master came to take her back to his plantation. He was dead set on taking you, too, but I snatched you from Maggie and ran." He paused and blinked before going on. "You were just a tiny thing, you fit real neat in my saddle bag, and you gave me no trouble on the ride out of town. I didn't stop riding for days. It was hard travel, but I had to get you as far away from that evil man as I could. When I finally got so dead tired I couldn't go on, I stopped at a Negro boarding house in St. Louis. After a spell, I got a job driving a wagon full of folks to Kansas. Had to leave you behind..."

"With Daisy Lincoln," Julee added, her voice soft and uncertain.

"Yep. I paid Daisy a good part of my wages to look after you, and I made her promise not to tell you who I was. She didn't know nothing about your mama."

"Why did you do that? That man who took my momma

was far away."

"Don't matter. The white man's reach is long, and his anger never dies. He said he'd find me, and take you from me, and I believed he would. I didn't want you to ever have to worry about that. So I had to keep you from knowing who your mamma and daddy were. Just until you'd understand better." He reached over and took Julee's free hand. "Do you understand, Julee? You ain't mad at me are you?"

Julee bored her gaze into Big Tim's misty eyes, clearly upset by what she had heard. "What you did wasn't right. Making me think I didn't have a momma or a daddy was powerful wrong."

"I know, I know, but I can't change it now." Big Tim scowled at Julee, sensing her rejection. He'd been a fool to believe it would be easy to tell a fifteen-year-old that she'd been lied to all her life, that she had not deserved to know the truth about who she was, or what he had done to keep her from knowing.

"I used to count the coins you gave me, over and over, hoping you'd show up at Daisy's. Then, when you did come, I used to pretend you were my daddy. I prayed every night that my daddy would come looking for me and take me away. All I wanted was *someone*. *Someone* other than Daisy. You shoulda told me the truth."

Shoulders sagging, Big Tim went limp. "Yes, I reckon you speak the truth, young lady. Guess all I can hope for now is that you try hard to forgive an old man for not doing right by his daughter because he loves her so much. Just let me make things better ... for both of us, all right?"

Julee wrapped her small fingers around Big Tim's large, rough ones and tilted back her head. Staring at the ceiling, she closed her eyes. "Guess the good Lord was listening to me after all. He's done brought me back my daddy." With a jerk, she widened her eyes and grinned at Big Tim. "And he's a dammed smart one, too."

Chapter 21

Thorne did not regret his decision to travel on the Overland Mail stage, but the frequent stops to drop off and pick up mail, coupled with severe storms that washed out roads and interrupted progress, added two weeks to his travel schedule. By the time he arrived at Fort Smith, Arkansas, he was exhausted, irritated, and anxious to get on with his search for Tama. However, in order to enter Indian Territory he needed written permission from Major James Fleming, who, unfortunately, was in Texas giving testimony at a hearing on the defection of two soldiers and would not return to Fort Smith for at least a week.

Though deeply aggravated by the disruption of his plan, Thorne remained calm. He spent his wait time holed up in a room above the soldiers' barracks, where he retooled his strategy to find Tama. When Major Fleming finally returned to Fort Smith and agreed to see him, Thorne was prepared to make his case.

"You say your daughter was taken by Indians against her will?" Fleming repeated after listening to Thorne's request.

"That's right," Thorne agreed.

"Guess that's a valid reason to grant permission for you to go look for her," Fleming stated. He was seated at a desk created from a thick oak plank placed atop two sawhorses. He removed a leather pouch from his shirt pocket and began to roll tobacco into a piece of brown paper, which his long knobby fingers twisted with an expert flip. He lit the cigarette from a lamp burning on his desk, leaned back, and sent a hazy trail of smoke away from Thorne.

"I think so," Thorne replied, trying to gauge the man's mood, hoping his story would hold up under intense questioning. He slid to the edge of his chair and folded both arms on the desk, as if preparing to negotiate the matter. "I have good reason to believe my daughter was swept up in a recent round-up of Creek Indians in Georgia. Along the Tallapoosa River."

"So far from your home? Didn't you say you're from North Carolina?" Fleming pressed.

With practiced ease, Thorne replied, "She ran away. I sent men to look for her, and that's how I learned she'd been taken by the Indians."

"Humm, what's she look like? Might be she's right here at Fort Smith. We recovered two white girls from the Comanche a few weeks ago. They won't talk. Won't do anything but stare into space and sleep. Maybe she's here."

"I don't think so," Thorne replied, prepared to launch into the next phase of his plan. "You see....my daughter is not white. She's mulatto." He waited for, and received, the reaction he expected.

Fleming tilted forward and squinted down his thin, sharp nose at Thorne, one eyebrow raised. "A mulatto, huh? You own slaves?"

"I do," Thorne admitted, seemingly proud. "I own one of the largest, and most profitable, cotton farms in the state of North Carolina, and I have fifty-six slaves to work it."

"This "daughter"... she's one of your slaves, I'm guessing?"

"She is," Thorne stated with defiance, as if challenging

Fleming to say something derogatory about the southern planter's way of life. It was not a crime, nor was it unusual, for a white planter to impregnate a female slave. In fact, among some circles, such behavior was seen as an economical way to increase a master's slave population, though that had certainly not been the reason Thorne slept with Maggie. The smirk of displeasure that tugged Fleming's lips spurred Thorne to add, "Owning slaves may be frowned upon by those who do not understand the economics of Southern planters, but slavery is a necessary and accepted form of labor where I come from, and I do not apologize for the way I run my plantation."

Fleming swiped a finger alongside his nose, and stated, "Well, Mister Royaltin, you'll not be going into Indian Territory to hunt for your slave daughter. Better turn around, go on back to North Carolina, and tend your plantation with the slaves you still have." Fleming took a hard draw on his cigarette. "I know what you're gonna say, that Indians bring their slaves right along with them and we allow them to be resettled. That's true. Even some of the blacks that come with them own slaves. If the government starts letting white men scour the territory to hunt for slaves, we'll have a revolution on our hands. Just leave it all alone; that's the way we keep the peace. Won't be any slave hunting going on out here."

"I'm not looking for my daughter so I can take her back to North Carolina," Thorne defended. He pulled from his coat pocket a brittle piece of paper that he'd folded in half and handed it to Fleming, then waited as the major read the document. "You see. That's her manumission paper. In it, I admit that Tama is my daughter and that I want to set her free. I want her to have this document. It would mean a lot to me ... letting her know she'll never have to worry about her freedom."

Fleming turned his eyes on the paper once again, then studied Thorne with a combination of suspicion and respect, then slipped the document beneath the black record book on his desk. "All right, Mr. Royaltin. You appear to be a gentleman, so I'm going to take you at your word. I'll give you ten days to find your half-breed daughter, but an Army escort is going along with you. You bring the girl to me and I will give this paper to her in person." Then he paused, as if considering saying more, and removed the paper from beneath the book. He spread it open on the table. "I want you to sign this again, Mr. Royaltin ... at the bottom of the page ... with me as a witness, just to make everything legal. I don't want any forgery or foolishness about this, understand?"

"I am more than happy to oblige," Thorne said, accepting the quill and ink that the captain offered.

* * * * *

Those living inside and around the timber-log walls of Fort Gibson were awakened each morning by a bugler sounding reveille. As the rising sun broke over the land, a soldier ran the flag up the tall pole in the center of the compound, and folks placed pots of coffee on wood-burning stoves or in campfires scattered across the grounds. After a typical breakfast of bacon, eggs, and biscuits smeared with raw honey, soldiers began their routine duty details: processing new Indian arrivals, patrolling the territory, performing maintenance on the grounds and the artillery, and settling disputes among tribes. The women generally remained close to the fort, tending children and tackling domestic chores that required strength, creativity, and patience.

Elinore had just finished clearing away the breakfast

dishes when she looked out her open door and saw Big Tim outside. She nearly dropped the iron skillet she was wiping clean when Julee emerged from behind him. For the past two weeks, Elinore had visited Julee at the hospital every day, bringing food, clean clothes, and news of what was happening at the fort. Elinore felt a keen sense of responsibility for the girl, and wished Julee could live with her and Paul. However, their one-room home was cramped, and Paul made it clear that he questioned Elinore's judgment in bringing the girl to the territory. They had a painful argument three days earlier, during which Paul referred to Elinore as a do-gooder, like her mother, who only wanted to ease her conscience for all the terrible things that abolitionists believed Southern whites had done to blacks. Elinore accused Paul of harboring racist attitudes he had confessed to discarding long ago. The argument created a rift between her and Paul that lasted for three days. However, Elinore eventually forgave him, reminding herself that she had knowingly married a Southern man who did not share her compassion and concern for people with whom she had little in common. Elinore felt it was her mission as a dutiful wife to stand by Paul and help him become a more tolerant and accepting person.

"Julee!" Elinore exclaimed, leaving Ben at the table chewing on a biscuit, to step outside and greet her visitors. Relieved that Paul had already left for duty, Elinore wiped her hands on her apron and then gave Julee a warm hug. Holding onto the girl's shoulders, she beamed her pleasure at seeing how well Julee looked. "I see you're up and about. You look well."

"I am," Julee replied, raising her injured arm to show off the small bandage covering her wound. "My arm feels just fine, and it's almost back to its regular size. Gives me no pain.

I'm grateful to the doctor, but I'm glad to get out of that hospital. Hope I never go back."

"What a relief..." Elinore said, shifting her attention to Big Tim. "You saved her life, you know?"

Big Tim shifted his weight to one side and nodded.

"So what are your plans, Julee?" Elinore asked. "Do you want to live with Widow

Marsh, the woman I told you about?"

"Naw," Big Tim spoke up before Julee could respond. "I got permission for both of us to stay in the territory. Julee's gonna come live with me. We're heading to Lone Grove right now."

"Lone Grove?" Elinore remarked. She had heard about the settlement west of the fort, established by slaves who had either been set free by their Indian masters or run away from them. It was little more than a tent camp on the Arkansas River, deep within the boundaries of the Creek Nation. Most of the residents of Lone Grove lived in shanties made of twigs and hides or in canvas tents supplied by the government. Slaves who registered with specific tribes were granted permission to fish, trap, and hunt on the restricted Indian hunting grounds, and many came to the fort to trade animal skins for domestic utensils and farming tools.

"Yep. We're going to Lone Grove," Big Tim said. "I know it's a bit rough out there, but we'll make out fine. I'm gonna build a nice little cabin for us, a place where Julee will be safe ... where she can grow a garden and keep house."

Elinore glanced questioningly at Julee, wondering what the girl thought about Big Tim's plans, but then she turned back to Big Tim and asked, "So you told her the truth?"

Seeming almost embarrassed at how happy he was, Big Tim pushed out his chest when he said, "I sure did." He placed an arm around Julee's shoulder and held her to his side. "She knows everything now. Hate I waited so long ta claim her, but now that I have, I don't plan ta let her out of my sight ... *non*, at least not for a long time."

"Julee," Elinore began, "what do you think? Now that you know who Big Tim is?"

"Makes me real happy," Julee replied, a pensive shimmer in her dark eyes as she graced Elinore with a pride-filled grin. "But you know what?" She hesitated; then let her shoulders drop. "I used to pray that one day I'd find my daddy, and he'd be just like Big Tim. So I guess the good Lord heard my prayers. What I been hoping for was always right here. You helped, Miss Elinore. You let me come along with you, and that's why things turned out this way." She glanced at Big Tim, who inclined his head, urging her to go on. "I appreciate you trying to get me a place to live with the widow woman," Julee told Elinore," but my place is with my ... father."

"I understand." Tears threatened to spill from Elinore's eyes, but she blinked them back. A warm glow of satisfaction flowed through her to see the joy on Julee's face. She gave the girl another stout embrace and then said, "Before you leave, please go inside and say good-by to Ben. He's been asking about you. I told him you were tired from the long trip and had to go to a special place to rest."

Julee chuckled and then went to see Ben. Once she was inside, Elinore focused on Big Tim. "So you and Julee will be together. That's good. Lone Grove is less than an hour's ride from the fort. I'll come to visit when I can."

"You don't have to make that promise," Big Tim warned.

"I know Captain Wardlaw would not want you to go to Lone Grove. I don't much blame him. There're dangerous folks there, livin' right alongside real friendly ones, but it's best if you stay close to the fort." He took Elinore's extended hand, shook it, and then said, "Good-bye ... and you take good care of that boy. He's gonna grow up to be a real strong young man. I'll be seeing you now and again when I come in for supplies, and I'll be sure to bring Julee sometime."

"Please do," Elinore said. Watching her newfound friends get into their wagon initiated a sense of impending loneliness that weighed heavily on her heart. The three of them had shared hardships as well as laughter on the trail, and she had trusted them completely. The ties that bound them could never be broken, even though the time had come to loosen them a bit.

Elinore tucked a strand of blonde hair behind her ear and sniffed back a tear, feeling as if members of her family were going away. With a final wave, she turned around, went inside, and picked up little Ben. "We'll see them soon," she promised, determined to visit Julee and Big Tim at Lone Grove in spite of her husband's warning.

Chapter 22

"Best read this." Canyon tapped the newspaper spread open on the desk. "News like that makes folks more scared than they ought to be," Canyon remarked, handing Paul a yellowed newspaper page torn from the *Arkansas Gazette*. He crossed the simply furnished room that served as the headquarters for processing new arrivals and leaned against the wall, waiting as Paul read the article. The sound of troops going through their early morning drills in the parade ground drifted through the open window.

Paul gave the brittle paper a shake and then held it up to his face. "Tribal feuds and general hostility toward the U. S. government continue to create grave danger in Indian Territory," he quoted from the story, written by the reporter he had welcomed to Fort Gibson a week ago. The journalist told Paul that he planned to write a story to reassure local citizens living along the Arkansas border that all was going smoothly with the Indian resettlement and that they had nothing to fear. "The Osage and Cherokee continue to wage a sporadic and brutal war that began when the Cherokee arrived and settled on land that had long been home to the Osage. In the eyes of the Osage, the Cherokee, as well as the Creek, must be purged from the territory. The Osage have vowed to fight for the return of their land, and the hunting rights they believe have been wrongfully taken from them. Fort Gibson is severely overcrowded as it has become a place of refuge for those caught up in this inter-tribal violence."

"Damn," Paul cursed, flinging the paper aside. "This is not

what that man said he was going to write. This kind of stuff makes folks nervous."

"Things around here been pretty calm lately. We sure don't need newspaper men spreading fear," Canyon agreed with concern. "Most of the chiefs are well informed and they regularly read the Arkansas papers. This kind of article might cause a lot of trouble."

"I hope not," Paul countered. "As long as the feuding tribes keep their raiding and fighting away from here, not much we can do."

"There's an awful lot of Cherokee living right outside these walls," Canyon remarked. "And they been agitating for the government to close this place and give 'em control of the boat landing."

"That'll never happen," Paul replied with a snap. "The government will never turn this fort over to Indians."

Canyon grunted skeptically. He had been a scout and interpreter for the Army for five years, spoke many of the Indian dialects, and knew how to gauge the natives' temperaments. He knew the Cherokee and the Creek were growing more fearful of the Osage every day, and that tensions were high. Many Cherokee were complaining that the army was not doing enough to protect them from their warring neighbor to the north, and they were making threats about taking over the fort. All Canyon could do was assure them that the soldiers were doing their best to keep the peace and that the fort was a refuge for any who needed it.

Born to black parents in east Texas, Canyon Tallboot grew up on a pig farm near an Alabama Indian village. When his mother died, his father took up with an Indian woman who moved into his home and raised Canyon and his two brothers in her ways. Canyon left home when he was eleven years old, wandered among various Indian tribes, and then hooked up with the Army as a scout. Now, at age twenty-three, he was content with his post in the territory, serving without incident under Captain Paul Wardlaw, even though the captain's tolerance for those who were not white, or Southern, was regularly put to the test. The first time Paul called Canyon, "boy," Canyon made it clear that he was a grown man and would not answer to any name other than the one his mother gave him at birth. It took a while for Paul to accept the fact that he could not boss the few black soldiers at Fort Gibson around as if they belonged to him. So he reserved his anti-abolitionist rhetoric for discussions with Southern men like himself.

Paul stuck the newspaper into a basket on his desk and looked at Canyon. "I asked Captain Rogers to hold things down here for a couple of hours," he informed Canyon while buttoning his jacket. "I promised Elinore I'd take Ben out for a ride while she goes to the market at Muscogee. I'll be back about noon."

"Sure thing. Me and Rogers can handle things around here."

Paul jammed his hat on his head, picked up a sheet of paper, and then added, "Check this supply list for the new arrivals in the Creek Nation. Take the wagon out today."

"Will do," Canyon replied, picking up Paul's list to review the order.

Canyon spent most of the morning in the storehouse, securing supplies and making sure he had the standard supplies for the Indians: salt pork, bacon, dried beef, flour, corn meal, rice, beans, green coffee, sugar, vinegar, candles, soap, and black salt. Those who farmed their land grew fresh fruit and vegetables, and raised hogs and chickens to add to the government staples.

When Canyon finished, he tied a tarp over the loaded wagon, and then headed toward the stables to check on his horse, which had thrown a shoe the previous day. However, when he rounded the storehouse and started down the path, he stopped short, shocked to see a woman, either asleep or dead, lying in a grassy patch not far from the stables. Her clothing, which was of typical Indian fashion, was torn and filthy. Mud caked her feet and streaked her skin, which was neither black nor white, but a soft buff color, rather like coffee laced with too much cream. Her black hair was a matted nest of ringlets that clung to her head and partially covered a face that Canyon stared at in disbelief. It was the most beautiful face he had ever seen, on any woman, white or black. He hurried toward the woman, knelt down, and gave her elbow a gentle tug. When she stirred, he expelled a breath of relief, and then watched her closely as she tried to sit up.

Tama looked up and was surprised to find a black man kneeling over her. He was wearing an Army uniform, but he was a Negro – the first she had ever seen dressed in blue and gold. She blinked at him, trying to get her bearings; then she slowly recalled where she was and why she was lying on the ground.

Traveling by foot, and following the directions that Cimpi's cousin provided, Tama had talked her way onto steamboats, begged for rides in wagons, and forded streams on foot until, at last, she stood outside the tall timber gates of Fort Gibson. Cautiously, she walked inside and nodded at the soldier who simply waved her in. The first thing she saw was an enormous gun on wheels, and the sight of its long dark barrel jolted her back to the raid on Great Oaks, to the guns the soldiers had leveled on the Fox to push them from their chickees. She recalled the people's screams, the terror in their cries, the sadness in their hearts as they were led away. The muscles in Tama's throat had tightened, and suddenly sick to her stomach, she fled behind the nearest building, heaved into the grass, and then fell to the ground in exhaustion.

Now, Tama cautiously observed the black soldier, whose eyes seemed kind and void of evil. She decided to let him speak first.

"You sick?" he asked, inching his face closer to hers.

Tama shook her head, no, not ready to speak.

"Who are you? Why're you here on the ground? Where'd you come from?" Canyon demanded in a tone that reflected his alarm.

The torrent of questions washed over Tama like a splash of cold water, snapping her back to the reality of her situation. The man appeared genuinely concerned, but she still wasn't certain she should trust him. Despite his appearance, he might turn out to be as mean and brutal as the soldiers who'd forced the Fox from Great Oaks.

"Do you know where you are?" Canyon continued to probe.

Tama hesitated, but then she asked, "Fort Gibson?"

Canyon inclined his head. "Yes, this is Fort Gibson, and I'm Sergeant Tallboot. Is this where you supposed to be?"

"Yes."

"You come alone?"

"Yes."

"Why?"

"Because the people from my village are here."

"Who're they?"

"The Muscogule Fox. From the Tallapoosa River."

"Their mico is Hakan, son of Blue Waters?"

Tama sagged back in relief. "Yes, you know him?"

"I was here when his people arrived. I took them to their assigned lands."

Tama pressed her hands together and leaned forward. "Take me to him. Please. I walked with the Fox, but a soldier named Fisko separated me from them ... and sold me to a man ...."

"Sold you? For a slave?" Canyon's eyebrows lifted and creased his brow as he examined Tama more closely. Clearly, the girl was Negro, with a good deal of white blood in her, but she didn't look as if she had lived long among the Creek.

"Yes, but I got away from him and been traveling ever since. Please, I must find Hakan." She touched the talisman hanging around her neck. "You see, I have this."

Canyon settled his gaze on the talisman, recognizing the symbol of the Fox clan. He knew enough about Native American charms and amulets to know that what the girl was wearing was authentic. "I believe you," Canyon began. "I can take you to your people, but you gotta register first." He reached down to help Tama stand, extending a hand to her. "Come on. We'll go see Captain Rogers so you can sign your name in the big green book. I got a wagon full of supplies that I have to deliver to the Creek. Guess you could tag along. "

"I'd be grateful for your help," Tama told him, relieved to

be, at last, so close to Hakan.

Rising, she followed Canyon into a rough-cut log building where a be-whiskered man was hunched over a book. He set it aside when Canyon entered and launched into an explanation about Tama's circumstances. When Canyon finished, Captain Rogers said, "All right, Canyon. You take her out when you deliver the supplies." He flipped open the green book. "What's your name?"

"Tama."

"Just Tama? You need a surname for the register," Captain Rogers stated with great authority.

Tama hesitated and looked to Canyon, who motioned for her to answer. "He means your last name."

"Well ... Royaltin," Tama replied in a whisper. "That was my father's name."

"Okay. Tama Royaltin. That'll do fine," Rogers replied as he wrote her name in the book. "From the looks of you, you came a long way," he told her, slipping his gaze from her head to her feet, while motioning for her to sign her name beneath his writing.

"Yes, a long distance," Tama agreed, wiping a hand across her cheek as she carefully printed letters on the line, grateful to Maggie for teaching her how to write her name.

A combination of fear, anticipation, and amazement came over Tama as she rode into the Creek Nation. She had not expected the newly formed settlement to be quite so civilized, with a school, a trading post, the Creek Council House, and a busy market place where Indians were actively bargaining for pelts of mink, rabbit, fox, and beaver.

On the outskirts of a village, they came upon a tipi constructed of buffalo hides draped around sturdy tree limbs. A gray-haired Indian was sitting in front of a smoky fire. He stared quizzically at Tama as the wagon rolled past, and in an instant, she recognized him: It was Natomee, the Fox storyteller who recounted the origin of the Creek at the Red Tail Dance. She lifted a hand in greeting, but he did not respond. His lack of recognition pained Tama but just seeing the storyteller gave her hope.

Traveling on, they rode deeper into the Fox settlement, where the sights that greeted Tama initiated waves of despair. It was clear that the Fox had dwindled to less than half the number that lived on the Tallapoosa. She had witnessed the death of many during the journey, but she had not comprehended the magnitude of the devastation. The tents, tipis, and lean-to shelters that dotted the area looked hastily constructed and barely strong enough to survive a summer storm. She could see that the clan was extremely impoverished, and she wondered how they managed to survive on the meager provisions provided by the government.

"Are these your people?" Canyon inquired as he pulled the wagon to a halt near the central log fire in the middle of the settlement.

"Yes," Tama replied, climbing down from the wagon.

"Well, you go on. I'll start unloading these supplies at the storehouse," he told her, pointing to a three-sided chickee beyond a cluster of tents. "Come get me if you need me."

Before Tama could decide whom to approach to ask about Hakan, Suja emerged from behind a wall of blankets and stood in the path, her eyes wide in surprise. Quickly, Suja marched over and planted herself in Tama's path.

"So the runaway zambo is back," Suja started right in, a cruel edge to her words.

Tama grimaced but sucked in her breath to keep from lashing out. "I didn't run away," she calmly informed Suja. "The soldier *took* me away... and sold me ... for fifty dollars."

Suja giggled, and then rolled her eyes, as if Tama's hard luck story held no interest for her. "You could have stayed wherever he left you because that's where you should be. Not here." Suja deliberately spoke loud enough for those nearby to hear what she had to say. "This is not your home!" She slid disapproving eyes over Tama. "And you dare to wear my mother's clothing, and her *culv?*" Reaching out, she ripped Spring Sky's talisman from around Tama's neck and fisted it in her hand. "You have no right to wear any symbol of the Fox!" She drew her teeth down over her lips. "You are not one of us. Leave our village and go live among your own kind."

As expected, Suja's outburst quickly drew the crowd of curious people even closer. They gathered around, eager to watch the exchange between the two women, listening to Suja's spiteful words with great interest and curiosity. However, they did not interfere. "You caused my mother's death," Suja continued to rant. "You are a curse to our clan. We don't want you here."

"That is not true," Hakan interjected, walking up behind his sister. He went to stand in front of Tama, smiling as he told her, "I am glad to see you, Tama. Long ago, I promised that you would be welcome to live among the Fox. That has not changed."

"Your sister thinks differently."

With a dismissive wave of his hand, Hakan told Tama, "I

know you did not cause my mother's death or bring hardship to my people. We are suffering because of the government's laws, which rule our lives." He assessed Tama boldly, and then said, "You appear well."

"I am," Tama replied, lifting the hem of her skirt to stick out a muddy foot. "Covered with dirt and scratched by thorns, but, yes, Hakan, I am well."

"You are brave to come this far alone."

"Hakan," Tama started, wishing she could touch him, hold him, and tell him how much she'd missed him. "I'm not brave. I had to find you. There was no other place to go."

"Come," he motioned, leading her away from the curious onlookers. "We must talk. I want to hear everything that happened."

After stopping beneath a leafy oak tree, Tama told Hakan what Fisko did to her, how she escaped, and how a forest-dweller named Cimpi helped guide her back to him. "Then Sergeant Tallboot, the man who delivers your supplies, agreed to bring me here. Hakan, everything will work out for us, won't it?" she finished.

Hakan remained silent, then turned his face away from her and gazed far down the road. "Things are different now, Tama. I am Mico Hakan, leader of the Fox. I must make important decisions, settle disputes, and represent my people at the Creek Council House. We live with the threat of attack by angry tribes to the north. They say this land is theirs. Life here is not easy, and my people have suffered greatly, but we will stay and begin to make new lives." He shifted his stance and watched Tama carefully, his face clouded with uneasiness. "I am not the same man that you met in the mountains, who only wanted to return to Great Oaks. I foolishly believed that being Mico of the Fox would not be so heavy a burden, but I was wrong. The demands of my people are great when borne alone."

"But I'm here now ... let me share your burdens, " Tama sympathized, suddenly cautious. Hakan sounded unusually tentative, as if unsure of himself, as if he wanted to test her reaction to seeing him again.

Hakan slowly shook his head back and forth, his eyes locked with Tama's. "Fisko told me that he sent you back to your master, across the great mountains. I believed him. I also believed you were lost to me forever. I wanted to go after you, but I could not leave my people. The boat arrived, I got on it, and it brought me to this place." He stopped talking, as if he had no words to explain what happened next. "In this time of sadness, Wyiana stood by me ...and now *she* shares my burdens."

Confused, Tama blinked, not wanting to understand what he was telling her. "What are you saying, Hakan?" To her dismay, her voice broke slightly.

"Wyiana is my wife."

"Your wife?" Tama stammered in bewilderment, unwilling to digest what he had just said.

"Yes. She shares my burdens and my tipi," he confessed.

"Why Hakan? I know you don't feel for her as you feel for me."

"Soon after our arrival the elders insisted I take a wife ... so I did as they wished. Wyiana and I share many things from the past, and we also share the promise of the future. We will keep the traditions of the Creek alive ... but ..." he paused, his expressive face becoming very somber. "I admit ...I do not yearn for her as I always will for you."

Stunned, Tama started backing away from Hakan, as if putting distance between them would lessen the sting of his confession. There was nothing she could say or do to change what he had done, and the overwhelming reality of his betrayal cut like the slash of a knife. Hakan was the leader of his clan, his traditions and customs did not apply to her. His decision to push her out of his heart created a deep well of disappointment.

As casually as she could manage, Tama swallowed the sob that moved quickly into her throat, and then turned around and walked away. Increasing her pace, she began to run, and did not stop until she was out of Hakan's sight. Standing in the road, Tama gasped for air, her fingers tensed into her palms.

He did not follow, she realized, glancing uneasily over her shoulder. Bending over, she sank to the ground and braced her head on her knees, trying not to imagine Hakan and Wyiana lying together, kissing, touching, laughing, and loving one another – as she had hoped to do with him. He had turned to Wyiana so quickly. How could he do such a thing after promising Tama he would keep her with him forever? Clearly, he was content with his decision, so she must be as well even though the pain of his actions cut deeply into her heart. Weak with disappointment, she lifted her head and glumly watched Canyon driving his near-empty wagon toward her. When he stopped, she turned her tear-stained face up to him and said, "I can't stay here."

"Get in," Canyon offered, as if aware of what had happened. "I'll take you to a place where you'll be safe."

Hakan lingered where Tama left him, staring down the road after her, devastated by the way things had turned out. He should have fought Fisko harder, made the soldier tell him where Tama was. He could have tried to rescue her, but if he had done that, his clan would have gone on without him and he would have lost their respect. The elders pressed him to take a wife, and he acquiesced without argument. Many of the elders had two, or even three, wives, but such an arrangement did not appeal to Hakan, and he was certain Tama would never settle for half of his heart. As the chief of his tribe, he had acted appropriately, but perhaps too hastily, and the sting of losing Tama pierced him anew, making him flinch with regret, though he yearned to hold her in his arms once more.

Chapter 23

Canyon drove the wagon up a steep embankment and onto a rutted road that rimmed the ridge above the river. The rush of fast-moving water at the bottom of the gorge mixed with the grind of the wagon wheels as he traveled on in silence.

Canyon glanced at Tama, who turned her face from him. He knew she pretended to watch the river, but realized she was crying. He suspected that her tears were those of a woman rejected by the man she loved.

In an attempt to rouse Tama from her despondent disposition, Canyon pointed to a crudely built footbridge spanning the widest part of the gorge. "That is the main connection between the Creek and the Seminole in the south. Used mainly by women going back and forth across the river. The Seminole built it real narrow, so only people on foot can use it. Keeps men on horseback from riding in."

Tama barely moved her head to look at the bridge, but Canyon was encouraged. At least she'd stopped crying. Canyon was about to tell Tama about the settlement he was taking her to when he was startled by a noise that made him gee-haw to the horses and pull them to a halt. All senses alert, he motioned for Tama to remain quiet, and then he stood up in the wagon and searched the tall grass. He was alarmed to see it rustling back and forth even though there was no wind. The snap of a broken twig cracked the silence. Canyon reached for his rifle, but before he could take it up and aim, two Indians stepped out of the grass and stood in the middle of the road. One of the men pointed a long knife at Canyon, while the other lifted a bow strung with an arrow. Undaunted, Canyon grabbed his rifle, leveled it on the two, and then shouted, "I have no whiskey, guns, or ammunition. Move out of the road!"

The Indian holding the bow and arrow had blue stripes painted on his face. He walked toward the wagon, ignoring Canyon's warning.

Determined to avoid a deadly confrontation, Canyon fired a shot above their heads and shouted, "Move out of the road! We have nothing you want." The man froze.

However, his knife-wielding companion raced forward and grabbed hold of the harness of one of Canyon's horses. Swiftly, Canyon jumped to the ground, smashed the butt of his rifle into the back of the man's head, and forced him to his knees. Keeping his gun trained on him, Canyon shouted to the man's companion, "Drop your weapon on the ground and I will let him go!"

However, instead, of complying, he turned and fled. Using the toe of his boot, Canyon prodded the one left behind. "Get up and get out of here, and don't try this again!" The defeated warrior jumped up and ran, desperate to get away.

Canyon turned to Tama, who had remained surprisingly calm throughout the encounter. "You all right?" he asked.

"Yes," Tama murmured, watching the sway of the grass as the men disappeared. "Who are they?"

"Osage. Becoming a real problem out here. They hate the government, the Cherokee, and the Creeks, who they say are living on land that belongs to them. Very hostile bunch. Their settlement is teeming with whiskey peddlers, horse thieves, murderers, and kidnappers. They raid villages and travelers for food, livestock, slaves, and children, too."

"There's nothing you can do to stop them?" Tama ventured.

"We've got one marshal to keep the peace in all of Osage Territory. He stays busy, but one man can't police all that space."

"You sure ran 'em off," Tama remarked with admiration.

"Standing up to 'em, and not backing down is the only way to do it," Canyon replied as he hefted his rifle and got back into the wagon.

They traveled on without talking until Canyon drove around a bend in the road and arrived at what looked like an encampment, not a village. The strong scent of wood smoke and roasting meat greeted them.

"What's this place called?" Tama asked as they passed a hodge-podge of shelters that fanned out from a slow-moving creek.

"This is Lone Grove," Canyon replied. "I know it don't look like much," he added as he moved along, nodding in familiar greeting to a few of the folks he passed. "The people here are struggling to survive, but they're peaceful. Don't want nothing but to be left alone." He pulled up beside a man carrying a freshly skinned rabbit and called out, "That for sale?"

The man turned, looked up, and grinned at Canyon. "Sure is."

Canyon dug into his pants pocket, removed a coin, and tossed it to the man. Then he took the rabbit, wrapped it in a piece of burlap and placed it in the back of the wagon. "Mighty kind of you," he remarked as he slapped the reins against the horses' backs and continued on. They passed through the center of the settlement and traveled down a near-deserted road until arriving at a partially completed cabin, built from freshly cut logs. The tiny house stood alone, no neighbors in sight. Canyon got down from the wagon and walked over to a man who stopped splitting a log and set his axe aside.

"Mr. Lester!" Canyon called out. "Good to see you again."

"And you," Big Tim acknowledged as the two men shook hands.

"The cabin's coming along real nice."

"Yep," Big Tim agreed. "Hope ta finish soon. Got the roof on the back part, so at least we got some shelter. Good thing the weather's been holding up."

"No rain in sight," Canyon agreed, tilting his face to the nearly cloudless sky. "Here, I brought you a rabbit, all ready to cook."

"Mighty good of you...we can use it," Big Tim said as he accepted the meat.

Canyon turned his eyes to Tama, motioned for her to come over, and then looked back at Big Tim. "I got a favor to ask."

"I'll do what I can," Big Tim replied.

"I'm hoping you might be able to help this young lady out."

Big Tim shifted his gaze to Tama, who moved up to stand beside Canyon. He scratched his head and asked, "How so?"

"She needs clothes, food, a place to stay for a while."

"Humm," Big Tim murmured, then asked Tama, "What's your name, girl?"

"Tama." She kept her eyes down, studying her torn, muddy dress as she picked at the fabric.

"Well, Tama, I'm Big Tim. Looks to me like you done traveled a far piece, huh?" he observed.

"Yes, I been on the road a while," Tama whispered, unsure about being left alone with this burly, rough-looking man.

"She's assigned to the Creek on the Canadian, but things didn't work out. Can she stay with you til I get permission for her to live somewhere else?"

"Don't see a problem with that."

"Good, but let's keep this between you and me, okay? I don't want Captain Wardlaw makin' a fuss about me putting her where she don't belong."

"I see," Big Tim remarked, and then added, "Sure she can stay."

When a young woman came from the back of the house and walked up to stand at his side, he said, "This is my daughter, Julee. And Julee, this is Tama. She's gonna stay with us a while."

Julee examined Tama with caution, but smiled her agreement. "Might be a bit cramped, but we'll manage okay."

"That's mighty nice of you. I brought along some flour, coffee, and a few blankets," Canyon said, sounding relieved.

"That's a blessin'," Big Tim replied before telling Julee, "Help this little gal get cleaned up. Maybe you got some clothes she can wear?"

"I sure do," Julee said, her features becoming even more animated as she grinned broadly at Tama. "Come on. I got some store bought soap you can use, too. The lady at the hospital gave it to me."

Tama looked Julee over, admiring her freshly braided hair, her clear dark skin, and the blue and white flowered pattern on her plain cotton dress. She looked happy and eager to help Tama. Leaving Canyon and Big Tim talking, Tama took Julee's outstretched hand and walked with her toward the cabin. Once inside, Julee sent Tama behind a blanket strung up to separate the single room in two. "You take off those raggedy clothes while I get a pail of water and that soap. I got something nice for you to wear, too."

Quickly, Tama removed her torn dress and stripped off her mud-caked moccasins, pondering her situation. She did not want to think about Hakan's betrayal, Suja's hurtful words, or the fact that Wyiana had stolen Hakan's heart from her. As far as Tama was concerned, she hoped never to see any of them again. All she wanted was to concentrate on building her life in this strange, wild place, and with Canyon's help, she was starting.

When Julee returned with a bundle of clothing flapping in her arms, Tama smiled. *Maybe we can be friends,* Tama thought. She had never had a real friend before, and the prospect made her feel warm all over.

Chapter 24

The market at Muscogee surged with life as traders from outlying areas and vendors from nearby towns competed for the attention of those who were buying food, skins, cloth, trinkets, and a variety of domestic goods.

Thorne Royaltin rode slowly through the bustling throng, his eyes darting over the faces of each young woman he passed. He saw white women, black women, Indian women, and those whose skin color reflected the racial mixtures now common on the frontier.

Accompanied by the escort provided by Major Fleming, Thorne had arrived at Fort Gibson four days earlier. The post commander cordially greeted him, reviewed the permit issued by Major Fleming, and then showed Thorne the Arrival Register, where Tama's name, complete with the last name, Royaltin, had been entered. Thorne learned that his daughter had been given permission to live among the Upper Creek on the Canadian River, and once his Army escort departed for Fort Smith, Thorne traveled on alone.

Now, as Thorne passed through the market at Muscogee, he directed his horse toward a knot of women crowded around a table heaped with colorful blankets, an air of calm, self-confidence radiating from his face.

Elinore shook out a vibrantly patterned blanket in shades of red and yellow, then held it high to inspect the weave. Since her arrival at Fort Gibson, she often visited the Muscogee market to purchase useful, decorative items to make her and Paul's quarters more like a home. As she examined the blanket, which would be perfect for little Ben's bed, she calculated how much to offer the solemn-faced Cherokee woman standing behind the table.

"I'd roll it up with poke root and give it a good airing before puttin' it on that child's bed," Widow Marsh advised Elinore with a cluck of her tongue. "Fleas. Get into everything if you're not careful. The Indians bring 'em to market along with their wares."

Elinore chuckled her understanding. "Poke root? I'll be sure to try it," she said. Holding up two fingers to indicate her price, she leveled a serious gaze on the vendor, who quickly responded by displaying four brown, wrinkled fingers in response. Elinore held up three. As soon as the woman nodded, Elinore placed three coins into her palm, making her smile at last. After folding the blanket into her straw bag, she noticed that Ben had wandered to a nearby table where a young man dressed in buckskin was selling animal figures carved of bone. Hurrying toward her son, Elinore stepped into the path of an approaching horse, and then quickly moved to the side. Glancing up at the rider, she gasped. There was no mistaking that smooth white skin or the thatch of black hair protruding from beneath the leather hat on his head. She had met him on the *Belle Ohio*. Thorne Royaltin. The man who owned Julee's mother.

Quickly, Elinore lowered her head, tugged down the brim of her sunbonnet, and moved beneath the shadows of a vendor's canvas canopy. Squinting in concern, she kept her gaze trained on Thorne's back as he rode through the marketplace, his head swiveling from side to side, his attention darting from face to face. He did not notice Elinore, and she was relieved. Clearly, he was looking for someone, and Elinore knew who it had to be. Royaltin must have recognized Big Tim when he saw him in St. Louis. He must have made inquiries and then tracked Big Tim into Indian Territory. Did Thorne know that Julee was with Big Tim, and if so, what would happen to the girl? Worried, Elinore hurriedly paid the vendor for the carved bear that Ben wanted and told Widow Marsh she was ready to go home.

That night, after dinner, Elinore told Paul about her near-encounter with Thorne Royaltin, detailing the history of bad blood between Royaltin and Big Tim. Poor Julee was caught in the middle, and Elinore was worried. "Thorne Royaltin owns Julee's mother, so he claims Julee as his property. He vowed to kill Big Tim to take her away, and I'm afraid that's why he's here."

"I doubt that," Paul commented, sounding extremely disinterested in Elinore's story about her newfound friends. He sat down at the table, placed his Colt .45 on it, and began to take the firearm apart.

"Oh, yes. I'm sure he's come after Julee," Elinore stated with a tinge of fear in her voice. "Why else would a cotton planter from North Carolina be riding through the Creek Nation?"

"I don't know why, but I do know it sure as hell doesn't concern us," Paul replied, clearly irritated by Elinore's desire to become involved in Big Tim and Julee's problems. He wiped the handle of his gun with a rag and blew into the barrel. "Royaltin can do as he pleases. And he does have a right to claim his property."

Elinore gasped. "How can you say that?" Her fury exploded with each word. "He has no right to own a human being."

"He's a southern planter protecting his labor. As any businessman would. He's not doing anything illegal."

"I don't understand how you can defend him ... or any slave-holder, for that matter," Elinore snapped, her temper flaring. "Big Tim deserves to know that Royaltin is here, so he can protect Julee." Elinore threw words at her husband like stones. "Someone needs to go to Lone Grove and warn him."

Paul looked up from the gun he was cleaning, an expression of shock on his face. He frowned at Elinore. "Someone? Who?" There was defiance in his voice, as well as a hint of challenge. "I'm not going into that nigger camp to warn him and neither are you."

"But Paul," Elinore protested, "Royaltin will take Julee back to his plantation and make her a slave."

"He'd be taking her back to her mother," Paul added with a dismissive sneer. "What's so bad about that?"

"Slavery, that's what's so bad." Elinore paused to take a breath and calm her nerves. Paul was a Southern man who grew up in a place where slavery was an accepted labor force in an economy that depended on it. While courting, they had discussed their views on the subject, and Paul had assured Elinore that he hated slavery and harbored no resentment toward her family for their abolitionist activities. They agreed not to debate the socio-economic structure of the South, though it lurked in the background of their relationship like a shadow lingering just beyond a patch of sunlight. He had assured Elinore that he was happy to leave the south and marry her, but now she wasn't so sure. Had she been foolish to believe their conflicting views on such an explosive moral issue would never come to a boiling point? Had Paul been naive to believe he could ignore his deeply embedded beliefs and forget the traditions he'd lived with so long?

"Paul," Elinore started. "You've met Julee. She's a good girl. She deserves a better life than picking cotton and serving a white master."

"Don't be so dramatic," Paul admonished, setting his gun aside. He studied his wife; then he stated, "Most likely, Royaltin's come here to trade for furs and most likely he will never come across Julee or Big Tim. I don't see any reason for you to be so alarmed." He holstered his gun and stood. "I want you to stay away from those people and keep out of their affairs. You're not to go to Lone Grove, and that's final."

Elinore went to sit in her rocking chair next to the hearth, little Ben on her lap. She pulled her son to her chest and placed her head on top of his, thinking that Julee's mother never had the chance to hold her child like that.

* * * * *

Julee placed a bowl of steaming fried potatoes on the table, then returned to the wood stove and removed pieces of rabbit from the pan of hot grease. She piled the meat on a wooden platter and set it at the head of the table, where Big Tim was already seated. Tama sat on one side, Julee on the other, and after joining hands while Big Tim said a short prayer of thanks, they began to eat.

"You're a real good cook," Tama told Julee, biting into a piece of rabbit. "Did you learn from your momma?"

Big Tim stiffened, the corners of his mouth turning down.

He lifted a brow at Julee, who shrugged and said, "No. Guess I just learned by myself." She looked at the food on her plate and said, "I never knew my momma." Lifting her gaze, she eyed Tama. "Far as I know she still living on a plantation in Carolina."

"Carolina? North or South?"

"North."

"Yeah? That's where I used to live," Tama stated with a less than enthusiastic tone. "But I ran away when my momma died. Old man Royaltin's probably still got the dogs out lookin' for me."

Big Tim gasped and tilted forward, as if to see Tama more clearly. He tapped the table with his fork. "Did you say Royaltin?"

Tama stabbed a chunk of meat and nodded. "Um hum. Thorne Royaltin is most likely mad as hell that I got away." She slowly chewed and then swallowed. "He has a big plantation with lots of slaves. Me and my mama, Maggie, worked in the kitchen house."

Big Tim jerked his head to one side, his lips slightly parted. "You say your momma's name was Maggie? You lived on Royaltin's place?"

Tama shrugged, as if that part of her life was not worth discussing. "Yeah, but like I said, my momma died in a fire ... the night I ran away."

"You tellin' me the truth, girl?" Big Tim's question was stern, his voice hard. He set down his fork and glared in confusion at Tama. "Tell me what you know!"

The force in Big Tim's voice made Tama jerk back and look at him in surprise. Startled by his interest in her past, she hesitated to answer.

"What's wrong, Big Tim?" Julee asked, puzzled by his reaction. "Why you so interested in Tama's momma?"

Placing a reassuring hand on Tama's shoulder, Big Tim spoke in a much calmer tone. "Just tell me all you know about your mother and the man who was your master."

Cautiously, Tama began to relate a brief version of her life at Royaltin Ridge, leading up to the night of the fire. "I left my momma in our cabin ... it was full of smoke. Couldn't hardly breathe. She didn't even try to get out. Just told me to run ... away from the sun ... not to the north like she did a long time ago. I ran until I got across the mountains and that's where I met Hakan .... and how I came to live with the Indians."

Big Tim pushed his chair away from the table and exhaled slowly, his bronzed brow easing low over his eyes as he took in what Tama had said. He stared at the fresh pinewood floor, thinking, calculating, absorbing all he'd heard. Finally, he poked out his jaw, as if daring Tama to give credence to what was filling his mind. "What'd your momma look like?"

"She was dark skinned, had big brown eyes. She was sweet, had a soft voice, and she was real tall, and strong, too."

"Did your momma have a scar on her arm? Kinda looked like a little half-moon?"

Tama threw back her head and looked down her nose at Big Tim. "How'd you know that?" she snapped, now tilting toward Big Tim.

"Did she have such a scar?" he pressed, ignoring Tama's question.

"She sure did. She told me that Master Thorne put it there the first day he bought her, when she fought to keep him off her. He was awful mean. When I was a little girl, momma even ran away, but Master found her and brought her back. After that, she stayed put. But I got away."

Big Tim blinked, as if to clear away the fog of confusion and disbelief that claimed his thoughts. His mind whirled with questions, with the impossibility that Maggie's daughter might be sitting at his table, across from her half-sister. He gave himself a mental shake to dislodge the image of Maggie cowering on the floor while Thorne Royaltin beat her with his lash. He struggled to mute the sound of her cries for help, which he had not been able to provide. All he'd been able to do was save their child from Royaltin's grasp and keep her safe for all these years. For the first time in his life, Big Tim sensed blood draining from his head, and he felt as if he might faint. The sensation exceeded the emptiness he'd suffered when he left Julee behind with Daisy Lincoln, and now, regaining his speech, he murmured, "It can't be...you can't be ..." he faltered, then expelled a long sigh, as if releasing the weight of a long-held burden.

"What's wrong?" Julee asked, looking from Big Tim to Tama and back several times.

Big Tim, ignoring his daughter's question, addressed Tama. "How old are you?" He knew that Maggie had borne a daughter for her master, and that she had left the five year-old girl behind when she fled. Could Tama be that child, now grown?

Tama moved her fingers along the edge of the rough table while silently calculating her age. "I passed my birthday while I was traveling, so I guess by now I'm twenty, maybe twenty-one."

"Tell me what else you know about your momma," Big

Tim said, accepting Tama's answer without comment.

Tama took a deep breath, and then began to relate the little she knew about her mother, including what she had been told about the time Maggie fled from Royaltin Ridge, and how she'd met a nice man who helped her, but how Master Thorne had found her, beaten her, and taken her back to the plantation.

"That man up North who helped your momma," Big Tim started. "She ever say his name?"

Tama shook her head no.

"Well, young lady .... I'm pretty sure it was me," Big Tim confessed, satisfied that Tama had just confirmed that Maggie, his Maggie, was the mother of both girls.

"You?" Julee and Tama repeated, nearly in unison, shocked by Big Tim's revelation. "Yes," Big Tim whispered, still trying to grasp what he'd just learned. "I believe what

Tama says is true...and if that's the case, you two gals are true blood sisters."

Chapter 25

Osage warriors thundered out of the north and bore down on the Fox while sunlight faded into dusk. Tearing into the Creek settlement, they shot arrows tipped with fire into tipis and log shanties, torching the homes of the unwelcome newcomers. The sound of horses' hooves stamping the ground did not drown out the shouts of hatred coming from the Osage as they struck down the first Creek they encountered. The thud of an axe, thrown with such force that it severed the right arm of a young man, initiated cries of elation from a painted man who swiftly took down another with a thrust of his lance. The slaughter gained momentum as wave after wave of Osage swamped the village, their war cries loud and sharp.

Wyiana ran out of the tipi she shared with Hakan and straight into the path of a wildly snorting horse that reared back and thrashed its legs at her, knocking her to the ground. Before she could recover and try to escape, the rider jumped down from his horse and pierced her heart with a fire-tipped arrow, then slit her throat with a hunting knife. Jumping back on his horse, he spun it around and pointed it toward Suja, who was screaming in terror after witnessing the slaughter of her best friend, who was lying face down in the dirt, blood spurting from her neck. Frantic to escape the massacre, Suja raced toward the forest. She shouted for Hakan, who was out of the village tracking a wild boar, to come and stop the slaughter of his people, to save them from the murdering Osage. However, Hakan did not emerge from the forest, and when Suja arrived at the edge of the tree line, her shouts for her brother abruptly stopped. A tomahawk, thrown from behind, smashed into the side of her head and sent her to her knees. Doubled over, she wavered for a moment and then collapsed. Lying on the ground, she inched trembling fingers over her throbbing flesh, and gasped to feel the edge of her cheekbone poking through the hole that had once been half of her face.

* * * * *

Along with morning reveille, disturbing news awakened those living at Fort Gibson: Overnight, a band of renegade Osage had attacked the Creek settlement at the Canadian River. Six Indian men and two women had been killed. Many others were severely injured. A white man and his son, who had been hunting in the area, had also been attacked. The Osage scalped the father, captured the child, and took him into Osage country. The renegade Indians were demanding guns and ammunition from the soldiers at Fort Gibson for the return of the boy.

Tama swished Big Tim's red flannel long johns in the river a final time, stood up, and wrung them out, glad to get an early morning start on her chores. She draped the dripping underwear over a tree limb, and reached for a coarse cotton shirt, which she plunged into the water, and then pounded against a wide, flat rock. Since moving into the cabin with Big Tim and Julee, Tama had taken over the chore of washing clothes while Julee did most of the cooking, an arrangement that suited both girls.

Learning that she and Julee were truly blood sisters

268

created a new sense of peace within Tama. The day of the revelation, she and Julee had talked for hours, sharing stores of their childhoods, learning everything they could about each other to strengthen their newfound relationship. The ties that bound them, with Big Tim, created the family that Tama longed for, allowing her to heal from the pain of Hakan's rejection. As long as she was with Julee and Big Tim, Tama felt loved and protected, as she had hoped to feel with Hakan's people.

Big Tim promised Tama that he would talk to the commander of the fort and make arrangements so she could live permanently with him and Julee at Lone Grove.

After hanging the wet shirt up to dry, Tama took a break to stretch her back while gazing toward the road leading to the center of Lone Grove. In the distance, she saw a man on a horse riding toward her, and the sight sent her heart racing. It was Hakan, and he was alone. She curled wet fingers into fists and watched his approach. *Why has he come here?* she wondered, relieved that Big Tim and Julee had gone fishing and were not around to witness his arrival. When Tama told Big Tim and Julee about Hakan's rejection, Julee had been sympathetic, but Big Tim had simply shrugged and murmured, "*C'est la vie.* You find another man who will treat you like you deserve."

Now, Tama lingered near the river as Hakan rode closer. She noticed that his body was taut, his arms were stiff, and his face was set into a grim expression. When he dismounted and began to walk toward her, Tama noticed that his clothing was splashed with blood, from his deerskin leggings to the sleeves of his shirt. A pang of fear sliced through Tama, and Hakan's solemn expression told her that something was terribly wrong.

She abandoned her washing, stepped into the road, and

looked into his face, recognizing the unmistakable sheen of sorrow that filled his deep brown eyes. A draining sense of apprehension swept through Tama, weakening her to her bones. She stood before Hakan, waiting for him to speak.

"The Osage raided our village last night," he said in a voice hoarse with pain. "They burned our homes, stole our animals, and took our food. Six Fox men and two women are dead ... Wyiana is among them."

Tama exhaled in regret, aware of how hard this tragedy hit Hakan. He'd lost his father and mother, and now the woman he'd taken to be his wife was dead, too. His burdens seemed to grow heavier by the day.

"I'm very sorry," Tama stated with genuine concern. "Wyiana did not deserve such a death. I'm sad for you, Hakan. I am sad the Fox have suffered so much."

"Suja saw the face of the Osage who killed Wyiana and then attacked her with his tomahawk. He wears the tattoo of the sun on his chin."

"Is Suja all right?" Tama inquired, truly hoping she had escaped injury.

"I found my sister bleeding on the ground near the forest, the side of her head split open."

"Oh, no," Tama gasped. "Where is she now?"

"She remains in her tipi, with only Natomee to tend her. She refuses to go with those who fled to safety among the Cherokee, who are giving my people shelter."

"What are you going to do, Hakan?"

"Find the one with the sun tattoo on his chin and settle with him for what he has done. Then I will lead the Fox back to our homes, and rebuild our settlement. The Fox are strong,"

270

he continued. "We will survive this hateful thing and go on."

"Be careful, Hakan," Tama warned, fearful that the rage she saw simmering beneath his controlled façade would spur him into danger.

"The Osage must suffer for this savage act." He lowered his gaze to Tama, who fanned a mosquito away from her face and then moved a step closer to Hakan. She wanted to embrace him, to let him know that she felt his pain. However, she also feared his rejection. Hadn't he turned away from her to lie with Wyiana. Hadn't he pushed her out of his life and his heart? What did he want from her now? Sympathy? Comfort? Surely, not her love. "I'm sorry about what has happened," she began, "but ...why did you come here ... to tell me about your people? We have no reason to talk, Hakan."

Without hesitating, Hakan countered, "That is not true. I will always want to talk to you, Tama." He glanced to the river as he struggled to confess his feelings to Tama. "I turned to Wyiana in a time of great upheaval and change. She was the comfort I needed when everything and everyone around me was strange. I come to you now because you are in my heart and always will be. I hope you hold me in yours."

Tama stood quietly, allowing his admission to settle in her mind. He was telling her exactly what she wanted to hear, but under the circumstances of his arrival, she dared not embrace his words too soon.

"I did not trust my heart to be patient," Hakan went on. "But now I must, and I hope you will, too. I am going to track the man who killed Wyiana and attacked my sister. When I return, I hope you will be here." He eased his shoulders back and wiped his hands on his buckskin shirt, uncertainty in his stance.

Tama was flooded with relief. She stood quietly, amazed, and shaken while her lips quivered with hope. All the disappointment and regret that had plagued her since she first left Hakan's village began to ease. The tears she had shed and the heartache she had suffered softened to hear these words from his heart, and in that moment she began to believe that a future might exist for them. "Yes," she told him in a clear, strong voice. "I will be here, waiting, if that is what you want."

"It is," he finished, in a tone of commitment that sent joy to Tama's heart.

Tama remained at the river for a long time after Hakan rode away, torn between her love for him and her fear of believing in their future. After all she had endured, Tama wanted to live among people who welcomed and accepted her, as Big Tim and Julee did. What if being with Hakan did not bring the happiness she hoped for? How would Suja react if Tama lived with Hakan in their village? The elders of the Muscogule owned many slaves...Tama was a mulatto, half-black, half white. Would she ever be truly accepted by Hakan's clan? Or would she simply be tolerated because he was their leader?

* * * * *

The wrinkled old Indian who emerged from the tipi peered at Thorne and slowly moved his head back and forth. "All gone," Natomee replied to Thorne's inquiry about the location of the Fox from the Tallapoosa River. "The Fox moved far away, to the east. To live among the Cherokee. The Osage say this is their land. They want to take it from us, but the Fox did not ask to live here," Natomee lamented. He snorted in disgust, then turned his back to Thorne and walked toward the center of the near-abandoned village, where horse tracks, shards of broken pottery, piles of rubble from burned out tipis, and scattered ashes littered the land. Streaks of blood remained etched into the dusty ground.

Thorne dismounted his horse and followed Natomee deeper into the ruins, where the scorched remains of dwellings simmered in smoky heaps and the acrid scent of burnt animal skins was thick. Thorne passed several old men who were squatting among what had once been their homes, but he saw no women, children, or young men. He tensed when Natomee pulled back the flap on a partially destroyed tipi and turned his watery eyes on him.

"The sister of our mico lies inside, a broken woman," Natomee told Thorne. He motioned for Thorne to move closer. "Look. See what the Osage have done. The Osage split the woman's face with a tomahawk, but she lives. And she refuses to leave her home."

Thorne bent low and stepped inside the dim enclosure. He blinked to adjust his eyes to the smoky gray light, but then he focused on the frail girl, whose swollen, red face was shiny with oil. She was lying on a bed of willow withes, covered with a buffalo robe. A low fire burned in the center of the tipi, creating a cloud of thick smoke that made Thorne begin to gag.

Quickly he stepped outside, swallowed hard, then said, "I'm looking for a slave girl...goes by the name, Tama." He watched as a flicker of recognition lit the old man's eyes. "Not black. Not white," Thorne continued as the glimmer of interest in Natomee's expression intensified. "She's a zambo runaway. Does she live here?"

Slowly, Natomee shook his head, no.

"But you do know of her, don't you?" Thorne pressed, certain the man knew something about Tama.

The corners of Natomee's mouth turned down as he inclined his head in an affirmative gesture and stared across Thorne's shoulder.

"Where is she?" Thorne demanded.

Natomee stretched his arm toward the winding road that led out of the village. "A half-day's ride from here. Where the blacks who flee their masters go to live. Follow the ridge above the river, away from the rising sun, and you will find her."

* * * * *

Elinore was frantic. She could barely keep her mind on her chores as she moved through her morning routine. The Osage attack, coupled with Thorne Royaltin's presence in the territory, occupied her mind. Nervous anxiety prevented Elinore from saying much to her husband as he prepared to join the search party going after the boy who had been captured by the Osage.

"I don't know how long we'll be out," Paul told her as he put on his hat and stood in the doorway, prepared to leave. "May be a few days. Depends on what we find."

"I know. You have a job to do."

"Do not leave the fort," Paul ordered. "Both whites and Indians are in danger until this matter is settled."

"I understand," Elinore replied, careful not to make a promise she might regret.

As Paul stood there looking at her, Elinore took in her

274

husband's trim, handsome figure, in his crisp uniform. Her heart swelled with love for him, while her mind whirled with confliction. She could tell from the tone in his voice that he was still upset with her about her desire to help Julee, but she refused to apologize for what she'd said to him the night before. "Don't worry. Ben and I will be fine. Take care," she told him.

"I will," Paul said in a flat tone as he started toward her, but then he stopped. Turning away, he walked out without kissing Elinore good-bye.

Paul's departure tore at Elinore's heart. She moved outside and watched as he mounted his horse, joined Canyon and the others, and rode away. When she thought about the captured boy and how frightened he must be, her thoughts turned to Julee, who was in danger and did not know it. Elinore did not move from her open door until the search party disappeared from sight; then she went inside and changed into a dress suitable for riding. If she didn't tell Big Tim about Royaltin's arrival and something happened to Julee, she'd never forgive herself.

After leaving Ben with Widow Marsh, she saddled her horse and started out toward Lone Grove, praying she had made the right decision and that Paul would forgive her for what she was about to do.

Elinore arrived at Lone Grove to find Big Tim sitting on a log outside his cabin, cleaning the fish he'd caught that morning.

"What you doing here, Miss Elinore?" Big Tim asked, wiping his hands before rushing to help her down from her horse.

Elinore shook her head, refusing to dismount. "I can't stay. I just came to warn you. Thorne Royaltin is here."

"Here? In the territory?"

Elinore nodded. "Yes, I'm sure."

"Where'd you see him?"

"At the market in Muscogee. He didn't see me, but I could tell he was searching for someone."

"That man's an evil devil. No telling what he's up to," Big Tim grumbled. "I bet he saw me in St. Louis and found out where I was headed."

"I don't know. But he's come for a reason, and I fear it's for Julee." Elinore yanked on the reins and spurred her antsy horse around. "Let Julee come home with me. Please. You don't want her here when Royaltin shows up. She can stay with me until you're sure it's safe for her to come back. Paul's out searching for the little boy taken by the Osage, and God only knows when he will return. Having Julee with me will be good company. Seems like everybody's on edge."

Big Tim pursed his lips, then said, "Yeah. I heard 'bout that trouble with the Osage. Hope they find the child alive."

"Me, too." Elinore dug her heels into the side of her horse. "Hurry, Big Tim, please get Julee."

Big Tim turned toward the cabin and yelled, "Julee!" calling her name two times before she came out, wiping her hands on her apron. "You gotta leave. Right now, with Miss Elinore. There's trouble coming, so don't ask me no questions, just do as I say."

"What for?" Julee spat, shaking her head as she stomped across the yard. "I'm in the middle of makin' biscuits."

"Just trust me. Go to the fort .... and stay with Miss

276

Elinore 'til I come for you," Big Tim commanded, urging her toward Elinore's horse.

"What kinda trouble's comin'?" Julee queried as she settled onto the back of Elinore's horse. "Trouble like what happened with those Indians up river?"

"I hope not," Big Tim hedged. "But whatever happens, you'll be safe at the fort." He reached up and touched Julee on the arm, then stepped away from the horse, shading his eyes with one hand as he silently bid her goodbye.

"Be careful, Big Tim," Elinore cautioned over her shoulder as pulled the reins taut. "I've got to hurry." Then she snapped the reins hard and took off down the road, headed back to Fort Gibson.

Elinore pressed her horse hard around the curved and narrow trail that would take her home. She had defied Paul's order to stay away from Lone Grove, and was not proud of her disobedience, but she was not sorry she had done what any true friend would do. In her opinion, both Julee and Big Tim were her friends whether Paul liked it or not. She ducked a low hanging branch and gripped the reins tighter, calculating the damage she'd done to her marriage by bringing Julee into her home. Once Paul returned, Elinore would stand her ground and put his tolerance of her friendship with Julee to the test.

Her mind remained on Paul, on how much he had changed since he arrived in Indian Territory. He was not the same man she'd married less than five years ago. Back then, he'd been more sensitive to the situations and feelings of the Negroes. He'd been patient and willing to accept the fact that he and Elinore had grown up in worlds that were far apart yet destined to collide. *Has his time among the Indians hardened him?* she worried. *Has his isolation in this wild, dangerous place created this hard edge he now carries in his voice?* His attitude and tone alarmed Elinore, and she wondered if this change was normal for military men who were constantly faced with danger. *That must be it,* Elinore assured herself. She had not expected her and Paul's relationship to be as it was when they first married. Time had passed. They'd been apart for nearly four years. They both had grown and changed, and now they had to accept those changes if they wanted to keep their marriage alive.

Preoccupied with her thoughts, Elinore did not see the rattlesnake that slithered from beneath the heavy brush alongside the trail, but her horse did. When the animal whinnied and reared back on its two hind legs, it sent both Elinore and Julee crashing to the ground. Julee landed in a clump of juniper bushes, but Elinore, who instinctively covered her head with her arms, rolled beneath the animal's thrashing legs and then tried to scramble away from the snake. However, she did not move fast enough to escape the rattler that sank its fangs into her leg.

Stunned, but unharmed, Julee thrashed through the bushes and pushed her way out, then ran to Elinore and crouched down beside the injured woman.

"Snake," Elinore mumbled, pointing to the two bright red spots on her upper calf.

Julee knew she had to act fast. Frantically, she ripped a strip of cloth from the hem of her dress and tied it just below Elinore's knee. Then she tore open the pouch of dried turtle blood that she never removed from around her neck and pressed the scaly poultice into the wound, praying it would save Elinore's life.

Chapter 26

Hakan rode north from Lone Grove and traveled for two days, passing into Osage territory at the point where Hominy Creek flowed into Skiatook Lake. There, tall pines and birch trees towered above crystal blue water, creating a landscape so serene that it belied the danger lurking within. Deep into his journey, Hakan came across two Pawnee hunters who told him that the Osage warriors who most likely raided the Creek were camped on the far side of Skiatook Lake. They were drinking the white man's whiskey, dancing, shouting, and fighting over the loot from their raid. They had a white boy with them, too.

Hakan told the Pawnee that he had no interest in rescuing the boy but thanked them for the information and rode on. It was revenge, not the urge to rescue, that inflamed his soul and spurred him around the edges of Skiatook Lake and up the sloping hill where he took cover among the trees high above the Osage camp. After securing his horse in a well-hidden spot beneath a jagged outcropping of rock, he crouched low and crept along the ridge of the rise until he found a spot that provided a clear view of the camp below. He swept the area with a slow glance and spotted the white boy sitting beneath a gnarled mesquite tree. He was apart from the men, who were shouting in drunken hoots while waving stolen Army rifles, feathered tomahawks, and long pointed spears, making gestures of bravery with their weapons.

Within moments, the man with the sun tattooed on his chin emerged from a tipi that faced a huge bonfire in the center of the camp. The Osage was wearing the same blue cloth vest and brown deerskin pants that Suja had described, and Hakan was certain that the vivid, dark spots on the warrior's clothing were the bloodstains of his people.

Settling in, Hakan waited until the silver, quarter moon tipped the tops of the trees and the white man's whiskey had pressed the Osage into a slumber so deep that his arrival would not be noticed. Rising, Hakan eased down the slope and crept into the camp, then went directly to the tipi facing the low-burning fire and stepped inside, relieved to see only one figure lying on the pallet in the center of the space. He leaned close, bent down, pulled his knife from its sheath, and with one swipe, slit the Indian's throat. A soft gurgle slid from the man's mouth as blood colored the sun tattoo and his body twitched with a jerk. Then he was still. Mission accomplished, Hakan pulled back the tipi flap and stepped out, but was startled to find the white boy standing in his path, as if waiting for him to finish his business and come out.

"Take me with you." The boy's whisper was as desperate as the pleading expression in his eyes.

Without comment, Hakan pushed past the boy and hurried up the slope toward the spot where he'd left his horse. He hadn't come to the Osage camp to rescue a white captive. He'd come to avenge the slaughter of his people, and he'd done it. Now, he had to get far away before his deed was discovered.

"Please don't leave me here," the boy continued, running after Hakan.

"The men are drunk on whiskey. You are free. You can go wherever you want," Hakan threw over his shoulder as he began to untie his horse.

280

"Go where? I don't know where I am," the boy whined, fear tightening his voice.

Ignoring the boy, Hakan mounted his horse and faced south, prepared to go back the same way he'd come. However, before he dug his heel into the side of his horse, he paused and leveled a hard look on the boy. "What's your name?"

"Charlie."

"Get on, Charlie." He waited until the boy jumped up and sat behind him. "Hold onto me. The ride will be fast and rough."

Hakan pressed his horse with urgency, riding without thought of anything other than putting this awful incident behind him, of returning to Tama, of setting things right with his people. Barreling southward, he did not stop until he was safely out of the Osage Nation and back on land assigned to the Creek, where he and Charlie made camp for the night.

The curve of the rising sun was peeking over the blue-streaked horizon when Hakan awakened the next morning. He looked over at Charlie, still asleep on the grass, lying on his stomach with his head on his arms. The trauma of having been a captive of the Osage, coupled with the hard ride the day before, had taken a toll on the child, but there was little time to rest. They had to move on quickly, before enraged Osage warriors arrived to avenge the death of the man with the sun tattoo.

Leaving the boy to rest a while longer, Hakan led his horse to water. He sank down on the riverbank and stared into the water, still shaken by what he'd done. Killing a man was not an easy thing to do, and Hakan had only done so once before: when a crazed fur trapper came at him with a hunting knife. Hakan took no pleasure in killing, but he did feel a sense of satisfaction that he'd settled the matter and could put thoughts of revenge aside. He turned his face upward and traced the flight of three vultures circling overhead as they wheeled and drifted on widespread wings. He closed his eyes against the emerging sun and shed tension from his body. Since the day he left Great Oaks, to the night of the Osage raid on the Fox, Hakan had been consumed with hatred and revenge. But now that he had spilt his anger, along with the blood of the Osage warrior, he wanted to empty his mind of sorrow and fill it with contentment. He'd lost many of his people to the hardships of the journey, to the hatred of the white man, and to the vengeful Osage, who seemed destined to fight forever. Hakan had no stomach for war. He wanted to live in peace, and, he hoped, with Tama at his side.

The rumble of approaching horses shattered Hakan's reflective mood. Rising, he slipped his knife from its sheath and watched the thicket where the sounds were coming from. Soon, two men emerged. One was white, the other, black, and both were dressed in military uniforms. Hakan recognized the white man as the officer who registered the Fox when they arrived, and the black man was Tallboot, the sergeant who escorted them to their new homeland.

"What're you doing up here so close to the Osage?" Paul demanded, rising in his stirrups to glance around.

"Watering my horse," Hakan casually responded, not about to give the officer any more information than necessary.

"Don't be smart with me. What are you up to?" Paul shot back.

"Exploring," Hakan hedged with a shrug.

"I doubt that," Paul snapped with authority. "If you came up here to start more trouble, go on back home. Leave it to the Army to keep the peace. You'll just make things worse."

Hakan looked at Paul with undisguised contempt. "For you or for my people? The Osage burned our homes and killed many, including my wife. My sister may now be dead, as well. A man cannot let such things pass without taking action."

"That's our job," Paul tossed back.

"And mine as well," Hakan countered. "The white man cannot settle trouble among the Indians. This fight is ours, not yours."

"So you crossed the border, then?" Paul asked, clearly not wanting to dance around the issue.

"I did," Hakan boldly admitted.

"And what happened?" Paul prompted, digging for more information.

Hakan merely stared at Paul, his expression conveying his answer.

"Did you see a white boy in the Osage camp?" Paul inquired, realizing that Hakan was not going to divulge much more.

"Yes. He's over there." Hakan pointed to the grassy spot where Charlie was lying, still asleep.

"How'd you get him away from the Osage?" Canyon wanted to know, dismounting to walk toward Charlie.

"It was easy," Hakan replied. "While the men who raided my village slept in drunken stupors, the boy simply walked away. I put him on my horse ... and we rode south. Wake him up and take him back to his mother."

* * * * *

The residents of Lone Grove, who had risen at daybreak to start their daily chores, graced Thorne Royaltin with apprehensive glances. Unfazed by his cool reception in the all-black settlement, he gave wide berth to a scrappy brown dog that snapped at his horse's legs and headed to a shanty where a sign outside read, Blacksmith, Abe Adams. A muscular black man wearing a leather apron was standing at a fire pit hammering a piece of iron.

"Can I help you mister?" the blacksmith asked, not looking up from his work.

Thorne didn't hesitate to state his business boldly. "Yes. I'm looking for a girl." He sniffed; then he expelled a short breath. "A mulatto girl. Very pretty. Black hair, fair skin. Her name is Tama."

"Why you lookin' for her?" the blacksmith deadpanned, continuing to pound the hot piece of iron.

"I have some news for her."

"That so?"

"Yes." Thorne paused, wanting to use the right words to get the man to help him. "You see, I've come a long way to find her."

"Why might that be?" the smithy asked; then he added, "You a bounty hunter?"

"No, I brought her emancipation papers. I want to give them to her."

"Hummm. Free papers?" Now he stopped hammering the hot iron and studied Thorne with more interest. "You speaking the truth, Mister?"

"Yes, I am," Thorne flatly replied. "Do you know where she lives?"

With a grunt, the blacksmith jerked his head toward the overgrown trail behind his shanty. "There's a man has a girl who might be her. Down that trail. It's far back in the woods, but that's where her folks be livin'."

Her folks? Thorne silently questioned, nodding his thanks as he rode off. I'm all the family she has. Whomever she's hooked up with is not going to have her around for long; I've come to take her back to the only home she has.

After rounding a deep bend in the road, Thorne saw a new pinewood cabin nestled in a grove of trees. The place was sturdy, isolated, and looked built with great care. A thorny wild rose bloomed outside the front door, softening the rough edges of the crudely planed logs. A man in the yard was tossing chunks of meat to an excited hound dog that yelped and jumped to catch the treats. Thorne slowed his pace, slipped off the main road, dismounted, and hid in the shadows to watch. Instantly, he recognized the man: It was Big Tim Lester, whom he had seen at the gunsmith's in St. Louis. The man who attacked Thorne when he reclaimed Maggie, fifteen years ago.

In a flash, the memories rushed into his mind: the struggle to pull Maggie away from Lester. Maggie had screamed to a man, begging for his help, and she'd called him by the name Big Tim. Thorne recalled her terror, the baby's cries, the feel of Lester's large hands around his neck, squeezing the life out of Thorne. He recalled the clip of the lash as it cut into Maggie's flesh, her punishment for running away. A fresh tremor of rage slithered through Thorne. It had taken him a year of searching to find Maggie, but he had ultimately been successful. He'd found her and Big Tim Lester living in a paper-thin shanty in a crowded free-black ghetto fifty miles from the Kentucky border. She was living in conditions much worse than the slave quarters Thorne provided for her. Maggie might have thought she was living in heaven because she was on free soil, but Thorne quickly put an end to her life in "paradise" when he dragged her back to his plantation. Thorne vowed on that day to find the nigger bold enough to attack him and make him pay for what he did.

Now, Thorne waited until Big Tim finished feeding the dog and went inside the cabin before he stepped onto the road and walked toward the house.

Inside, Big Tim slammed the door with a bang. He'd seen Thorne Royaltin lurking in the shadows and knew trouble was on its way. He reached into his holster, which was hanging on a hook beside his bed, gripped his Colt six-shooter, and then yanked the door open to stand face to face with the man he wanted so badly to kill.

Instantly, Thorne pulled his gun and fired, knocking Big Tim's pistol from his hand. "Stay where you are, Nigger! You won't get away this time!"

Big Tim narrowed his eyes into slits and flexed his injured hand. "Royaltin," was all he said.

"That's right," Thorne confirmed. "Step out here in the open."

Big Tim grimaced, then took a few steps forward as the cabin door swung shut behind him. The hound dog trotted up and stood alert at his master's side.

"I came for what's mine," Thorne called out. "And you're not going to stop me."

At Thorne's booming voice, the startled hound dog growled and bared its teeth. Big Tim reached down and patted the dog's head, urging it to quiet.

"I came for Tama. I know she's here. Where is she?" Thorne demanded.

"Tama? Not ..." Big Tim stopped short of mentioning Julee, realizing that Thorne had no idea that Maggie's other daughter lived there as well. "Tama's gone to live with the Creek," Big Tim calmly lied, knowing she was at the river washing clothes.

"You're lying! I've been there, the old Indian said she's here. The blacksmith said so, too. Go get her and tell her that daddy's come to take her home."

"If she *was* here, she wouldn't be goin nowhere with you, Royaltin," Big Tim challenged. "Best clear out before you get hurt."

Thorne gave up a guttural laugh, a sneer of disregard on his face. "You don't tell me what to do. I thought you learned that the last time I saw you. Now, get outta my way."

Thorne took a step forward. Big Tim snapped his fingers. The hound flew at Thorne and sank its teeth into the calf of Royaltin's leg.

"What the hell? Get off me!" Thorne shouted, striking the dog with the handle of his gun, frantic to dislodge it from his leg. When that didn't work, he flipped his pistol around, aimed, and fired off a shot that split the dog's head in two and splattered blood all over the cabin door.

Big Tim rushed at Thorne, knocked him to the ground, and pummeled him with his fists, determined to finish what he'd left undone fifteen years ago.

Tama heard the gunshot and froze, realizing it had come from the cabin. Dropping the quilt she was hanging on a tree branch, she raced up the trail and into the yard, stunned to see Big Tim and Thorne Royaltin locked in a fistfight on the ground. The dead hound dog lay nearby in a bloody heap, and Julee was nowhere to be seen. Tama grabbed a large rock, ran toward the men, and then struck Thorne on the side of the head. He fell back, looked into her face, and then shouted, "Damn you! You ain't nothing but trouble. Just like your whore of a momma." He lunged to his feet, took hold of his rifle, smashed it across Big Tim's face, and shouted at Tama, "You're coming with me. If you give me any more trouble, I'll kill this nigger, then I'll kill you. Don't test me. I got good reason to kill both of you right now."

Flooded with fear, Tama looked at Big Tim, who was lying in a pool of blood, a deep gash across his forehead. She turned, attempted to run, but Thorne grabbed her by the arm, spun her around, and jammed the tip of his rifle barrel into the wound on Big Tim's forehead.

"Cooperate or he's dead."

"Don't kill him," Tama pled. "Please. I'll go with you. Just leave him be."

Thorne gave Big Tim a hard kick in the ribs, twisted Tama's arm to her back, and pushed her toward his horse. He tied her hands together, shoved her onto the back of his steed, attached the rope to his saddle, and took off, leaving a cloud of dust that blocked out his image as he exploded down the road.

Big Tim groaned, spit a mouthful of blood into the dirt, and then struggled to his feet. Painfully, he stumbled into the cabin and snatched his rifle from the hooks that held it above the hearth. His head felt as if a thousand pins of fire were shooting into his brain, and the flesh wound in his hand, where Royaltin had shot him, burned hot as hell. *He came for Tama, and he got her*, Big Tim silently raged as he pushed bullets into his holster. He had fought Royaltin once before and lost, but this time he was not going to back down from the fight that was fifteen years overdue. He saddled his horse and tore out of the yard, thundering down the road in Thorne Royaltin's cloudy wake.

Chapter 27

Storm clouds crowded the morning sky and blocked out the sun, turning day into dusk. Paul and Canyon arrived back at the fort after delivering Charlie safely to his mother, and now Paul was finally home. Upon entering his quarters he found Julee sitting in a rocking chair holding little Ben.

"What's going on?" he asked, pausing just inside the door. "What are *you* doing here?"

He scowled at Julee, who looked down at Ben, who had fallen asleep in her arms.

"Miss Elinore got snake bit, but the doctor's been here and he says she's gonna be fine," Julee informed Paul.

"What are you talking about? Snake bit? Where did all this happen?" he snapped, pushing past Julee to get to Elinore. He flung back the curtain that separated their bed from the living quarters and sank to his knees at Elinore's bedside.

Julee placed Ben in his crib, then stood behind Paul and finished explaining what had happened.

"It's all your fault!" Paul growled, shooting a hate-filled look over his shoulder at Julee. "Damn you to hell. I told Elinore to stay away from that rat-hole of a place where you live. Look at her. You did this to my wife, you foolish, stupid girl. She's pale. Weak. How long has she been like this?"

"Ever since I brought her home, but Doc Stewart's sure she's not gonna die," Julee tried to explain.

"What did the doctor do for her? Why did he leave?"

"Wasn't much he could do. He said the turtle blood I put on the bite marks as soon as I saw she was snakebit was working just fine. He said to make sure she drinks lots of water and stays in bed." Julee nervously clasped her hands together; then went on. "I got to Miss Elinore just in time, Mr. Wardlaw. A minute later and the turtle blood might not of worked so fast."

Paul's head swiveled around as he shot a look of confusion at Julee. "Turtle blood? What kind of nonsense is that? "

"No, it's not nonsense," Julee countered. "Big Tim made me and Miss Elinore carry it with us all the way from St. Louis. She took hers off, but I never step outside without that pouch tied 'round my neck."

"Get out, you black devil!" Paul thundered. "Get out of my house and don't ever come near my wife or son again."

Julee backed away, clearly shaken by Paul's eruption.

"I said go!"

Without a word, Julee opened the door and left, but she stood outside only a few feet away.

Visible tears rose in Paul's eyes, filling him with an acute sense of impending loss. He couldn't lose Elinore, now. Not after waiting so long to have her here with him. He refused to believe she might die. His shoulders dropped and a nauseating wave of despair engulfed Paul as he examined his wife's pale, still form. Taking her hand, he pressed it to his lips. "Elinore. I'm here. Elinore, open your eyes." He kissed her forehead, her cheek, and then traced his gaze over her face. "Elinore, can you hear me?" he whispered. When she stirred, he inched closer. When she squeezed his fingers and murmured, "Paul," he placed his head on her shoulder and inhaled in relief, desperately needing to feel her close to him.

Elinore opened her eyes then closed them. Taking in a shallow breath, she managed to say, in a breathy voice, "Julee. Get Julee."

"Later," Paul responded, not wanting to leave his wife's side.

"No, Paul. Please, get Julee now."

Slowly Paul stood, opened the door, and found Julee standing outside, the wind whipping her skirt around her legs as large drops of rain splashed the ground.

"A big storm's coming," she said to Paul, as if he had never shouted at her.

"I know. It's been brewing all day," Paul replied. He bit his lip, sucked in a long breath and then said, "She's calling for you. Will you go in to see her?" A stab of guilt pierced his chest to see the look of relief on Julee's face.

"I sure will," she said, but when she started to go in, Paul stopped her. "I owe you an apology, Julee. You saved my wife's life, and I was wrong to speak to you as I did."

"That's all right," Julee replied. "You got a lot on your mind. I know you been worried, being out all night looking for the boy. Did you find him?"

"We did. He's safe .... back with his mother right now."

"That's good," Julee replied, moving inside the house. She went to the bed, touched Elinore's arm, then smiled at her and said, "Good to see you awake, Miss Elinore. Now that you're coming around and Mr. Wardlaw is back home, I'll be going."

"You don't have to leave," Paul interjected, resigned to the fact that he needed Julee now, more than ever. "I want you to stay. You've been a good friend to Elinore, and I've been so unfriendly to you."

"Mr. Wardlaw, I'll only stay if you really want me to."

"I do," Paul assured Julee. "And for as long as Elinore needs you."

"Then I'll stay." Julee tucked the blanket around Elinore's shoulders, and then went to sit in the rocking chair. "Mr. Wardlaw, can I ask you something?"

"Yes, what is it?" Paul replied as he removed his holster and hung it on a peg on the wall.

"I don't know what's going on, but Big Tim made me come here with Miss Elinore. Said there's trouble at Lone Grove. Think you can you send somebody out there to make sure Big Tim's all right?"

"Of course," Paul agreed without hesitation. "I'll send Canyon out but not until the storm has passed. But don't worry, I'm sure everything is fine."

* * * * *

Deep purple shadows streaked the sky, painting elongated fingers across the storm-filled horizon. Great pulses of lightning flashed behind the clouds, creating bursts of white fire gone astray. The rumbling thunder called back and forth with deafening layers of intensity while huge droplets of rain splashed to the ground.

Tama stared down into the deep ravine below the footbridge, recalling what Canyon had told her. The Seminole bridge was simply a footpath, made of tree limbs held together with strips of leather cord, and it wasn't sturdy enough to support the weight of two people on a horse.

"Stop! Go back! You can't get across," she shouted above the storm-driven winds.

Ignoring her plea, Thorne, shouted, "Shut up!" and then whipped the animal to move faster, and when the horse stopped cold and refused to move, he jumped down, grabbed the bit, and yanked the stallion forward.

The bridge groaned from the weight of the horse and its riders, swaying precariously from side to side above dark water that tumbled over sharp rocks protruding from the riverbank.

Tama tugged on the rope that bound her hands, desperate to get away, horrified by Thorne's crazy attempt to flee into Seminole country. Loud cracks of thunder drowned out the next crack of Thorne's whip as he lashed the horse unmercifully. The sharp slaps against the animal's side sent Tama's mind reeling back to Royaltin Ridge, to the whippings she'd been forced to watch as Master Royaltin punished his slaves. The slashing rain pummeled her face and soaked her clothing, nearly blinding her to the scene that she did not want to witness. As the fury of the storm increased, so did Royaltin's rage.

Tama struggled against the rope around her hands, thinking she'd rather jump into the ravine below and die than go back to the plantation to be enslaved by Royaltin for the rest of her life. If she jumped into the river, her death would be swift and sweet, taking her back to her mother. But did she really want to die? What about Hakan? He had come to her, and he wanted her with him. And what about Julee... the sister she had been lucky to find and still hardly knew. They were worth living for, weren't they? A sob of desperation wrenched her soul as she threw back her head and let the rain wash over her face.

When the horse's front legs shot through the slats in the bridge, Tama jolted forward. Gripping the saddle for support, she shouted at Thorne, "Stop! He's stuck! Untie my hands and take me down so I can walk!"

"You'll stay where you are!" Thorne shouted, slapping the horse even harder.

His brutal whipping sent the stallion into a jerky reaction that dislodged Tama from its back. She fell from the horse but remained dangling by the rope, screaming for Thorne to pull her up. He paid her no attention.

Tama braced her feet against the railing of the bridge and held on, facing the hillside that sloped to the river.

Hakan shielded his eyes from the rain with his right hand as he stared down at the blacksmith at Lone Grove.

"I saw 'em ride off down toward the Seminole footbridge," the blacksmith told Hakan. "I could tell the girl was tied up, and she was shoutin' something awful. Been gone a spell, though."

Swiftly, Hakan whipped his horse around and plunged into the rain.

Through the curtain of water that nearly blinded her, Tama saw a man standing at the point where Thorne had entered the bridge. She prayed her mind wasn't playing tricks on her because from the outline of the image, she felt sure it was Big Tim.

Big Tim had no choice but to fire on Royaltin and chance killing Tama if he missed. The bridge was swaying back and forth and the rain had clouded his view. His injured hand throbbed and pain from the beating he'd taken at Royaltin's hand consumed his body. Unsteady on his feet, but firm in his mission, Big Tim lifted his trusty muzzle-loader Hawkins and set his sight on Thorne Royaltin.

When Tama saw Big Tim raise his rifle, she looked straight into the barrel, praying he would hit his mark, not her. Cringing, she shut her eyes, prepared to absorb the pain of the blast. When she heard the crack of the gunshot, she gasped and recoiled.

The bridge jolted dangerously. Thorne Royaltin collapsed, spun off the bridge and plunged into the ravine. The thud of his body as it hit the rocks and then splashed into the water told Tama that Big Tim's aim had held true. Her slave master was gone. She was alive, though hanging by a rope. Cautiously, she opened her eyes and lifted her chin, relieved to see Big Tim, followed by Hakan, racing across the bridge toward her. When she began to sob, the frightened horse whinnied, but she rubbed her cheek against the animal's sleek side and murmured, "It's okay, boy. It's all over. Soon, we'll be home."

Chapter 28

At first, Hakan's touch was gentle, his hands creating silken trails on Tama's shoulder as he lay next to her once more. He stroked her face, her arms, her breasts, stirring her desire to become one with him as he explored the surface of her flesh. A full moon illuminated the bedroom of the two-room cabin Hakan had built for them. Celebrating their reunion, they took each other fiercely, with a possessiveness that underscored the permanent connection between their hearts. His lovemaking was swift but not brusque. Tama intensified her grip on his shoulders and brought his face close to hers, releasing a low sigh of contentment.

Lying in Hakan's arms, Tama touched the *culv* that Hakan had placed around her neck and released her hold on her emotions, clearing her mind of everything except Hakan's presence as she savored the exquisite serenity of their reunion. She and Hakan had lost, and gained, so much, and in a very short period of time. But now they were determined to banish their days of anguish with their kisses, erasing each other's suffering in their caresses. At last, Tama's fears about the outcome of their journey toward togetherness no longer plagued her. She knew their love would survive whatever losses and setbacks might come. Together, they would survive the deep wounds inflicted on their people and find the courage and strength they needed to journey on in their new homeland.

Epilogue

One year later

Elinore handed little Ben up to Paul and then climbed up to sit beside him. The covered wagon, which would be their home for many weeks, was piled high with all of their possessions. The humpback trunk that Elinore had so carefully packed when she left Cincinnati almost two years ago was, once again, strapped into place, filled with china plates and lace tablecloths, ready to journey along with her. The interior of the canvas-topped vehicle was arranged exactly like the one in which she had come to Fort Gibson, but this time she was riding with her husband and her son, her family united at last.

Looking down at Julee, Elinore smiled. "Fort Point is on the ocean. Paul says it's a very pretty spot. And it's not so far. You and Big Tim must come to visit us."

"All the way to California?" Julee remarked, shaking her head. "That sounds awful far away to me. It'd take forever to get there."

"Ah, *non*," Big Tim chided. "It's not so far. I been to Fort Point twice, but I'm not wanting to go there again. You'll find Fort Point to be a solid place, Miss Elinore. Made completely of stone. Built to protect all that gold coming in and out of the state." He turned to Canyon and gave him a devilish grin. "Now that I got somebody who seems to want to watch over Julee, I'm thinking of gettin' back on the road myself. Maybe I'll head out to Colorado where I hear there's plenty of work. I guess I been in one place too long."

"If you go, I'd take real pride in watching over Julee while you're gone," Canyon quickly remarked, shyly placing his arm around Julee's shoulder. "No need to worry about her. She's grown enough to get along without her poppa."

Paul gave Big Tim a knowing nod; then he chuckled in his throat. "Big Tim, if you go off and leave that girl of yours alone with Canyon, she might be a married woman when you get back."

"Aw, ain't nothin' wrong with that," Big Tim tossed back. "As long as my Julee is happy."

"We've got to start now," Paul said, cutting off the good-bye chatter. He picked up the reins to the team of horses that would pull them on to California and held them loosely in his hands.

"Wait a minute," Elinore told her husband, reaching under her seat. She removed the new breech-loading Henry that Big Tim bought for her in St. Louis and handed it down to him. "I have no need for it now that I have my own Army escort," she jokingly told him. "I want you to have it."

Big Tim accepted the gift with tentative hands, and he shook his head in disbelief. "Mighty fine piece. I do thank you and wish you well," he stated, stroking the length of the gun.

"Now, wave good-bye to everybody," Elinore prompted little Ben, who lifted his chubby arm and moved it back and forth. "Take care of yourselves," she called out, and then she turned her face to the west, excited about setting down roots with her family in a new place called San Francisco.

* * * * *

When Tama entered the rough log house at the center of the Fox compound, she found Suja sitting in a rocker by her fire, wearing traditional Muscogule dress. Her hair was piled high and swept to the front in a tall pompadour, just as Tama had styled it on the day of the Red Tail Dance, so long ago at Great Oaks.

Tama removed the dust flap covering the baby's face and approached Suja, who turned, and without speaking, opened her arms to take the child from its mother. Tama smiled when Suja nuzzled the baby's nose with hers, and smoothed its curly black hair with her hand.

After getting a cup of coffee from the pot simmering on Suja's potbellied stove, Tama pulled a straight back chair up beside her sister-in-law, placed a hand on Suja's arm and gave it a gentle squeeze of hello. The scar on the side of Suja's face was wrinkled, red, and ugly. The angry welts of raised bronze skin ran from her temple down to her chin, covering nearly half her face. However, she never tried to hide her disfigurement, and among her clan it was said that her scars symbolized the strength of the Fox, who rebuilt their ravished settlement in spite of continued threats from the Osage.

Tama listened closely when Suja began to speak, eager to know what story Suja would tell her three-month-old nephew this time. In gentle, yet animated words, Suja launched into the tale of the origin of the Muscogule Creek, describing how her ancestors emerged from caves on the Red River in Texas and traveled east to settle on the Tallapoosa River, where they established Great Oaks and lived proudly for many years.

"And," Suja said to her brother's firstborn son, whose tiny hand was curled tightly around her thumb, "no matter where you go or who you choose to live among, your Indian soul will be constant. You will be a Fox forever, just like your father...

and your mother."